CHILDREN
of
VALE

D. A. ANDERSON

Copy editing by Laura Hawkins
Cover and book design by the author
Source Image: "Light-Toned Deposits in Noctis Labyrinthus"
NASA/JPL/University of Arizona
Author photo by Anita Roach

Published by the author
author@childrenofvale.com

Visit www.childrenofvale.com

To my parents

CHILDREN

of

VALE

LEUM SEKTA VORANUM ISETURE TANOSIS-INSESAM,
ISETU THALOK NATIVUMIR, SIN TA ET VARE,
SE LEUMES ASHEPELA SUN SOLU RAKISARA
SELUANUM ET VALELANE.

You who walk as aliens in a strange land,
born into this world, yet not from it,
I seek your love and light,
children of My hand.

MATER VALE'S FIRST PLEA 1:1

As Interpreted by Her Sibyl

1

SHE WAKES UP. She opens her eyes for the first time. She hears muffled sounds at first: a low hum and a rhythmic pounding.

Everything is warm and wet. Her mouth opens. Wetness runs in. She inhales; fluid fills her lungs. She exhales and breathes it in again.

She reaches out. She feels her hands. Her fingers are long and pale as gypsum. She brings them close, touching her face. She feels her nose, her brow, moving up her forehead, up to her scalp. It is bald and smooth.

Everything is blue and blurry. She squints. Limply, with untested limbs, she swims through the fog.

Then—bump! Her head and hands hit something hard and smooth. It is the first time she feels pain.

Surprised, she stops. She doesn't see what she touched, but curiosity gradually outgrows the pain. She carefully reaches forward. The fog ends in something invisible, cold, and hard. She presses her hands to it, then her face. She peers through the fog.

There are round forms in the distance. They look like bubbles, but they are frozen in place. Inside each one is a pearly-white form with a head, two arms, and two legs. Some look like her, but some are smaller. Some are nothing but tiny pinpricks. The wombs encapsulating the embryos are arranged in rows, stretching endlessly in a perfect receding pattern.

An immense whirring sounds. The waters around her quiver.

She feels something move in the water. She darts away, her newborn eyes struggling to focus. Long, serpent-like forms appear in the water. They flash a series of colored lights, pulsating brightly down their black bodies.

They swim toward her. She darts away from them, hitting the hard, invisible boundary. They advance. She traverses the curved surface behind her, but there is nowhere to go.

When they are very close, she can see them clearly. They don't have eyes or a mouth—only a vertical slit at their front. One swims right up to her and its slit opens. Inside is a large, white iris.

She presses herself against the boundary behind her. Her eyes never waver from the creature as its iris flickers and pulsates.

It slowly places its iris on her forehead. It is not painful —it is warm and soft, even pleasant. Its phosphorescent body pulsates rhythmically and the others respond, each opening their own colored iris: first sapphire, then gold, then violet, then crimson.

Each creature attaches itself to the crown of her skull. She feels numbness work its way into her body; a wave of panic rises through her. The creatures brighten and synchronize. Before she can struggle, a profound relaxation comes over her. She goes limp. A warm, electric energy builds at the base of her spine. It rises up her back, through her neck and into the cavity of her head. The warmth builds in waves and fills her vision. It releases a shock; her back arcs reflexively and her vision changes.

II

THE HORIZON IS pink with sunrise. Bright stars form constellations, and auroras slowly dance, leaving luminous green and blue blushes against a black sky. Two moons, one dark and ominous, the other serene and white, hover overhead. A meteor shoots by, cutting the sky with a fading violet line.

Her back is wet. It's dew from the grass.

She sits up. She is nude. She is an adult, but has the torso of an adolescent boy and the hips of a girl.

Ahead of her is a cliff dropping into the sea. The sun is resting halfway on the horizon. Distant storm clouds silently pass thunderbolts between each other, glowing briefly.

She stands. She is alone. Walking feels new to her but comes naturally. Her legs obey her intent without protest. She approaches the cliff. The long grass terminates and falls at the precipice. She lowers to her hands and knees, peering over the edge. Dangling vines point to a craggy, sandless cliffside where waves crash against standing rocks. The rocks are black and shine like glass: obsidian.

She breathes in the cool air and looks up. A breeze blows over her hairless scalp. A storm cloud draws near.

The cloud billows closer, darkening. In moments, it engulfs the cliffside and becomes a tempest. It casts bolts of static like a ship about to land. The wind around her grows wild, circling around her like a vortex, flattening the grass. She withdraws from the precipice and falls backward.

A pale figure splits the clouds in two. She is tall, with flowing white hair that whips in the wind. A colorless tunic dresses her and two outstretched hands peer out from underneath it.

The girl covers her eyes with the crook of her arm, shielding her face from the wind. The long grass, driven wild, slaps her body.

The figure's feet touch the tips of the grass on the precipice, hovering effortlessly. A slender hand rises, opens; the storm dies, becoming a cool breeze. The grass stills. A voice speaks to the girl, but the figure's mouth remains motionless.

"I am Vale, maker of this world."

The girl lowers her arm, peering up at Vale. Her face is long, regal, with wide-set eyes holding large, cyan irises that glow against the storm. Vale's hand lowers and stretches out toward her.

"You are my daughter. Your name is Tyana. I love you and have faith in you."

Tyana looks at Vale's outstretched hand. Vale's fingers are long, with pearl-white skin, like her own.

She is overwhelmed, but Tyana forces herself to stand. Curious, she walks toward the cliff's edge. She stretches out her hand and places it on Vale's massive palm. It tingles with electricity. Tyana's body grows warm with the touch. Vale smiles serenely at her.

The wind whips up. Vale's smile fades, and her hand slips out from under Tyana's. Tyana follows her to the precipice, reaching for her. Vale falls downward beyond Tyana's view, disappearing into the sea.

Tyana stares, confused. The thundercloud dissolves, and Vale is gone.

The wind stills and the sea groans. A dark shape grows in the water. Waves hurl themselves against the cliff and their spray reaches the vines below. Tyana backs away from the precipice. The ocean breaks and water sprays upward. A wet, black figure rises from the sea.

The figure's face looks down at her. It is a face like Vale's, but it is not Vale's. It is made of glowing, molten metal. Her hair is black and slick with oil. She wears a burnt sash of fading colors. It is dripping water that is boiling hot and steaming.

She stares down at Tyana and smiles. Black liquid dribbles from her lips.

"I am Thea. You will obey and worship me."

Tyana is terrified.

Thea raises her right hand, holding a scepter in the form of a double-helix. At its top is the head of a tan-skinned man. The man's eyes open and he looks at Tyana. He says something in a language Tyana doesn't understand.

Thea repeats:

"Worship me."

Pain shoots through Tyana's abdomen. She falls to her hands and knees. Something warm makes its way to her mouth. She touches her lips. Black liquid drips from their corners.

Thea smiles. She raises her massive left hand. In it are seven girls carrying a bowl on their backs. Thea lowers them onto the ground, and they walk toward Tyana with the bowl. Their hair is black, and they are naked. The girls lower the bowl onto the grass. Thea leans over it and spits. A stream of black oil pours from her mouth.

"Take this," says Thea.

Tyana leans toward the bowl. The liquid is thick and smells like burnt earth. It causes her to heave a little, and she tastes it in the back of her mouth.

She looks away. She looks down at the servant girls, prostrated at the bowl. One of them looks up at her. Her face is blank and featureless; erased.

Tyana looks up at Thea, asking:

"Did you do this?"

Thea's smoldering face only smiles in response.

Fear rises up in Tyana. Fear that turns to anger.

She runs at the bowl and pushes upward with her whole body. It tips a little, then spills, spreading the oil-like fluid into the grass. The grass withers and dies. Thea stops smiling. The faceless girls rush Tyana, tackling her to the ground. She feels intense pain and pleasure wherever they touch. Their fingers are like hot irons piercing her skin, and they paralyze her with overwhelming sensation.

"Destroy her," Thea says.

One girl grabs Tyana's throat and begins to press. Something gurgles into her mouth. Unable to breathe, Tyana gathers what she has in her mouth and spits.

Black liquid sprays into the face of her attacker. It steams and sizzles. The girl releases her grip and Tyana throws her freed hand at the girl's head. It goes through, her fingers plunging into the girl's face. They are like hot irons in liquid rubber. The attacker's face begins to boil.

Thea frowns.

"I will make you obey."

Thea raises her scepter high over Tyana. At its top, the tan-skinned man repeats his foreign words like a chant. Thea brings the scepter sharply down.

III

THE DREAM STOPS; warmth and wetness return. Tyana feels herself floating again. The heat from the serpents attached to her falters and their lights flicker out. They detach, limp and lifeless.

A great pounding echoes through the womb. It turns into a roar. The waters stir and begin to spin in a vortex. The bottom gives out and Tyana feels herself sucked in. She falls through a wide tube, bumping against its surface. She is frightened and claws at the walls, but there is nothing to hold onto. She is pulled by the force of a vacuum.

Light breaks and she is thrown through an opening. Cold, dry air embraces her. She lands and rolls down something hard and metallic. She comes to a stop and coughs. Water spurts from her mouth.

She opens her eyes and they begin to adjust. Everything is cold and white. She can make out a gray, overcast sky. The ground is blanketed with snow. She starts to shiver.

In the distance she sees a black, blurry form. It is above the horizon, flying, moving beneath the cloudy sky toward her.

She commands her limbs to move, but they are weak. Her naked, wet body is shivering in the cold. She crawls backward, moving back up the incline she rolled down. The surface is smooth and freezing to the touch.

A sound now accompanies the dark form in the sky. It is a dull, melodic hum. Tyana looks back. It is getting closer.

She turns to run. At the top of the incline she can see the oval-shaped opening from which she fell. It is inside a tall, metallic cave. She is just at its entrance. She attempts to stand again, but fumbles, slipping on ice and snow. Behind her, the flying machine's hum grows louder.

She finally gains traction. With freezing fingers she reaches the entrance and attempts to pry it open. It is sealed shut. There is no mechanism nearby that she can find to open it with.

The machine's hum is now a loud roar. She turns—it is a ship hovering at the entrance of the cave. It is covered in spines. It releases a loud, hissing pop, and a pair of tethered cords fly toward her feet. They wrap around her body, sticking to her skin like glue.

The tether pulls and she is dragged toward the ship. She claws at the surface as she falls down. Snow gives way in her hands. The ship rises and she is lifted up into the cold air.

Hanging by her ankles, she looks down at the landscape receding beneath her. She can see the mouth of the cave. It is literally a mouth, a white maw carved in an obsidian cliffside. The mouth recedes into a face, and she recognizes the face: Vale, the same Vale from her dream. Her likeness, open-mouthed, is massive, partially obscured by snow, jutting from the side of a mountain.

Looking up, Tyana sees the tether reeling her into the belly of the ship. An aperture opens. She is drawn up into it.

The interior is white and clean. Around her stand four pale-skinned forms clothed in black, glossy attire. Two have crimson-colored hair. Another has braided, sapphire-colored hair. Another, taller and built, wears no gown but holds a long, bladed instrument with a barrel. Her hair is deep violet.

They stare at Tyana as she hangs upside down. The aperture closes under her head.

"Release the tether," says one. The glue around Tyana's body dissolves and she is lowered to the floor.

"Clothe her—gently."

A crimson-haired girl puts a thick blanket over Tyana, wrapping it around her shivering body.

"Determine her caste."

Tyana watches the girl approach with a metal tool. It carries a small needle at its tip. She reaches for Tyana's neck.

Her hand snaps to the girl's wrist and the tool drops onto the floor. Tyana pulls, yanking the girl toward her. They are face to face—the girl is stricken with a mixture of pain and pleasure. She cries:

"Sister—I ... I can't move!"

Tyana, still shivering, yanks again with all her strength. The girl is thrown to the floor. She crumples as if she had suffered a blow to her chest.

"That's not possible," says one.

Tyana stands and fumbles forward. She collides with a rack of tools and pushes it away. Containers fall to the floor.

"Restrain her!"

Tyana runs toward the nearest door. She collides with it and grasps desperately for any opening mechanism. She hears a loud pop behind her and a brief pain shoots up her spine, followed by an intense numbness. She falls limply to the floor.

The tall one with the violet hair stands over her, holding her weapon in the air.

"You have a Warrior today, Sister."

"Not possible. You saw what happened when she touched her."

Tyana hears a shrill moaning nearby on the floor.

"She threw her across the room," says the violet-haired one. "She is a Warrior. How else do you explain her strength?"

The one with sapphire braids comes into Tyana's view, standing over her.

"Bring us to the Mater's City. Take her to a cell for now. We'll determine her caste there. I won't wait for her hair to grow in." That one walks away.

The violet-haired one scowls, but says nothing. She looks down at Tyana and kneels next to her. She is fearsome-looking, with ornate, charcoal-colored tattoos that trace her neck and jaw. They seem burnt into her skin.

"Relax, sister. Let us do our work. You'll be home soon."

Tyana's vision fades. Consciousness slips away.

IV

T YANA AWOKE TO a bright light and an awful headache. She was on a firm bed. The numbness was gone, but her muscles protested as she moved. Her eyes adjusted slowly. She looked to her right, ignoring the fading pain.

The room opened into a long hallway. At its entrance stood a blurry figure with violet hair. In the blur she could make out that the figure's back was turned.

She carefully looked around the room. It was empty and featureless except for what she lay on. No tools, no containers, no other exit of any kind. Careful not to make a sound, she sat up slowly. The figure idled, back still turned. Tyana recognized the bladed, barreled weapon at the figure's side. It was holstered.

Tyana's feet touched the cold floor. She quietly moved across to the wall nearest to her captor, ignoring the protests of her aching body. She came up close to the figure's back. She took one deep, quiet breath—and lunged for the weapon.

An electric shock threw her backward. Sparks

sputtered from the weapon, and it glowed brightly where she had touched it. The figure turned.

"Good. You're awake."

Tyana nursed her hand. It spasmed from the shock. She flexed it gently and looked up.

"They didn't believe me when I said you were a Warrior. You move like one and think like one. They haven't delivered one of our caste yet, so I can forgive them this time. Fools, still."

The guard raised her bladed rifle lazily.

"Feeling better?"

Tyana scowled.

"It's a good thing for you I was here. Their tranquilizers aren't as measured as mine. You might've suffered real injury. I understand if you won't forgive me right away, of course. Don't worry—you're a prisoner only temporarily. We're on our way to the Mater's City. A hot meal and drink waits for you there."

The Warrior peered at Tyana's scalp.

"Your hair is growing in. Good. It means you're healthy."

Tyana touched the top of her head. Little filaments protruded from the skin.

"It will grow quickly. Don't pull it out. Violet, too. I was right—foolish Keeper. Higher castes never listen to lower ones, even though one knows her own kind. What's your name, sister?"

" ... Tyana."

"Tyana. A fair name for a Warrior. Mine is Kersa."

Tyana said nothing.

"Perhaps you'd like a view."

Kersa touched something on the wall. A small hiss sounded from behind, and Tyana turned.

The wall behind her dissolved into a window. They were moving. She saw a grand ocean, set beneath a gray sky and a foggy horizon. Craggy rocks rose up like thin, black spires. Bright-green mosses dotted their tips, and waves lapped at their foundations, frothing.

"Welcome to Valen."

Tyana approached the transparent wall, peering farther. The crags moved quickly, gradually increasing in density as they passed by.

"This is our home planet. There are seventy-two cities, each of which are populated by millions of Keepers, Scribes, Warriors, and lowly Artificers, all working together. We've colonized two other planets in our system, both of which have similar environments to this. Mater Vale prepared our way."

Tyana turned.

"Vale?"

"Mater Vale is our Mother, our creator. You already know Her—as you do Mater Thea."

"Thea—," Tyana shivered.

"Mater Thea is the Sister of Vale and Her Vicar. She rules over us from Her capital city. We're heading there now."

The image of Thea's steaming, oil-covered face returned in Tyana's mind. She looked back to the view.

The craggy rocks rose and joined together. Fog drifted away to reveal a cliffside rising sharply from the sea. Set in the cliffside was an obsidian face, massive, mouth gaping, swallowing up the water.

"That is the city," said Kersa.

They headed toward the gaping maw slowly, low to the water. Tyana watched as waves crashed against the lips; the teeth were hidden and the pupil-less eyes opened wide. They passed under the cliff's shadow and into the maw.

More fog parted. Huge machines and catacomb-like hives rose up on either side. Catwalks criss-crossed haphazardly. Steam rose up through huge vents.

"The Artificers work in these lower levels. It's forbidden for higher castes like ours to sink to these places. Unfortunately, even in the Mater's City, we must endure viewing them as we enter—I suppose to remind us of the necessity of their work."

Tyana watched closely as hovering vehicles rose up from the waters below, loaded with cargo. Occasionally, a red and white form would appear on a balcony or catwalk. Crimson-haired, dirty, and wearing blackened jumpsuits, they disappeared as quickly as they were seen.

Tyana heard a hiss behind her at the far end of the hall. She turned. At its end, walking toward them was the sapphire-haired Keeper flanked by two small, red-haired Artificers.

"We are making the final approach," the Keeper said, walking up to Kersa, paying no attention to Tyana. One of the Artificers eyed Tyana nervously—the same one Tyana had grabbed. "The newborn is to meet with her teacher. You will accompany us."

"I'm sure she'd appreciate a hot meal first," Kersa said.

"That is to the teacher's liking, not yours," the Keeper retorted. She looked briefly at Tyana. "Be sure to bind her hands as well. I have specific instructions. You are not to touch her, nor allow her to be touched."

"We are Warriors, Vesha. We need not be treated like prisoners."

"You have your instruction," Vesha snapped. "I will

16

take no further protests from you."

Kersa, fingering her bladed weapon, stepped toward Vesha. Kersa was a head taller and more built.

"I think your authority is inflating your arrogance, Keeper."

Something whirred to life in Vesha's hand. She raised a small, mechanical pistol with a wide barrel and a needle. It glowed in her hand. A red dot showed at its tip.

"Do not tempt me to use this again, sister. Would you risk another mark for your insolence?"

Kersa scowled. She lowered her rifle, replacing it in its holster at her side.

"By your command, Sister."

Vesha lowered the pistol. Its whine faded. Kersa took a pair of bracelets from her side.

"Forgive me once more, Tyana. You are a prisoner still."

Kersa placed the bracelets on Tyana's wrists. Strength drained from her arms as the cuffs attracted each other, binding her wrists.

Tyana looked at the Keeper. She and her crimson-haired assistant eyed her hands nervously.

"Make sure she does not touch you."

V

Tyana was led, hands bound, by Vesha and flanked by Kersa. A lift brought them up out of the ship and through the heart of the city. Tyana watched through its window as tier after tier passed by. Black stone walkways stretched onward while spires rose upward, resting on the shoulders of sculpted stone bodies. Her guardians said nothing, but Tyana stretched her neck to see.

Opulently dressed figures with cobalt-colored hair discussed matters in pairs openly. Elsewhere, hooded figures with golden braids walked in lines, never lingering. Warriors wandered alone, seemingly aimless. Tyana saw no crimson-haired Artificers.

The lift slowed, coming to a halt. Vesha turned to her.

"Your teacher's name is Vershil. She is a highly ranked Keeper. Treat her with the utmost respect, and she will give you fair instruction. Do not speak unless spoken to; do not take anything unless offered."

Tyana nodded. Vesha turned to face the lift door, and it opened.

Overcast light flooded a small but opulent courtyard. It was open to the air. Pink and green curtains fluttered in the chilled breeze. Veined marble columns supported a second floor. To the right was an atrium with a wide, low table, atop which sat stone rods, all ornately decorated. Some had dust covering them. On either end of the table lay two stone faces: one in alabaster, mouth closed and serene; the other, formed from obsidian, mouth gaping, eyes wide.

Ahead, at the far end, a figure in a long, shimmering black dress stood on the balcony. Royal blue coils sat on her head, terminating in braids that fell down her back.

Vesha moved ahead of them.

"May the blessings of the Maters rest on you, Sister Vershil." Vesha bowed at the motionless figure, who did not turn. "I've come to deliver your new student."

"Thank you, Vesha. Please save your pleasantries."

Kersa tapped Tyana on the shoulder to step forward. She did.

Vershil turned. Her face was serious, sculpted, with high cheekbones. Between her brows rested a small black diamond, burnt into the skin.

She walked toward Vesha, paying no attention to Tyana.

"Do you have her profile?"

Vesha gave Vershil a round, flattened object. Vershil peered at it as if it were a mirror. Her eyes glazed over. She stood motionless for a few moments, then came out of her reverie. She handed the disk back to Vesha wordlessly. Vershil addressed Tyana directly:

"What is your name?" Her azure eyes pierced Tyana. Only a gentle nose mitigated Vershil's gaze.

"Tyana," she said.

"*Tyana*. Interesting name for a Warrior. Do you like it?"

Tyana hesitated.

"It suits me," she said. Vershil paced around her slowly, examining her physique.

"I understand you have not yet had anything to eat. I suppose you are hungry. And thirsty."

Tyana said nothing. Vershil snapped her fingers.

"Vesha. Bring my student a dish from my table. You will find it prepared."

Vesha bowed and disappeared. Vershil continued to pace, inspecting Tyana. Tyana met her gaze as she passed by. Tyana's eyes flicked to the diamond above those eyes, and she felt Vershil's gaze bore deeper. She glanced away.

Vesha brought out a stool and a tray on which lay a bowl of what looked like seaweed. A glass of steaming water stood next to it. Tyana's eyes locked onto the food but she stood still.

The faintest smile crossed Vershil's thin lips.

"Good. You are obedient."

She addressed Vesha:

"Undo her wrist-cuffs, then leave us."

Vesha bowed and Kersa undid the cuffs. Kersa and Tyana exchanged glances silently. Tyana felt strength flow back into her arms, and she flexed her hands.

Kersa and Vesha walked back to the lift. Tyana glanced carefully back at the Warrior. Kersa was expressionless as the door closed.

Vershil paused her pacing.

"Sit. Eat."

Tyana sat on the stool. Two metal chopsticks lay next to the plate. Vershil watched as Tyana hesitated, then attempted to pick up the utensils in one hand, then in two. She fumbled both. She instead lifted the bowl with her hands to her mouth. The smell, though foreign, made her ravenous. She quietly slurped up the seaweed as Vershil watched.

Seeing no protest, Tyana continued. She slid the rest of the bowl down and quickly devoured its contents. Putting it down empty, she picked up the glass of hot water and drank it until it too was empty.

Vershil smiled again, making her lips thinner.

"Thank you," Tyana said.

"Do not thank me for what is not kindness, but necessities met."

Tyana said nothing. Vershil spoke:

"My role as your teacher is not to render affection to you. My role is simple: to instruct you in the ways of our society. Much of what you know you learned in the womb, such as our language. You already speak it; I did not have to teach it to you. This knowledge is given by Mater Vale to every newborn. Other knowledge is not so easily gained. Such knowledge is unique to your caste, and is earned. You will have another instructor of your own caste, a Warrior, for this purpose. I, however, am a Keeper. My caste's role is to govern and to instruct. We keep the society for Mater Thea who rules in Her sister's place. Your caste's role is to defend our colonies and wage war against the enemies of Mater Thea. Do you understand?"

Tyana hesitated, then said:

"Yes."

"My caste is higher than yours. For this reason, when you speak to me, you will not use the casual form 'sister'. You will speak to me with the proper form, 'Sister'. Do you understand?"

"Yes, Sister."

"Good."

Vershil paused.

"I should tell you, sister Tyana, that you are rare among the rare. This is no cause for personal pride. Rather, this will make your life difficult. The blessings of the Maters also come with burdens. Each caste has its own burden, and you will learn your own fully in time."

Vershil paused again.

"I have a gift for you on the occasion of your birth."

Tyana looked at her inquisitively. Vershil turned, walking behind the sheer curtains. She returned carrying a small box. Tyana looked at it, then at her.

"Open it."

Tyana did. Inside was a pair of long, black gloves.

"Put them on," she said.

"Do I have a choice, Sister?" Tyana asked.

"No," Vershil said flatly.

Tyana took the gloves and slid them on. They fit comfortably, reaching past her wrists.

"You are never to remove these gloves. Do not touch anyone without them. For you, it is forbidden. This is part of your caste-burden. Do you understand?"

She flexed her hands in the gloves. The fabric creaked.

"I am a Warrior, Sister?"

"Yes."

"Kersa is also a Warrior?"

"Also true."

"Kersa wears no such gloves, Sister," Tyana said, opening her hands toward Vershil. "Why must I?"

"You share Kersa's caste-burden, but she does not share all of yours. This is because you belong to two castes. You are twice-blessed by Vale, and thus twice-burdened by Thea. These gloves are for your protection and the protection of others. Should you break your burden by illicitly touching a sister without your gloves, or should one of lower caste touch your bare skin, both of you will be punished."

"Punished, Sister?"

Vershil parted her coat. Inside, Tyana noticed the dull gleam of a stout pistol, the same that Vesha carried.

"If you break your caste-burden, you will be marked for your sin—," she raised a finger up to her forehead, pointing to the black diamond resting between her brows, "—as I once was."

Vershil paused, hiding the pistol again.

"Marked—to what end, Sister?" Tyana asked.

"Your status will lower until you are shunned from society. Should your marks accrue without remedy, you will be banished—and likely perish."

Tyana was silent.

"As I said, you, Tyana, are exceedingly rare. Daughters of Vale belong solely to one caste, but there are exceptions. Mixed-burden sisters have been born throughout history: Warriors among Artificers, Scribes among Keepers, and so on. But a newborn of your particular mixture has never been seen. I have taught many sisters in my lifetime, and you are my student for a reason. Your full burden will be apparent to all once your hair grows in, and they will know you by your colors. Until then, your caste-sisters will not realize your true nature. I suggest you do not offer it idly. On that day they may become jealous of you; they may even despise you."

"How do you know all this?"

"I reviewed your bodily profile. It was collected by

Vesha when you were retrieved."

Tyana paused, looking at her gloved hands.

"If I am not solely a Warrior, Sister, what else am I?"

She felt Vershil's gaze on her.

"You are one of the Vestal caste, and thus inherited the Vestal touch, which is a power that must never be shared with the other castes. The Vestals belong to Mater Thea alone; their powers are Hers, and Hers are theirs. Their hair is black. Only seven exist at a time, and the seventh will be taken by Thea soon. You are her replacement."

Tyana stared at her gloved hands. They slowly closed into fists. The leather in them creaked.

"Do you need more to drink and eat?"

"Yes, Sister."

"I will prepare it for you."

VI

TYANA STAYED WITH Vershil, sleeping in quarters provided for her. She ate breakfast each morning and studied during the day, afternoon, and evening. She was not allowed to leave.

She learned that their race consisted of five castes, each with its associated color and duties. Every task was determined by caste, and no caste was allowed to share in another's work.

Industry consisted of oceanic agriculture, mining, and engineering. Nearly all of this was done by Artificers, the worker caste. Artificers produced machines and tools for the other castes, and also produced fine goods and architecture. There were few exceptions to this.

During all this Tyana was not allowed to remove her gloves, even when not in Vershil's presence.

On some evenings, while Vershil was away for reasons she would not explain, Tyana left her studies to stand on the balcony. She leaned against the railing, watching waves crash against the cliffside below. Ships flew into the city's mouth to port.

At night, she slept restlessly. She had persistent, recurring dreams. Each was a reprise of her birth dream. Mater Vale would appear, but was always blown away with the wind and replaced by Mater Thea, rising from the ocean. Mater Thea would crash her scepter on Tyana, and Tyana would wake up in bed, sweating.

One of those nights, deciding not to sleep because she knew the same dreams would come, Tyana turned on her night-lamp and sat up in bed. She still wore her gloves.

She threw off the covers and stood, walking over to the full-length mirror on the wall.

Her body was pale, white—almost colorless. Her eyes were bright cyan. Her legs and arms were long and slender. Her hair was starting to grow in; a violet halo surrounded her head now, and she ran her hand over it. Each follicle sensed her touch. She traced her form with her hands, still gloved.

She was breastless and androgynous, with no nipples or navel.

Her fingers traveled down her torso, toward her hip. At its termination, between her thighs, she felt the skin. She felt no sensation except for pressure where her fingers touched. She had no genitalia; the crux of her hips consisted of only thick muscle.

Hesitantly, she took one hand to the other. She took one glove off and let it drop to the floor. Her hand felt strange without it.

She placed her hand on the skin of her torso. Its touch felt warm, even hot, as she traced it downward. A tingle mounted as she did so, building wherever it went. She reached downward at her hips. The heat rose gradually as she pressed. It grew into a tingling ecstasy. Hallucinations appeared; swirling colors mounted at the edges of her vision. They faded as soon as she stopped.

She paused, staring at herself in the mirror. She looked at her hand again, flexing it. She took a deep breath and brought her fingers down again to the base of her hip. This time she pressed harder. The colors returned. A wave of sensation rippled outward from her core. The visions changed; patterns formed and motifs appeared at her vision's edges, working their way in. They echoed on each other and built up in intensity, complexity, and brightness.

Tyana removed her hand and, just as quickly as they came, the hallucinations faded.

After a while, she reached down and picked up the second glove. She replaced it on her naked hand.

She crawled back into the covers and hoped for dreamless sleep.

VII

IN THE MORNING, Vershil said to her:

"I have news for you, young one. Mater Thea is dead."

Tyana stood, apprehensive.

"I arranged for you to attend Her funeral tonight at the Mater's Cathedral."

"Funeral?"

"Yes. Even the Mater's body dies. You will witness Her passing, along with the other sistren that will be there."

"Who will be there?"

"Sistren of all colors, all castes. On the occasion of the Mater's death, all castes come to worship alike. You will stand side by side with Artificers, Scribes, and Keepers. It is a rare and strenuous affair. Witnessing a new Vicar's possession affects all who come to worship."

"Possession?"

"On the occasion of a Vicar's passing, the Vestals will carry Her body to a pyre. The body will be burned in view of all. Before the body is burned, one of the Vestals

28

will offer herself to Thea. At that moment, the Vestal will produce the holy liquid *ichor*. This is the sign of Mater Thea's possession. Once she is possessed, she will be crowned. A Vestal's anointing happens once per generation. Once she is anointed, she is Thea's, through and through. You should go and witness this."

Tyana stood silent and, against her first impulses, nodded in agreement.

"Very well. Go to the cathedral at the center of the city. Follow the crowds." Vershil approached, studying Tyana's growing follicles, still visibly violet. "I do not think that others will suspect your unique caste-burden. However—"

Vershil paused.

"In case you meet another Vestal—it is rare—but if you do, treat her with respect. She is of a higher caste. Withhold yourself; if she touches you, do not resist her, but do not offer her your own. Do you understand?"

Tyana nodded. Her gloved hands clenched reflexively, then relaxed.

"Very good. Prepare yourself at sundown. I will let you know when to leave."

VIII

THAT NIGHT, TYANA departed.

Nights on Valen were not always overcast like days were. Tonight was clear. The stars were visible.

Tyana started out, wrapped up in a long robe. A thick scarf hid most of her nascent violet hair. She exited Vershil's apartment. Grand city staircases connected the downward-sloping architecture of the city. Ominous statues of long-departed sistren dotted the medians.

As Tyana descended, others poured in from the alleyways of the city—slowly at first, but then so many that she had to slow her pace. From tall and built Warriors to slight and sullen Scribes, all were dressed in garments devoid of caste and status.

As she entered the main thoroughfare, shoulder to shoulder with other sistren, the crowded group became a thronging mass. She clutched her robe as others pushed in from all sides.

The cathedral loomed ahead. It was massive. Seven-sided and twisting upward, it towered over other buildings. Ornate sculptures of bodies covered it, grasping each other, holding up the walls and buttresses. Cauldrons on either side of its entrance roared with fire. The flames, reaching high over the silent crowd, cast shadows across its architecture; stone faces gasped at Tyana as she passed underneath them.

When she reached the threshold, she looked up. The building soared upward. Sculpted faces, mouths, and torsos bulged from its corners. Stained glass windows were clutched by stone hands. Seven-sided columns held up balcony after balcony as candles ran up their sides, disappearing into tiny pinpricks. Ornate details were everywhere.

Then singing. Tyana could hear chanting voices. On the balconies stood hooded figures huddled near the columns. Their sound was melodic, wailing, and their voices amplified throughout the cathedral. High tones pierced the air and low tones shook the floor.

In the heart of the cathedral was a bronze altar. On the altar was a body with sheer fabric draped over it. Its features showed through the fabric. Long, black hair dripped over the altar's side. Tyana, even from a distance, could make out the face. Images from her birth dream flashed before her. But this face was not made of molten metal … it was flesh. Unmoving.

Behind the altar was a wide platform. On it stood seven robed figures, their faces occluded. Between them and the altar was a bronze basin.

The crowd pressed in as more gathered. The balconies filled. The chanting paused.

One of the hooded figures walked toward the basin. She lifted her hood. Her hair was black, and her face was soft and fragile.

The crowd was silent.

As she approached the basin, she stopped in front of it. Slowly, gripping its rim, she looked down below at the body.

She convulsed. Still gripping the basin, as if in pain, she stood up again. Gently, she regained her composure. Then she convulsed again. The crowd watched.

Finally, after one heavy convulsion, she stood. But this time, a black liquid dripped from the corners of her lips. She spit; a stream of it fell from her mouth and into the basin.

Tyana felt a pain in her own chest. A heat rose up into her head. She looked and saw others in the crowd nodding downward. Some gripped their sides. Visions at the corners of her eyes began to grow, black and pearlescent like oil, accumulating in a tessellated pattern.

The Vestal at the altar produced stream after stream of black *ichor*, pouring from her mouth. As she did so, the crowd was affected. Many fell over, stricken. Some sat down and prostrated themselves. Tyana herself felt overcome with discomfort and doubled over. Visions invaded her sight, building from the corners of her eyes —when she closed them, they only became sharper and clearer.

The rest of the Vestals disrobed. They approached the one at the basin. It was filling with *ichor*. Each one dipped her hands in the thick, oily substance and caressed the Vestal's hair. She was visibly weakened, gripping the basin's rim to stand.

Tyana's sight became distorted with hallucination. Her night visions appeared: Vale's face twisted, breaking into molten iron; a great, black mouth, swallowing up the sea; closed eyes belonging to an oil-slick body, opening. A ripple started from Tyana's belly and moved upward; she felt a warm liquid enter her mouth.

In desperation, she turned. She was surrounded by others on their knees or prostrating. She clambered over them, fumbling for the nearest wall. When she reached it, she clenched her abdomen and forced it to be still. Hiding against the stone, she brought her fingers to her lips. Traces of black liquid emerged at their corners.

She looked back up to the front of the cathedral. The Vestal's scalp was coated now. It was slick and black. Her eyes seemed to look far away at something distant as her body shivered.

Her eyes lowered and fixated on the body on the altar. With *ichor* dripping down her neck, back, and face, the Vestal approached it. She knelt down at Thea's body and placed her hands on it. Black drips fell on the sheer fabric. The Vestal paused and then rose again.

Addressing the crowd, she announced:

"I am your Mater. Fall down at me, children, and worship."

The chanting voices wailed. The crowds threw themselves to the floor. Tyana shivered, gripping the stone wall as she watched. She closed her eyes.

IX

TYANA STOOD AT the mouth of the cathedral where the Mater's old body burned on its pyre. The crowds were gone; only she and a few straggling onlookers remained.

She watched the flames lick the corpse. Thea's features were still clear even as they faded into embers and ash. She expected the face to turn to her, silent in its moment of death, and stare at her with flame-ridden eyes. But the face did not move. It was expressionless; it faded in clarity with each minute as the flames did their work.

She felt someone approach from her left.

"What do you think of this sacred pyre, sister?"

"What will happen when it burns down?" she replied in question, still watching the flames.

"Her body will be encased with stone," said the other, "—or, what remains of it."

"And then?" Tyana asked.

"The stone visage will be laid to rest in the cathedral walls. Her bodily remains will be sculpted as they were in

34

life, and they will be counted as one of the Vicar's many incarnations."

"Does she always look the same when she burns?"

The hooded onlooker paused.

"*She* will always remain the same," she said, emphasizing the Mater's correct pronoun, "even though each Vestal She possesses is unique." She paused again. "In the end, we are overcome by the same spirit."

Tyana said, under her breath:

"And me?"

The onlooker turned to her.

"You are a Warrior, aren't you? You belong to Thea, but you are Her tool, Her weapon. You are here to keep Her dominion safe from those marauding barbarians outside our space. Or are you too young to have learned that yet?"

Tyana, antagonized, turned to the hooded figure at her left.

"I see the Mater in dreams. I do not need you to tell me what She says, nor to tell me what She desires of me."

The hooded figure paused.

"In dreams?"

Tyana turned away again.

"It is nothing you could know. They are my own."

"It is everything I should know," said the other. "I, too, hear and see the Mater—even when She is gone."

"Give me a reason to believe you can know my mind."

The companion paused, seeming to look about them. They were alone. She removed her hood.

"My mind belongs to the Mater. Tell me, how do you know Hers?"

Tyana looked. Standing next to her was a fragile,

beautiful girl, shorter than her, with nascent hair. It was black.

Tyana stopped short:

"You're a Vestal—"

The girl replaced the hood.

"You can tell even in this dim light. I hear Warriors have the sharpest sight among the castes."

Tyana paused.

"My apologies—I suppose I came coldly," Tyana said. The girl waved her hand.

"What is your name, sister?"

"Tyana."

"I am Ahnsair." The girl moved closer to Tyana. "How old are you?"

"I am three months," Tyana said.

"Two, myself. Who is your teacher?"

"Vershil, the Keeper."

"A fine Keeper and instructor—first in rank among her caste. I have heard only good things about her wisdom and guidance on the War Council."

Tyana said nothing.

"Tell me, Tyana—if you are a Warrior, how do you know Thea's mind?"

Tyana watched the embers on the pyre.

"I do not know how, nor why I know it. It was always there."

"Always there—from birth?"

Tyana paused.

"Isn't it the same for all of us?"

"It is for my caste only," Ahnsair said, moving closer. "We Vestals belong solely to Thea. We purify ourselves and perform rituals daily with Her and before Her, constantly reminded that we are to remain free and clear of Vale so we can be fully possessed by her sister, Thea. No other caste needs such dedication."

Tyana said nothing and Ahnsair continued:

"Even Warriors—while you defend Thea's dominion, you don't know Thea's mind—only her instruction and eternal desire for recompense. So I ask you again: how do you, a Warrior, hear the Mater in dreams, or know Her desires without instruction?"

Tyana huddled inside her robe.

"Something only I can know."

"It would be easy enough to ask your teacher, since she confers with the Mater personally on the War Council—" Ahnsair paused. "Yet something tells me there is another reason."

Tyana felt Ahnsair reach up toward her. Tyana darted away, but Ahnsair's fingers landed on Tyana's neck. Instantly, a pleasurable and tingling sensation radiated from the spot. Tyana felt her muscles seize; her voice faltered.

"Our power may be subtler than the Warriors'," Ahnsair said, "but it is stronger."

Ahnsair reached with a full grip over Tyana's scalp. Tyana thought to resist, but her muscles refused her intent. Ahnsair's fingers moved up her ear, near Tyana's temple, parting the roots of her hair. Lines and colors sharpened at the corners of Tyana's vision, and she closed her eyes to push them away. It did not work.

Ahnsair let out a small gasp:

"You have black in your hair, Tyana."

She retracted her grip. Tyana shuddered as she did so.

"Your poor eyesight deceives you," she said, recovering herself.

"Do not insult me," said Ahnsair. "The firelight shows

your colors; you're burnt with the Mater's holy presence. Your colors are clear to me; I can see both violet and black on your scalp—and I have no explanation for it."

"Neither do I."

"Your teacher will," Ahnsair said. "Fair chance I have asking her at the Council, since she will tell me."

"My matters are my own, Sister Ahnsair," Tyana said, drawing up her full height. "I ask you not to pry."

"I will pry only in what will be common knowledge if I'm right. And if I'm wrong, nothing will come of it. Who are you to protest?"

Tyana wanted to, but no words came to her. She turned to the pyre, tugging at her hood.

"You may not admit it, but you have a special relationship to my caste and to our Mater. You cannot ignore it forever. Perhaps I will see you again?"

"Perhaps," Tyana said.

Ahnsair laughed quietly. Then she left Tyana alone.

X

Tyana delayed returning to Vershil's apartment. Instead, she walked away from the cathedral, following the moonlight along the empty streets. The city was devoid of activity. The funeral-goers had left for sleep.

She followed the stone streets, down past the city's main plaza. As she went farther, the buildings became old and decrepit. Some were crumbling at their foundations, covered in vines and grass.

The moonlit streets led her close to the cliff's face, downward toward the foot of the city. When the streets finally ended, their stone-paved surfaces gave way to encroaching grass. The edge of the city faded into black mounds held fast by long grass and crooked, windswept trees.

Tyana could hear the crash of the sea below. She peered close to the edge. Beyond the grassy precipice, the thick, black sea crashed against the crags below. The moonlight glinted off the glassy, shattered rocks.

Testing one tree, Tyana placed her foot on its trunk,

then its nearest, thickest branch. She pulled and nestled herself up into it. Its coniferous branches brushed gently against her hood with the wind.

She inhaled and closed her eyes. She listened to the waves. No unwelcome visions appeared as she listened. Embracing the silent, unmoving blackness behind her eyelids, she smiled. The air was still.

Then something rustled in the grass. Her eyes snapped open.

Looking behind her, Tyana saw a flash of red and white. She slid down from the tree branch, holding herself low to the ground.

She peered above the grass. Everything was quiet.

"Who's there?" she announced.

Nothing replied. The grass was still.

Slowly, Tyana walked forward. She drew her robes close and scanned ahead. She stepped forward, watching the grass closely.

Something brushed against her ankle. She heard a sharp inhale. Someone scurried away from her.

Tyana instinctively reached out and instantly caught something: a handful of long, thick, crimson hair.

"Let go!"

"Why were you watching me?" Tyana said.

"I wasn't! Why're you watching me?"

"I'm not," she said.

"Then let go!"

"Only if you will tell me why you are here," Tyana said.

The red-haired girl, shorter than Tyana by a head, strained against her, cupping the wrist that held her hair.

"I'll tell you only if you tell no one I was here," she said.

Tyana paused. The girl's speech was strange and halting, even broken. She caught a glimpse of the girl's bright blue eyes. The girl was holding her breath.

Tyana relaxed her grip. As soon as she did, the girl darted away.

"Stop!"

Tyana outran her easily. She caught up and tackled her. They tumbled into the grass with a struggle. As they fought, Tyana felt her skin brush briefly against the girl's.

Finally, with some effort, Tyana grabbed both of the girl's wrists and held them in place, her body pinning down the other's easily. She pulled the girl's arms tight, restraining her. Tyana was naturally stronger and heavier.

"Stop it," Tyana said.

"Promise you won't hurt me, Warrior!"

"Why would I do that?"

"Because that's what you always do when you get the chance."

The girl tired and Tyana got a look at her face. Her features were nestled within a sculpted but subtle jawline set by wide cheekbones. She looked younger than Tyana, and had brilliant, vermillion-colored hair bursting from her scalp. It was collected in twisted, fraying locks.

"I am not like every one of my kind."

"Aren't you a Warrior?"

"At least."

Tyana watched as the girl peered at Tyana's scalp. Tyana said:

"What's your name?"

"You tell me yours first."

Tyana paused.

"Mine is Tyana."

"—Numa," the sister said, flexing her wrists. "My name's Numa. Now will you let me go?"

"As long as you tell me what this place is."

"Fine!"

Tyana let go and stood up. The sister scurried a few paces but then paused, looking up at Tyana. Tyana didn't move.

"Are you an Artificer?" Tyana asked.

"If you couldn't tell," said Numa.

"You're the first of your kind I've met."

Numa relaxed a little and got up on her feet.

"You shouldn't be here. It's not right for you," Numa said.

"What if I prefer it here?" Tyana replied. "Besides, you're here."

"Easier for me than a Warrior. These are the city's ends. It's forbidden for your Sistren to come here."

"We are outside," said Tyana. "Isn't it also forbidden for Artificers to leave the lower depths?"

Numa glared at Tyana.

"So we're both in a place we shouldn't be," Numa said. "What now?"

"Tell me about this place," said Tyana.

"What is there to tell? We're beyond the old city. There's nothing but ruins here now. This is where my sisters used to live before we were banned to the city below."

Tyana looked around. Mounds lay underneath the trees, squeezed into dust by the roots. Some betrayed themselves as the foundations to forgotten buildings.

"Why were the Artificers sent below?"

"An edict of Her black crown, Mater Thea," Numa sneered. "Long ago. It's how it's always been for us."

"Is that why you come here now?"

"I like the fresh air," Numa said. "And I like being alone. Is that so much to ask from an Artificer?"

"It is all I was looking for myself," Tyana said, sitting down in the grass.

"Weren't you worshipping at Thea's funeral?" asked Numa. "I think I saw you there."

Tyana looked up at the sky. The smaller moon was shining bright, standing in front of the larger, dark one.

"I was there. I would not call it worship."

"What would you call it, then?"

Tyana said nothing and instead glared at Numa.

"Fine, I see your mood. Why did you come here? Were you looking for something?"

"I'm not sure," Tyana said. "I recognize this place, but without the city. Without the ruins. Everything else—the cliffs, the grass, the sky. Even the moons. I recognize them from my dreams."

Numa paused, studying her.

"How old are you, Tyana?"

"What of it?"

"Your hair is short. You have a Warrior's strength, but you don't talk or act like one."

Tyana pulled her scarf over her scalp a little further.

"Is it so uncommon for a Warrior to go searching for peace?"

"Every Warrior I've met just wanted to break my bones so they could brag about it later. They look for violence, not peace. That's their burden."

"I'm not sure I share that burden," Tyana said, looking up at the moons. Numa watched her carefully. Tyana continued: "What do your sisters say about this place? Do they know what it was like before Thea sent you below?"

"My Elders might tell me a different story than your Keepers."

Tyana looked at her.

"What do they say?" she pressed.

"They say that when Mater Vale made this planet, She left Her ship in the sky. In time, it broke up and turned into the smaller, white moon. Thea, when She arrived to rule over us, also left a ship, and it too broke up and it became the black moon. Some nights, Thea's moon is closer and eclipses Vale's. Other nights, like tonight, Vale's is closer. They orbit each other."

"Do you believe it?"

"My Elders have their own interpretation. Keepers tell us anything if it suits their authority."

Tyana watched above them.

"Where is Vale now?"

Numa shook her head.

"No one knows. The Keepers might say they know from the scriptures. They say She's gone to the ends of the world to sleep until Thea's rule is complete. Then She'll wake up."

"Do you believe them?"

"Why should I? There's no way to tell, anyway. We can't read the scriptures for ourselves. Only Keepers can do that."

"Why did Thea consign your sisters to the lower city?" Tyana said, changing the subject. Numa scowled.

"Thea says it is because our work is unclean. We make machines. We build tools. We gather food. We do the menial things no other caste is fit to do. Even though we sing the hymns in the cathedrals for Vestals and serve Keepers their dinner, Thea hides us from the other castes, and we never see the benefit of our arts. Otherwise, I suppose we might remind them of how easy their burdens are."

"How long ago was that?" Tyana asked.

"Ages," said Numa. "As far back as our generations can remember." Numa furrowed her brow, pausing. "You're not really a Warrior, are you?"

"What makes you say that?"

"No Warrior hides her scalp. They show off their hair every chance they get. It is their pride—even for newborns."

Tyana huddled in her scarf, saying:

"My caste is my own business. Why not mind yours?"

Numa scowled again.

"Maybe I will."

She stood up, brushing bits of grass off her stained clothes.

"I bid you well, Sister Tyana. May you find your solitude." She turned to go.

"—Where can I find you again?" Tyana said haltingly.

Numa stopped, hesitating.

"If you find yourself in the lower levels, you can ask for me. But I don't recommend going there. After all, it is beneath a Warrior such as yourself."

Tyana said nothing and watched as Numa retreated through the grass. Her pace quickened in the distance until she disappeared.

XI

TYANA FOUND HER way back to Vershil's apartment before morning. She snuck in quietly so she would not alert her teacher.

On waking and descending from her room, she saw her teacher standing on the balcony, sullen.

"I did not hear you return last night," Vershil said.

"The funeral was long," Tyana returned. "I watched the pyre until there was nothing left."

"And?" Vershil said. Tyana paused.

"I met one of the Vestals."

Vershil turned to her, expectant.

"What did she say to you?"

Tyana joined her teacher on the balcony. The seas below the city frothed and the fog rolled in, obscuring the city's spires below.

"She may know my true colors."

"That is inevitable," said Vershil. "In time, your hair will grow out. Warriors pride themselves in showing their hair—it is up to you how to wear it."

Vershil gestured to a table behind them on which were two cups of steaming water.

"There is tea I brewed."

Tyana retrieved the mugs of warm water. They contained whole seaweed leaves, steeping until the water turned green. She handed one to her teacher.

"When sisters are multi-colored," said Vershil, "their colors are not balanced. There is a primary and a secondary color. You are a Warrior first, a Vestal second."

"You know this because..." Tyana began.

"Your biological profile was handed to me when you arrived," said Vershil.

"Which you can read?" Tyana asked.

"In a way." Vershil sipped her tea. "My role as a Keeper is to divine knowledge from images. When images are certain, so is the interpretation. The Scribes long ago received a system from Vale that creates these images with certainty. It is the foundation of our reading."

"But you cannot write?"

"Of course not. That power belongs to the Scribes. And in the same way that I can only read what I do not write, so they can only write what they do not read."

"What purpose does that serve?" Tyana asked.

"Knowledge is power, Tyana," said Vershil. "Vale separated the two castes who can read and write because of this; it takes both abilities to gain knowledge. One caste cannot corrupt the other this way."

Tyana took a sip of her tea.

"Come," Vershil said. "There is something I must show you."

XII

VERSHIL LED TYANA down to the library. It was nestled in the city's heart, past the main plaza and the Mater's Cathedral. Keepers watched Tyana as she followed behind Vershil. Some of their hushed conversations slowed or paused as they passed. Others paid no attention, gliding across the marbled floors silently in opulent gowns. Occasionally a group of Scribes would pass by, hooded and downcast, traveling in a single file or two abreast.

"The libraries are some of the oldest structures in the Mater's City," explained Vershil. "Only the Mater's Cathedral is more ancient."

They descended a set of gilded, spiraling staircases. At the bottom they came to a set of tall, heavy doors that seemed older than everything else around them.

Vershil pressed on the doors. They heaved and slowly opened, revealing a huge inner space. A massive glass mandala let light pour in from the outside, coloring it gold and cobalt blue.

"These are the libraries in the eyes of the city," Vershil explained. She turned to Tyana, beckoning, and the doors closed behind them. The mandala was large enough to span down to the floor below; a balcony allowed a view to its bottom. The oceans were visible through the mandala's aged, rippled glass. Tyana realized she was looking through the iris of the city's facade.

"Mater Vale taught the first Keepers to read in this room," said Vershil. "It is where we keep the stone scrolls once they are finished by the Scribes."

"Every stone scroll?" asked Tyana.

"No," said Vershil. "Only the most important ones."

Freestanding shelves surrounded them, filled to the brim with stone cylinders engraved with the insignia of the Scribes and Keepers. Some were larger than others. Some appeared to be untouched for ages.

"A Scribe's time is often spent recording the mundane details of transactions, statements, and deliveries. So is my time, as a Keeper, spent reading this information and counseling based on it."

Vershil approached one shelf that contained the largest, seemingly oldest cylinders. She carefully chose one and picked it up with some struggle. She placed it on a central table before Tyana. On either end of the cylinder Tyana saw the sculpted faces of the Maters: Vale on one side, her eyes closed and her expression serene; Thea on the other side, her eyes open and mouth gaping.

"This is one of the scriptures," Vershil said. Tyana looked at her.

"The ones written by Vale?"

Vershil shook her head.

"These particular scrolls do not date to that time. They are copies; the originals are lost. Stone is good at preserving the images, but they degrade eventually. They are transcribed only once every few generations. Transcription is the highest honor for a Scribe. They say the language of the scriptures is also the most difficult."

Vershil gestured to Tyana.

"Go ahead, sister Tyana. Touch it. I'll only allow this once."

Tyana looked at the stone cylinder. She approached it and, with her gloved hand, slowly ran her finger along its decorative inlays. It rapidly became too hot to the touch and the inlays flashed an angry blue and yellow light. Tyana withdrew her hand. The insignia in its center slowly faded like a lasting warning.

Tyana looked at Vershil, hurt more that her teacher would tempt her. Vershil said:

"By my word, you are clear of wrongdoing, Tyana. I beckoned you so that you would know what happens when one who is of another caste handles the scrolls. Any other time, touching one would be a sin that requires branding."

Vershil walked to the table. She traced her finger down the center line of the scroll. No insignia flashed at her. Then, with both hands, she twisted it from either side. The cylinder hissed and popped, as if a mechanical fire were lit inside. She spread the two halves apart and they glowed at their seams. Pieces of the stone lay suspended, hovering between the two poles, and light arced between each piece. Finally, with a crackle and hum, the light exploded, engulfing the room. Tyana shielded her eyes.

When Tyana lowered her gloved hands, she saw they

were surrounded by a sphere of golden letters. The letters threaded and combined among themselves, mutating from one kind of symbol to another. She reached out at one. It dissolved at her fingertips like luminous dust.

"How is this possible?" she asked.

"The work of the Maters is profound and mysterious," answered Vershil in a voice that was not entirely hers. Tyana turned—Vershil was facing her, but her eyes were nearly white, rolled into the back of her head. *"They gave us power over stone for writing, for reading, and for the mechanisms to control each."*

The symbols congealed. They turned into images of oceans, trees, and barren cliffsides. It looked like Valen to Tyana, but perhaps when it was devoid of life. It was like witnessing a memory projected around them.

"I saw fit to create a pure race, a race of children," Vershil recited, *"sequestered from the barbarism of humanity that plagued us."*

Tyana saw flashes of faces, bodies. Bodies that reminded her of what she saw in the dark, cavernous space of the womb before she was born.

"I, Vale, took it upon myself to do this. I claimed this planet and razed it. I created new life and gave birth to new civilization."

Tyana saw Vale herself, naked, stretched out on black, smoldering dirt. Her limbs turned colors, working from the veins outward. Her fingers on one arm turned blue; her opposite arm turned yellow. Her one foot turned deep red, and dark purple spread from the other.

"I formed the castes to divide my children. I gave each a burden to bear."

The colors met in her torso, moving up her head, which turned black.

"I gave them my sister, who rules with ichor *and cunning. They will suckle at my soul. They will see me in dreams and seek the praise of my sister. By her rule, they will live forever."*

Tyana watched with growing dread as Vale's features turned into Thea's. Vale's body slowly dissolved, leaving only her head.

"Here we learn," said Vershil, now in her own voice, "the Rule of Obedience, which staves off our burdens. This is obedience to Vale's holy sister, Thea. In order to fulfill our longing for Vale, we must obey the Vicar."

Tyana looked at Vershil, whose eyes had returned to normal.

"Where is Mater Vale now?"

"She is gone. She lies atop the world. As it says—"

Vershil's eyes disappeared again.

"I was whipped up by wind and stolen from my daughters so that my sister may return and conquer all."

"Conquer whom?" Tyana asked.

"Humanity," answered Vershil.

The images shifted again. Tyana saw four bodies now, again naked, standing on the blackened earth. Their colored hair showed their castes. They encircled a fifth, huddled in a pool of *ichor*.

"I colored each: vermillion, violet, amber, and sapphire, according to their burdens. Their conscience is perfect. In their perfection I lost myself. I laid my spirit in them so I could guide their fate. I gave them my sister who rules with sacred sin. I will call on them through dreams in the final days."

Vershil paused, then explained:

"We are all made in the image of Vale, but where She is whole and one, we are disparate and many. The castes make up Her new body for the sake of all living things. To be a child of Vale is to realize your place in that body, and to take up your burden: the sacred duty that cures the sin that binds you."

"Why does the text speak of sin and—dreams?"

"You hesitate, Warrior," said Vershil inquisitively. "Why? Do you fear your dreams?"

Tyana paused. Then:

"Yes."

"That is good. Your Warrior instructors will teach you not to fear. Fear of dreams is different from fear of the enemy. Fear of dreams shows reverence to Mater Thea. We all fear the dream that comes to us at birth. It reveals the original sin that becomes our burden for life. That burden is staved off by carrying out our duties to our caste. That obedience leads us back to Vale."

Tyana stared at the luminous image around them. The girl in the pool of *ichor* was weeping. Her tears were black.

"I don't understand," Tyana said.

"Most do not," replied Vershil. "That is why I am here to interpret it for you."

Tyana's brow turned sharp. She asked:

"If each caste is disparate, then are their burdens also different?"

"Yes—good. Do you know them?"

"I know only one."

"Say it," said Vershil.

Tyana remembered her birth dream: the burning, molten image of Thea; the faceless girls; the head of the tan-skinned man atop Thea's scepter.

"Violence—?" she whispered.

Vershil's eyes bored into Tyana.

"Tell me what happened in your dream. Each detail."

Tyana hesitated. What would Vershil make of her

dream—her refusal to worship Thea? Her spilling the basin of *ichor*? Her defense against the faceless girls? The tan man was like nothing she'd seen since.

"In my dream," she began, "I saw Mater Vale. She was taken away from me. When Mater Thea came, She came with a group of young sisters who had no faces."

Vershil's gaze held steady.

"They presented me with a knife," Tyana said, lying. "When Thea asked for my worship, I took it in my hands and I cut myself with it. I remember my white blood dripping on the grass."

Tyana looked Vershil in the eye. Vershil's gaze relented—she even smiled.

"Good. Your dream is like I expected. Self-mutilation in the presence of Thea is a common response for a Warrior in the birth dream. The faceless sisters you saw, however, were the seven Vestals. Only the Vestals encounter them in their dreams. Since you are of both castes, your dream contains both."

Vershil paced, continuing, as Tyana let out a quiet exhale.

"The source of the Warrior's affliction is self-hatred. The Warrior will blame herself for the loss of Vale. She will commit violence against herself because of this. Your transgression must be turned away from yourself and toward Thea's enemies. As long as you do that, you will stave off your sin and fulfill your burden."

"What happens if I don't?"

"Then your own sin will consume you. As a Warrior, it may even kill you."

"And the faceless ones?"

"They are faceless because the Vestals are vessels for Thea and Her identity, not their own. Their presence in your dream shows a special relationship to their caste, even while you are a Warrior. It only makes sense they would present a knife to you."

Tyana didn't say anything.

"The dreams are different for each caste, and the caste for a newborn is dictated by her response to Thea in the dream. The sin of the Artificers is madness. They become manic at the sight of Thea in their dreams, so they spend their lives working machines and building tools, toiling for the greater society. Without the focus and regimen of their work, they would go insane.

"For Scribes, it is ignorance. They do not recognize Thea at first sight. So their burden is to write, record, and memorize. They defeat their sin not only by copying the scriptures, but by recording every activity, every note of trade, and every piece of history. Without this, without the regimen of writing, they would wander away from society, listless, disengaged, and eventually they would decay.

"For Keepers, like myself, it is arrogance. We govern cities, preside over councils, and safeguard knowledge. We are the highest caste after the Vestals, yet we are bound to Thea's laws like any other sister. Were a Keeper to claim more power than she should, she would encroach on the powers of the Vicar Herself and be destroyed. For all the knowledge and power we have, Thea's presence casts a shadow over us that elicits our humility."

"And Vestals?" Tyana asked.

"For the Vestals, it is lewdness. They must remain untainted vessels for Thea's possession. For them, any kind of sin is contagious. This is why they are isolated from other castes."

"If lewdness is their sin, then what is their burden?" Tyana asked. Vershil stopped.

"You already know," she said, looking at Tyana's hands.

Tyana flexed her hands, feeling the creak of the gloves. Vershil continued:

"When the time comes, the Vestals themselves will instruct you in how to use your burden. I as a scholar have limited help for you in this matter. But know that when the time is right, you will understand its use."

Tyana brought her hands up and rubbed one within the other. Some of the creases in her gloves were beginning to show their wear.

"You said that I was the only sister who ever had these two colors."

Vershil nodded solemnly.

"How do I carry these burdens, then? If each caste knows its burden and they are so clear, how do I interpret my colors? What purpose did the Maters give me?"

"No one can tell you why the Maters chose these colors for you. This is the added trouble of the multi-burdened. You must find it out for yourself."

"What do the scriptures say?"

Vershil paused, hesitating. Then the images around them changed. The vistas and smoldering earth faded. Replacing them was a pearlescent oil slick, full of all colors, abstract and seemingly formless, but slowly moving. It surrounded them on all sides. Vershil's eyes disappeared again.

"The children of many colors are fit to me because they fulfill my special tasks set unto them. You will recognize their colors readily, but not their burdens."

Vershil's eyes reappeared.

"That's all?" Tyana asked.

"That is all."

"Surely there must be more."

Vershil sighed.

"The mention of multi-burdened ones only appears once in the scriptures. The passage itself is murky and hard to interpret. Many Keepers do not even believe there are multi-burdened ones simply because there are so few verses that cite it."

"Have they not seen me?" Tyana scoffed.

"No, they haven't, *sister*," Vershil replied sharply, emphasizing the lesser form of address. "Multi-burdened sisters almost never occur in a generation. There are so few that, if they are born, they are often spectacles for the rest of their caste. Worse, your colors are an artifact no scholar can recall, even if they read every scroll in this room. Have you seen the sisters stare while you walk with me? They don't long for your newborn youth. They see your nascent hair and don't know whether to greet you with a Warrior's embrace or stay away for fear of spreading their sin like a plague."

Tyana bowed her head.

"Forgive me, Sister."

Vershil sighed again.

"I accept your apology. Your burden is simply not as clear according to the traditional rules. With the little history we have of the multi-burdened, yours is a puzzle —even to me."

Vershil's gaze softened and she approached Tyana.

"I will tell you this, at least. I have lived long enough to see many generations and mentor many newborns. But when I was young and still a student I knew a multi-burdened sister. She was my teacher."

"Your teacher was multi-burdened?"

Vershil nodded.

"Her name was Weira. Her colors were blue and yellow, all but evenly mixed—a Keeper and a Scribe. She could both copy words and read them. Imagine it— whatever she wrote, she could interpret. She oversaw the transcription of many scrolls. Libraries across the hemisphere are populated by her work alone. She controlled the shipping of those scrolls personally, and if there was any failure or damage, she could repair the scrolls herself. She is gone now. But when she lived, she made a name for herself, even though she was heckled in her youth."

Vershil hesitated, then gently clasped Tyana's gloved hands in her own.

"I cannot tell you how your burdens will help you stave off your sin. That is your journey and yours alone. But I can tell you that I believe the more grievous the sin, the greater Vale's redemption is for us. If you strive for it, She will grant it to you. I witnessed what one multi-burdened Sister was capable of, and I chose you as my student for a reason."

She let Tyana's hands go.

"Come. That's enough of a lesson for today."

XIII

THE GRASS WAS soft underneath Tyana's feet. She looked up at the clear night sky. The stars were brighter than normal, and Valen's two moons hovered overhead. The larger, darker one eclipsed the white one.

She peered over the cliffside. It was devoid of life. Trees had not grown yet nor been swept crooked by the wind. The craggy spires on the coast still had their obsidian, glassy sheen. They hadn't yet been eroded by years of water and salt crashing against their foundations.

She heard a whimper in the distance behind her.

She turned around. Off in the grassy field was a white figure hunched over, sitting. Tyana walked toward her.

As she got closer the grass parted; the figure was naked and bald. She was holding her face in her hands, surrounded by a pool of *ichor*.

"Who are you?" Tyana asked the girl. She didn't respond. She was weeping.

Tyana squatted down next to her just beyond the pool

of black liquid.

"What's wrong?" Tyana asked.

"She watches," said the girl in the pool.

"Who watches?"

"Thea. Thea watches," said the girl, whimpering. Her tears seeped through her fingers. They were black.

Tyana hesitated, wondering how she could comfort her.

"Why? What does Thea watch for?"

The girl looked up, and Tyana's breath caught in her throat. The girl's face was Tyana's own.

"You," said the girl. "Thea watches for *you*."

Tyana faltered backward. The pool of *ichor* quivered and began to move up the skin of the girl. It covered her like tar. It engulfed her torso, her neck, and finally her face. The girl stood up. She opened her mouth, then her eyes. They glowed like cyan-colored fire. She let out an inhuman cry—

Tyana sat up in bed, covered in sweat. Her body tingled with remnants of the dream. The sensation of grass faded into the touch of silk covers at her feet.

She got up. Her little room in Vershil's apartment was lit only by a blue night-light. She looked up through the small skylight in the ceiling. The night sky was overcast. No stars were visible. She ran a hand through her hair, grown enough now to be visibly purple with sections of black.

It was then that Vershil walked in unceremoniously, holding a lantern for light. It cast shadows everywhere.

"Tyana," said Vershil.

"Yes, Sister?" Tyana responded.

"Come with me."

Vershil left, leaving the door open. Bemused and in

her nightclothes, Tyana followed.

She descended the spiraling staircase of the apartment where Vershil waited below. When she got to the bottom, Tyana saw a cadre of Warriors waiting there.

"Vershil?" Tyana said, concerned. Vershil turned to her:

"Tyana, your time under my tutelage has ended. It is time for you to begin training for the caste you were born into."

Tyana looked at the Warriors. They were fearsome and tall; many had tattoos over their faces.

"You are to study under Verikash, First Warrior and representative of your caste to the War Council."

"Vershil—"

"There is no discussion here," Vershil interrupted. "You will be taken to the city where all Warriors are trained. You will stay there until you come back a true member of your caste."

Vershil motioned to the group. Two of them came forward. They clutched Tyana by the arms.

"Vershil, please—"

One holding Tyana interrupted:

"If she really does belong to our caste."

"You must never touch her unclothed hands," Vershil said to the Warrior. "Do not remove her gloves."

"It is the only part of her we will not remove," retorted the other.

They forced Tyana to the exit. Tyana looked back at Vershil; her stern gaze was tempered by a subtle softness, but she said nothing. Then the door closed.

XIV

THE WARRIORS BOARDED a ship with Tyana in tow. They sat her in a curved antechamber that reminded her of the cell she was brought to the city in. The only difference was that she was free to wander the ship under the watchful eyes of other Warriors. Based on their looks, she decided to stay put. She instead watched the landscape pass by through the antechamber windows. Rocky cliffsides turned into an endless horizon of foggy seas. She wondered what waited on the other side.

Footsteps down the hall preceded someone's presence.

"So you weren't just a Warrior after all," said one, joining her. Tyana recognized her. It was the same one who first brought her to Vershil.

"Kersa," Tyana said.

Kersa grinned. She was dressed in the standard garb of a Warrior: part segmented armor, part tunic.

"Here I thought those Keepers were being overly cautious. Now I know why they treated you like expensive cargo."

"Has much changed?" Tyana asked.

"Not that I can see."

Kersa sat opposite Tyana.

"Can't hide the hair much more, can you?"

Tyana tugged at her hood. Her hair and its mixed colors were easily discernible without it.

"Has anyone mentioned it to you?" Kersa asked.

"No," Tyana said.

"They will," Kersa said, her grin disappearing. "And you—," Kersa said, looking Tyana up and down, "—you are smaller compared to most. Don't expect Verikash to go easy on you just because you're mixed with a higher caste."

"I don't expect it."

"Vershil may have given you a charmed life at the Mater's City. All those readings from scrolls and fine food —you'll have none of that where we are going. Training is meant to break your body and mind. It is possible to fail."

"What happens to those who fail?"

"They are never coronated—and what good to the Mater is a Warrior who doesn't reach coronation?"

Kersa stood and came close to Tyana.

"I don't know what purpose or powers you have, little one. But I know a Warrior when I meet one. Whatever reason the Mater gave you this color, hold onto that reason. Hold onto it especially when you think you can't hold on any longer."

Kersa gazed sternly at Tyana. With trepidation, Tyana finally nodded. Then Kersa walked away.

Tyana looked back out the window. She could see the city breaking into view. It was carved into a cliffside, but its similarity to the Mater's City ended there. A series of harsh, geometric cubes jutted from the cliff face. They faded into the side of the cliff and waves lapped at their edges. Inside, slits and crevasses gave off pinpricks of light. The facade had none of the organic presence of the Mater's City. Instead, it was brutal and austere, jutting out against the black cliffs.

Tyana watched as they entered the city's shadow, heading for its center. Its darkness filled the antechamber and surrounded Tyana.

Then a knock on the wall came behind her. She turned to face a different Warrior, who said:

"It's time for you to meet your new teacher."

XV

AFTER THEY DOCKED, the group of Warriors led Tyana, cloaked with a hood, out of the ship. Kersa led them. The docking platform extended out a long, undecorated causeway. Tyana could see over its edge. The sea here was choppy, frothing against the cliffs below. The air was colder than that at the Mater's City and it carried salt up from the spray.

When they reached the entrance, two Warriors stood guard with weapons at a wide gate. A third, whose armor was slightly different, stood center and ahead of them, watching the incoming group.

They reached the gate. Tyana was surrounded by Warriors on all sides and was the shortest among them. The center guard gave her a stern look up and down. She addressed Kersa:

"Who comes?"

"The initiate Tyana," she said, "who was accepted by her teacher Verikash."

Tyana watched silently. The guard looked from Kersa

to Tyana, then back. The guard unceremoniously nodded in the direction of the gate. The group moved forward. As they did so, Tyana peered at the guard's armor. She had a stone collar around her neck. She carried no visible weapons.

Tyana looked ahead as they entered the gate. They entered a narrow hallway, black and undecorated from floor to ceiling. Tyana could see it branched off to her left and right into similarly dark, featureless hallways.

They kept going. Tyana could see a clearing and light ahead. When they entered it, the space overwhelmed her. It was a massive open arena with raised platforms like an amphitheater. They were stacked with rows and rows of Warriors. There was another in the center alone, sitting.

The group led Tyana toward the center. They stopped and Kersa stepped aside, looking at Tyana. She gestured subtly with her head toward the central platform. Tyana took a step forward.

"Who comes?" said the lone Warrior. She wore no armor and her tunic appeared to be incomplete, even in tatters. Tattoos were thick all over her body. Tyana hesitated.

Kersa poked Tyana in the back, pushing her forward. Tyana walked, regaining her composure.

"Tyana—the initiate," she said finally, a few paces from the platform. The Warrior stood.

"*Tyana*," she repeated. "Interesting name."

The Warrior stepped down from the platform. She was barefoot.

"I've never heard of a Warrior with a name like that. Are you sure it's a Warrior's name?"

Tyana didn't answer.

"My Sister Vershil who sits on the War Council sent

you to me. She told me you were a Warrior. Was she wrong?"

She approached Tyana. Her hair was long and thick. In some places it was matted and locked together.

Tyana didn't answer.

"Let me tell you my name," she said as she got close. "It's Verikash. That's a Warrior's name."

Tyana tried to meet Verikash's gaze. When she did, Verikash's full lips spread in a wide grin across her face, full of teeth.

"See me? Good."

Verikash paced around Tyana, addressing the room:

"No need to hide here. We are proud Warriors. We wear our hair openly, however we wish. You should as well."

Tyana's reflex sprang into action, but Verikash was faster. She had already pulled Tyana's hood down.

"What's this?" Verikash feigned surprise. The room murmured. She reached out and touched Tyana's hair, flattening and parting it. "Is this a Warrior's hair? Are these a Warrior's colors?"

Tyana's body clenched, holding back the urge to brush away Verikash's hand. Then the hand gripped the hair.

"I said," Verikash hissed into Tyana's ear, "are these *colors*—?"

Verikash emphasized the plurality. Then she let go. Tyana answered:

"Vershil isn't the only one who calls me a Warrior."

Tyana thought of Kersa, but dared not look behind at her.

Verikash paused, then paced again. Her grin reappeared.

"Do you know I sit on the War Council? Across from

Vershil, next to Mater Thea's hand?"

Tyana didn't answer.

"Every war operation is conducted under my review. Every raid. Every battle. If I ground a warbird, it does not fly. If I stay your blade, you do not draw it. But this place—"

Verikash raised her hands, gesturing to the Warriors around them.

"This place is *our* hall. We are free to do as we wish here. Free to fight each other—as we wish." The room murmured again in agreement. She turned back to Tyana:

"I do not care what my sisters do here as long as they do not deprive each other of life or ability. I do not care what colors you have in your hair as long as one of them is ours. I make only one requirement: that if you walk through our hall's gates, you are a Warrior, through and through."

Verikash gestured to a Warrior off to the side. She brought over two short staffs.

"Having a Warrior's color is only proof Mater Vale bore you to be one. You must prove to me you can walk the path."

Verikash took the staffs and threw one toward Tyana. She caught it.

"Prove it."

Tyana looked around, aware of all the eyes boring into her. Verikash held her staff crosswise in front of her. Her whole body seemed ready to pounce.

"Come on—I'll even go without the staff. Make it easy for you." She threw down the staff, kicking it away. She gestured at herself. "Prove it."

Tyana hesitated at first, then lunged forward. Verikash

dodged, matching Tyana's movement.

Tyana lunged again, this time downward with the staff. Verikash deftly moved out of the way. Someone laughed.

Tyana circled around the tattooed Warrior, swinging the staff but contacting nothing but air. Verikash matched Tyana's movements without strain.

Then Verikash caught the staff and, with a lurch, sent it back up into Tyana's face. It contacted Tyana's cheekbone just below the eye, knocking her downward. The shock and speed of it kept Tyana down until Verikash said:

"You have to prove it to me."

Tyana looked up, clutching the staff. She assumed a stronger stance. She lunged, but Verikash caught it again. With a pivot of her body, she sent it back, striking Tyana in the collarbone. Tyana went down again, the first blow already stinging.

Verikash grinned.

"Come on—one more try before I pick up my staff."

Tyana, now in trepidation of making any movement, stood up, still clutching her staff. She steadied herself and, after a pause, aimed at Verikash from a different direction. Verikash caught the blow and redirected the staff out of Tyana's hands and into her own, landing its end in rapid succession against Tyana's diaphragm, shoulder, and jaw.

Tyana was now on the ground, gasping for breath and bleeding. Verikash frowned. She dropped the staff.

"These weapons bore me. Maybe I'll use mine another time. Looks like that's all you can take for now."

Verikash walked up to Tyana, who was getting up to her knees. She whispered into her ear:

"Remember, Tyana—you have to prove you're a Warrior. If you can't, you're no use to me."

Tyana coughed.

Verikash, still frowning, briskly walked away, announcing to the room:

"Be gentle with her, sisters. She seems fragile."

XVI

"I TOLD YOU she wouldn't go easy on you."

Kersa sponged away the dried blood from Tyana's cheek.

"I was hardly a match for her."

"Your smaller size won't earn you pity."

"Does she instruct only by way of beatings?" Tyana asked.

Kersa pressed the sponge a bit. It stung and Tyana tried not to wince.

"It's not a beating. She teaches you right movements from wrong movements. Wrong movements hurt."

Kersa sighed quietly.

"Verikash is a strong Warrior. If you show any weakness of will, it'll only embolden her—and others."

"I have to learn to fight in order to fight."

"You will. You will learn from her. You will learn from all of us. Sometimes it's with words, sometimes it's without."

"For how long?"

"For as long as necessary."

Kersa rinsed the sponge in the basin, then moved onto suturing Tyana's jaw. She winced visibly as Kersa began, who only scowled in response.

"Pain is familiar to a Warrior, Tyana. You should embrace it—and hold still."

When Kersa finished, Tyana looked at her, and said:

"Thank you."

"Give me none of it," Kersa said, washing her hands with a rag. "Remember what I told you. We try to break each other here. As far as you know, I may be giving you a new set of bruises tomorrow."

"What's the use in that?"

"To build each other up," Kersa said. "Our bodies respond to stress and adapt. This place is designed to draw out your strength. It challenges you. It happens with all initiates—you'll see."

Kersa collected the suturing kit and said:

"Now stop asking questions and follow me. I'm supposed to show you to your new quarters."

Tyana followed Kersa. She led her through another long, narrow hallway, turning a few corners along the way until they came to an unassuming door that was little more than a slit in the wall. Kersa pressed her open palm against it and it opened. She motioned to Tyana to follow her inside.

Tyana's quarters were a sparse, square room. Their only defining feature aside from a bed and storage for garments was a wide but short window open to the air outside.

"How do I find my way back?" Tyana asked.

"That is up to you," Kersa said.

"Every hallway looks the same. I'm not sure where we

are."

Kersa paused, then said:

"That is the point. Good dreams, Tyana. I wish it sincerely."

Then Kersa exited through the door. It closed behind her.

Tyana felt engulfed by the darkness of the room. It was smaller than her room at Vershil's apartment. The bed sheets were simpler. But there was still a blue night-light and, as she looked through the drawers, changes of clothes.

She walked up to the window. It was high up and only tall enough to provide a view of the sky if she peered over its edge. Cool air blew in. Tyana could hear the distant ocean below and even smell its salt spray.

The sky was overcast tonight. Though the horizon glowed with their light, Tyana could not see either of the moons from her window.

XVII

Tyana woke to a loud knock at the door. It had been a dreamless sleep.

A Warrior was standing at the entrance.

"Your teacher is ready."

The Warrior departed, leaving the door open. Tyana got up and searched for her garments. They consisted of simple black pants and a short tunic.

Once she dressed, she looked outside the door. No one was nearby.

The hallways ran in both directions and seemed to be identical. She was barefoot. She stepped outside her room—the door shut behind her.

She went left first. That part of the hallway ended in a right. She followed it, which ended in another right.

After a few turns she realized that she was either going in circles or traveling toward an eventual dead end. She altered her path, noticing that some hallways were narrower than others. She followed these and fewer and fewer junctions appeared, offering only one alternate pathway.

Finally, after turning one corner, almost by chance, she entered a clearing. The opening led to a wider hallway. She breathed a sigh of relief as she recognized the arena. Her relief, however, faded nearly as quickly as it came.

She recognized Verikash ahead of her. She was not wearing the same tattered tunic Tyana saw yesterday. Today it seemed to be proper, if light, armor with a thick stone collar. Verikash was accompanied by another guard dressed in the same. Next to them both was Kersa.

"Good morning, Tyana," Verikash announced. "I see you made it to our main hall without incident?"

Tyana walked forward, apprehensive. The floor of the arena was made of thick canvas. It felt warm against her feet, even though the air was cold.

"I made my way," Tyana said.

"You'll find that these hallways are not as straightforward as one's first impression," Verikash said, walking toward Tyana. She smiled and her wide lips spread across her square jaw, revealing her teeth. Tyana said nothing. Verikash began to pace around her.

"Today is your first lesson. I will give you the same lessons as they were given to the first Warrior by Mater Vale. Do you understand?"

"Yes," said Tyana.

"Show me your stance."

Tyana looked at her feet. She spread them at an angle and sunk her weight into them.

Verikash walked around Tyana, analyzing her.

"How many legs do you have, Tyana?"

Tyana paused then, with some trepidation, answered: "Two—?"

Verikash grabbed Tyana's tunic from the back and,

with a forceful tug, Tyana was on the ground.

"Wrong. You have three legs. I just took the third one away. You may be bipedal, but the structure of a balanced stance has a third point extending from the back of your hips to the ground. It's invisible, but you can't stand without it. A Warrior must understand her body in all its parts, seen and unseen, to be effective. To do this, you must understand not only what your body is capable of, but what its limitations are."

Tyana got up.

"Where are your hands, Tyana?"

Tyana raised her hands.

Verikash's wrists came down on Tyana as a coordinated blow aimed for her collarbone. Tyana's hands were in the right place. She blocked Verikash's blow and its force sank into Tyana's feet.

"Good," Verikash said. "You followed my force and blocked it. But what if I give you more force?"

Verikash's wrists tilted toward Tyana's center. Tyana buckled as Verikash leaned in. Verikash said:

"You can't hold me, sister. Get out of my way."

Tyana shifted her weight and stepped away, allowing Verikash to follow through. Verikash smiled.

"Good. Remember to get off your prey's line of attack. Once you make contact, you can redirect their energy back into them. But if you stay put, you'll receive their full force."

Verikash gestured to the Warrior standing near Kersa.

"Try it out with our sister," Verikash said.

Tyana assumed her stance again, watching the other Warrior who was still half a head taller than her. The Warrior made a slow pass with both arms, as if she was aiming for Tyana's collarbones. Tyana blocked and deflected both of them, moving off the line of attack.

"Good. You have the right sense of balance and power. But this is much slower than usual."

Verikash pushed the Warrior aside and stood in front of Tyana.

"From now on your hands must be wherever my hands are. Follow mine—or else they might get past yours."

Verikash made the same movement again. Tyana met her wrists with her own.

"Good. Again—faster."

They did it again. Verikash repeated, again and again. The more they did it and the more force and speed Verikash gave Tyana, the more Tyana buckled. Then Verikash stopped.

"Stop. You are tense." She shook Tyana by the shoulders and slapped parts of her torso, buttocks, and legs. "Wake up the parts of your body that aren't listening. Relax them. Let your weight sink into the earth."

Tyana took a breath and readied her stance. Verikash stepped aside, assigning the Warrior again to Tyana.

"Practice."

The Warrior struck at Tyana, and Tyana blocked the blow, straining less this time. Verikash paced around them as they continued, watching Tyana's stance. She came to stop next to Kersa.

"Stop," Verikash said. "Try it with our sister, now," she said, gesturing to Kersa.

Kersa looked at Verikash, then at Tyana. Kersa stood in front of Tyana.

"Continue," Verikash said. Kersa struck at Tyana; Tyana blocked it again, moving off the line.

"Switch," said Verikash. "Tyana, you strike Kersa."

Tyana hesitated. She sank her feet into the ground, and then lunged. Kersa blocked her strike.

"Again."

Tyana did it again, and Kersa blocked, deflecting her again.

"Kersa, show our sister Tyana here what you can do with that movement."

Kersa looked at Verikash in tacit acknowledgment. Tyana struck Kersa—Kersa got off the line of the attack and redirected the force of Tyana's blow back onto her. Tyana found herself lying on her back.

Kersa offered her a hand to get back up, which Tyana accepted.

"Kersa is one of our finest grapplers," Verikash said. "You'll come to tangle with her in time—I'm sure she won't mind." Kersa shot a quizzical look at Verikash, who ignored it. "But there is more to our art than grappling. There is weaponry—staff, blade, spear, and pistol—all of which you will become proficient in. When you are ready, you may even come to use our most potent weapon, which is the very reason why Mater Thea still has Her dominion."

Tyana tried to hide her curiosity, now piqued.

"But first, we must train your stance."

XVIII

TYANA'S PERSONAL LESSONS with Verikash, often with Kersa present, were her only marker during the day. Days began to blur together, and lessons became increasingly grueling.

"Train on your own when you can," Kersa advised. "Once you join the general lessons, you'll have to keep up with everyone."

The city itself was a shifting labyrinth that created profound disorientation. Walls and hallways transformed themselves seemingly at random. Each morning, Tyana had to find her way anew. At night, Tyana could feel the floors shifting deep beneath her. Sometimes she felt them right beyond her walls.

Once, awakened at night by the sound, she opened her entrance to see a smooth, black wall shifting in front of her. As it slowed, a narrow hallway appeared, one she had never seen before. A great locking mechanism seemed to groan aloud as the hallway slid into place in front of her. Lights appeared, illuminating the floor.

Tyana, curious, stepped onto the fresh pathway.

She followed it for a few turns, memorizing it at each one so she could follow her way back. At one junction, the hallway to her left dropped down into a chasm far enough to be dangerous if not scaled carefully. To her opposite, the hallway had broken into a disjointed staircase, steadily rising upward.

At its top was a cadre of Warriors. They were dressed in training garb. One had her head partially shaved. She said:

"Are you Tyana?"

Tyana hesitated, then said:

"Yes—?"

"I am Sek," said the other Warrior, answering Tyana's oncoming question.

"What do you want?"

"To see you," said Sek casually. She began to walk down the staircase, bounding down from the steeper steps until she was at Tyana's level. The other Warriors followed, three in total. "We heard about your unique ... qualities. Naturally, we wanted to test them."

Tyana began to back away—then made a break toward the path from which she came. One of the other Warriors, with surprising speed, got there first and cut her off. She grinned as Tyana stopped in her tracks. Behind Tyana, the hallway dropped downward sharply.

"Come on now. We're not that bad," said Sek. "We just wanted to see you for ourselves. After all, Verikash told us all you aren't quite a Warrior through and through."

Sek came close to Tyana. Violet hair sprouted and fell down her face on one side. She had one noticeable tattoo along her jawline.

"Are you afraid?" she said.

"It's true," said one of the Warriors. "Look at her scalp." Sek looked at Tyana's nascent hair, now an easily visible mixture of violet and black. Sek began to reach for it; Tyana swatted her hand away.

"Feisty," said Sek.

"Maybe a Warrior after all?" replied one.

"Even pesky Artificers don't like being touched," retorted another.

"Let's take her gloves," Sek teased.

"Don't touch me," Tyana interjected, holding back a tremble in her voice. "You wouldn't want to." She clenched her hands, and the leather in her gloves creaked.

"Is that a challenge?" Sek asked. "Or is it the Vestal in you talking—afraid to be contaminated by our filth?"

"It was meant for your sake," Tyana growled.

"She *does* want a challenge," said one.

"I didn't come here for that," Tyana retorted. Sek reached for Tyana's hair, faster now, and Tyana blocked her, harder. Sek countered, following through. Tyana blocked the counterattack, but the force of it sent her tumbling backward, onto the floor, and over the lip of the chasm behind her.

She felt weightless for a moment. The world seemed to spin around her at least once. Then a hard thud echoed across her whole body.

Stunned, she lay still. She opened her eyes. Above, she could see Sek and the other Warriors peering over the edge. They seemed to say something, but it didn't register. An intense ringing enveloped her, and after a moment, Tyana lost consciousness.

When she came to, Sek and the others were gone, and

instead Kersa was standing over her. She felt herself being lifted up. Tyana felt Kersa's voice resonating in her chest as she huddled against it, but she couldn't make out what Kersa said. It didn't matter. Tyana didn't say anything in return.

XIX

WHEN TYANA CAME to, she saw Kersa talking with an Artificer in medical garb. She must have let out a groan, because Kersa came over to her quickly.

"Tyana? You're awake?"

Tyana didn't respond immediately. She struggled to focus her eyes. The Artificer came over to her and applied an injection. Tyana's vision cleared quickly and she felt more awake, and also felt more aware of pain throughout her body.

"Kersa—," she managed.

"What happened?" Kersa asked.

"Some Warriors and I had a fight. One was named Sek. She threw me off a ledge."

"You could have just avoided them by staying inside your quarters."

The door opened. Verikash entered, wearing her tattered tunic without armor. Behind her, Tyana could recognize the group of Warriors she confronted—including Sek.

"Explain this to me," Verikash demanded.

Kersa stepped forward:

"Sister—our medic has stabilized your initiate and she will recover."

"What do you mean stabilized? What's her state?"

Kersa looked at the medic, gesturing, who explained:

"Minor concussion, major bruising on the back and sprains across the left side of the body."

"She was pushed off a ledge, Sister," Kersa interjected.

"I dispute that," Sek argued.

"Enough," Verikash roared. "Artificer—how long will it take for my initiate to recover?"

"About three days," she said. "We'll give her some medicines to accelerate the healing process."

"Did she break any bones in the fall?" Verikash demanded.

"No," said the Artificer medic. "She needs to rest for a few days to let her body heal from the impact. That's all."

This seemed to placate Verikash. She looked at Kersa, then Sek, then turned to go.

"You won't brand her for this?" Kersa protested, gesturing at Sek.

Verikash stopped in her stride and turned.

"Did Sek deprive my initiate of life?"

Kersa stood silently.

"Did Sek deprive Mater Thea of Tyana's ability as a Warrior?"

Again, Kersa stood silently.

"Answer!"

"No," Kersa admitted, breaking gaze with Verikash.

"That's right. Tyana is not dead, nor does she have a

broken limb or a vital organ damaged beyond repair. She is not coronated yet. This setback will not deprive Mater Thea of her abilities as a Warrior; if she has any, they aren't fully developed yet. Therefore, I cannot justify giving Sek a mark for this."

Sek's lips spread wide, stopping short of breaking a smile.

"She will heal," Verikash said, "and I make that your personal responsibility from now on, Kersa, since you take such a strong interest in her."

Kersa bristled in her place, but did not protest.

Verikash approached Tyana. She came up close and said, whispering in her ear:

"Remember, Tyana—you must prove it to me."

Tyana met Verikash's eyes but said nothing in response.

As Verikash exited with the rest of the Warriors and Sek, Tyana watched her stern gaze turn from her to Kersa. The door closed, and they were gone.

XX

TYANA STAYED IN her quarters for three days. She recovered quickly, receiving daily treatments from an Artificer medic. The first day, she was bedridden; she spent it watching the shadows change in the skylight as day turned to night. From her bed she could not see the stars nor the moons—she had just a vague sense of time passing.

On the second day, she felt well enough to leave her bed and stretch. Her whole body ached, but she pushed through the pain.

After the third day, at night, she peered up at the skylight from her bed. Her body did not ache as badly. She got out of bed and tried to look down the skylight from the far end of her quarters. If she peered hard enough, she could see that the skylight opened onto a seemingly larger platform outside.

She wondered if she could climb up to it.

With a jump and some straining, she was able to get a hold on the skylight's edge. She hoisted herself up, ignoring the aches in her shoulders. The skylight was small and at a slight incline, so she crawled forward on her belly. When she reached the end, it opened up to a larger platform and into the air.

The drop wasn't far. It was close enough that Tyana could get back in without jumping. So she crawled out onto the platform.

She was standing on one section of the city's outer facade. There were no barriers to her left or right—only other sheer, rectangular nodules like the edge of the one she stood on now. Above, the sky was clear. She could even see the stars. The two moons hung overhead. Tonight, the white one eclipsed the black one. She peered over the edge. Below was nothing but a long drop to the frothing ocean.

She reclined. She stayed there a long while, smelling the salt spray wafting below, drawing lines between the stars with her eyes. She recalled feeling this way on the cliffs in the Mater's City—at the place she met that Artificer.

What was her name? Numa.

She wondered if there was any truth in what she said about her Elders' stories. What would Vershil have to say about them? Were there other things the Artificers knew, but wouldn't talk openly about?

"Tyana!"

Tyana recognized the voice instantly—it was Kersa. She was standing behind her, just beyond the skylight's exit.

"What are you doing here?" Tyana asked.

"I should ask you the same," Kersa said, steadily approaching.

"How did you find me? You're not here to push me

over, are you?"

Kersa stopped.

"I'm here to keep that from happening. Remember—Verikash's word? She wanted me to personally ensure your health. That also includes your safety." Kersa broke a grin. "Otherwise, who knows?"

Tyana faked a smile in response, turning back to look up at the moons. Kersa approached closer.

"You're obviously feeling better. Maybe you can tell me why you're out here alone."

Tyana grimaced, saying:

"You may be here now, but I'm still alone. Maybe it's easier for you when there are others like you here."

Kersa rolled her eyes.

"That attitude will get you nowhere." She sat down next to Tyana. "You still have a Warrior's color."

"Verikash says I'm not a Warrior through and through. Maybe she is right."

"No initiate is a full Warrior until coronation," Kersa chided. "She's goading you. The others are just following suit."

"So they threw me off a ledge in order to test me?"

"It is their way. They'll only stop if you prove to them it's not in their best interest to attack you."

Tyana showed little comfort.

"Do you know how I found you after you fell?" Kersa asked. "Sek came to me and told me what happened. She didn't want to throw you off. She came to brawl with you. The way you fell was just an accident. Besides, Verikash was right: nothing untoward happened," Kersa said, looking Tyana up and down. "Your body is already healed—if anything, this will draw out your strength."

"How do I know that strength you talk about is in me?

I'm not fully from this caste, so why should I believe I'm fully like it?"

Kersa looked at Tyana hard.

"Do you remember what happened when we first met? When you were born?"

Tyana was silent.

"You hadn't taken your first step. You grabbed one of the midwives—some poor Artificer—and threw her straight across the room. The others couldn't restrain you. It took a dart from my rifle to put you out."

Tyana did recall.

"That was when you were an *infant*," Kersa hissed. "I've seen other Warrior births, but not like yours. Think of what you'll be like as an adult."

Tyana looked down at her hands, gloved.

"That was before I had these on," she said.

"You're just beginning now, and you don't know your full abilities," Kersa continued. "After you've gone through training, you'll know your own strength and will be able to wield it properly."

Tyana started to work at the fingertips of her right hand's glove.

"Maybe you're right, Kersa," Tyana said. "Maybe being mixed with a higher caste isn't a disadvantage." Kersa paused, watching as Tyana revealed her bare hand. She continued: "Maybe it's just a strength I don't understand."

The wind on her open palm was soft and cold. Tyana and Kersa both contemplated it, saying nothing. Finally, Kersa asked, almost furtively:

"What does it do?"

Tyana's eyes flicked up to her. "Will you help me find out?"

Kersa seemed at a loss for words. She hesitated. Tyana began to reach for her.

"Tyana—"

"Just don't tell anyone," Tyana said. "Please."

Kersa held still, a mixture of curiosity and apprehension, as Tyana rested her palm on her cheek. Electricity lit from Tyana's fingertips, traveling into them both. Kersa's breathing halted. Hallucinations appeared at the corners of Tyana's eyes, building every moment she lingered. She relaxed and closed them, putting aside her fears, engaging the visions. She tried to divine their pattern. They seemed to form faces, faces like nothing Tyana had seen.

Kersa suddenly gripped Tyana's wrist. Tyana could sense Kersa's pulse racing and her breath faltering. Kersa was pushing her away but her hand had no strength in it. The connection between them held fast like glue. Tyana opened her eyes. Kersa's were rolled back into her head.

"Sister..." she said breathlessly, "...*let go*..."

Tyana let go. Kersa fell, slumped over. Her eyes reappeared and she blinked. Sweat was beginning to bead on her brow.

"Kersa—how are you—what did you see?" Tyana asked.

Kersa was stricken. She looked from Tyana's ungloved hand back to her face.

"Nothing. I saw nothing." She stood and turned, almost hurriedly.

Tyana, bemused, called after her: "Kersa...?"

"I don't know what powers you have, Tyana," Kersa said anxiously, stopping on her heel. "But you may face things I'll never see. Never share this with me again. Never tell anyone this happened."

She stared at Tyana for a moment, then continued up the skylight. She left without another word.

Tyana looked down at her hand and the glove at her side. The ocean groaned below, and the wind swept up its salty spray.

XXI

THE NEXT DAY, Tyana joined the training hall during the general lessons. She no longer received personal instruction from Verikash. Instead, she paired off with other Warriors, repeating movements as demonstrated by Verikash. She noticed Kersa off to the far side. Kersa avoided her at all costs, refusing to make eye contact. She noticed Sek as well—her gaze lingered on Tyana.

Tyana ignored them both.

From then on she applied her whole self to Warrior training. The first weeks were hard. She came back to her quarters consistently sore and bruised. She healed quickly, however, and often spent time outside her quarters at night, soaking in the wind and moonlight.

Occasionally, while outside, she would unglove her hands and explore the power of touch on herself. She could trigger hallucinations and modulate their intensity based on where and how hard she touched—moving from her chest, to her temples, to the crux of her hips. As she grew more comfortable with the visions, she sat with them longer. Some nights they would be nothing more than geometric patterns folding in on themselves; other nights, something like what she saw with Vershil in the libraries appeared: golden glyphs swirling in the air, or prismatic oil slicks that seemed to breathe and respond to her will.

Things from her night terrors would appear. The oil slicks would form a face. She could recognize it: Mater Thea's, her mouth gaping wide. Tyana would break the connection then. She tried to produce Mater Vale's face, but couldn't.

She sighed to herself. Frustrated by her lack of control over the visions, she retired to bed, rehearsing the movements of the past day's lesson in her mind, anticipating the next.

XXII

NIGHT, BEFORE SUNRISE. The sky was an inky purple, fading into the darkest forest green toward the direction of the oncoming sun. The sky was clear, and the moons weren't visible.

Tyana flexed her feet, grass underfoot. She was in her training garb. Ahead of her, the long grass parted and gave way to a clearing. She recognized she was dreaming.

Heading toward the clearing, she saw the nude girl hunched over, surrounded by a pool of *ichor*. She wasn't weeping, but she still hid her face against her knees.

Tyana knelt down at the edge of the pool, careful not to touch it.

"Why are you here?" Tyana asked.

"To warn you," said the girl, rocking on her haunches.

"About what?" Tyana asked.

"About the monster," said the girl.

Perplexed, Tyana leaned in.

"What monster?"

The girl didn't respond. She just kept rocking on her haunches.

"What monster?" Tyana asked again. Still the girl didn't reply. Tyana sighed—then asked:

"How do I kill the monster?"

"You can't," said the girl.

"Why not?"

"You can only wound it," retorted the girl, disturbed. Tyana sighed again. Then, leaning as far as she could toward the girl, she asked:

"Why can I only wound it?"

"Because you *are it*," said the girl, looking up at her. She looked like Tyana did when she was a newborn: bald, without hair.

The pool around her quivered. The *ichor* crawled up her body like a viscous skin, forming scales as it did so. It covered her face, erasing her features—then, Mater Thea's face pushed through, overtaking her. Her jaw opened wide, revealing obsidian teeth and an oil-coated tongue; she opened her eyes, revealing molten pools of metal for pupils—

Tyana woke in a cold sweat. She hadn't had a night terror since first leaving Vershil's. Even while touching, she could still withdraw and stop the vision.

She slowed her breath. She threw off the sheets and sat on the floor. She centered herself, waiting for her pulse to fall back down to normal. Her hair stuck to her brow and temple. With a finger, she swept it away. It was long enough now she could see it without a mirror— bundles of black hair mixed in with wider swaths of violet.

She looked up at the skylight. She wondered which moons were out tonight. Seeking fresh air, she climbed up, making her way outside and into the open air.

The moons were not out tonight. The sky wasn't overcast—they simply weren't there. Like in her dream.

XXIII

THAT DAY, TYANA was called on to spar by Verikash.

"You've improved, little initiate." Verikash took to addressing Tyana by her slighter build now. "Show us what you're capable of."

The training hall cleared a space. Verikash looked around; she stopped, grinned, and pointed: "Kersa. Spar with your sister Tyana. Show us what she's made of."

Tyana looked. At first, no one moved, then Kersa stepped forward from the crowd.

They still hadn't spoken since that night. Kersa appeared confident, but when she looked at Tyana, Tyana could see it in her eyes: apprehension, a kind Tyana didn't recognize when written on Kersa's face.

They approached each other in the center of the circle and assumed a stance. Kersa circled around Tyana —Tyana mirrored her. For a moment, it seemed like Kersa would strike, but she didn't. Instead, she reversed directions, her eyes still locked on Tyana. Tyana mirrored her again. Tyana stole a look at Verikash—she was watching Kersa, frowning.

Tyana took the initiative and advanced a step, as if she were about to strike. Kersa mirrored her, stepping back —then stepping forward again as Tyana relented. Verikash didn't hide her disappointment:

"Kersa, strike Tyana," she commanded.

Immediately, Kersa lunged forward, aiming for Tyana's center. Tyana moved off the line, deflecting Kersa's blow on her wrists, just at the ends of her gloves. Kersa, instead of countering, simply followed through, creating more distance between her and Tyana.

"Again!" Verikash roared.

Kersa turned and lunged again. Again, Tyana easily deflected it. She even left an opening for Kersa to counter—but Kersa followed through, denying any opportunity to encroach on her.

Verikash sighed audibly.

"Kersa! Relax."

Kersa removed herself from the spar, joining the circle. She ignored Tyana's gaze.

"Sek!"

Sek stepped forward from the circle, a quizzical look on her face. Verikash pointed at her:

"Give our initiate Tyana a fair spar—would you?"

"Gladly," said Sek, breaking into a grin. She stepped forward, approaching Tyana, her shock of violet hair bobbing across her face.

"Don't worry, I won't go easy on you," she said, assuming a stance.

Tyana assumed hers.

Sek lunged forward confidently. Tyana caught the blow, moving off the line. Sek countered, and Tyana followed through. Sek disengaged, reassuming her stance.

"Better," she teased, "but good enough?"

She encroached on Tyana again, releasing a series of strikes that Tyana blocked, then countered in rapid succession. Tyana disengaged this time. Sek grinned.

"Someone take someone," Verikash taunted, unimpressed. Sek shot her a look, then looked back at Tyana, enlivened.

Tyana centered herself, reassuming her stance. She noticed Kersa in her peripheral vision, but kept her sight trained on her opponent.

Sek let out a shriek and leapt at Tyana. Tyana countered the oncoming flurry of blows and, on the last one, went for a strike toward her temple—except she grazed it instead, making contact with the bare skin just beyond her glove.

Tyana followed through, but it looked like Sek had taken a blow to the temple. She stumbled, clutching her head where Tyana made contact. She blinked wildly and, for a moment, stopped to catch her breath.

Verikash raised an eyebrow.

Sek shook it off and reassumed her stance. Tyana reassumed hers—wider, more confident this time.

Sek unleashed herself on Tyana again, but Tyana countered each blow, searching for an opportunity. When she found it, she feinted, and instead of striking at Sek's temple again, she slid her bare arm under Sek's jaw, across the jugular, and close to her spine. A flash of hallucination invaded Tyana's vision and she poured her will into it. The contact was brief, and it fled as quickly as it came.

Sek went down. Her breath faltered and she spasmed, losing coordination in her upper body. It appeared as if

Tyana had struck her in the throat. In truth, she had just glanced it.

The other Warriors gathered around Sek. The veins in her neck bulged while she gasped. Verikash barked orders to get the Artificer medics. Across the way, Tyana could see Kersa, staring at her.

Gone was that curious apprehension Kersa had during the fight. Now, it was something else. Kersa turned and walked away, exiting the training hall.

That's when Tyana recognized it: fear.

XXIV

TYANA DID NOT spar again that day; other Warriors took turns instead. Sek was taken away for treatment and did not reappear afterward. The other Warriors eyed her strangely. Did they think she took Sek down legitimately or did they think she performed some kind of trick?

The remaining lessons finished. Tyana was sore, but in good spirits. She left the training hall, heading for her quarters. The labyrinthine hallways shifted again, creating new inclines and pits. The hallways always grew narrower close to the great hall, however. Knowing this, Tyana could find her way to the barracks without trouble.

She had gotten through the worst of the maze and was nearly there. She turned the corner and stopped mid-stride.

It was Sek.

She was bruised along the neck where Tyana led her arm across it. There was a rash and her veins were visibly discolored.

"What did you do to me?" she hissed.

Tyana retreated backward, slowly, and stopped. She looked behind her—three Warriors stepped into view.

"I want you to face me," Sek said.

"I already faced you," Tyana said.

"No, not like a true Warrior," she said, pointing at her neck. "What is this? This isn't a bruise. You cheated."

Tyana looked at her potential exits. They were all blocked by Sek's cadre.

"At first I felt bad for you when you fell off that ledge. I'll be sure to rout that pity in me from now on."

"If you fight me, Sek, I won't give you the benefit of the doubt."

Sek assumed a stance. So did the other Warriors. She fumed at Tyana:

"I'm counting on it."

She rushed Tyana with a shriek, unleashing a flurry of blows. Tyana countered, surprised at her speed. With significant effort, Tyana locked and threw Sek to the ground. The other Warriors made their rush; Tyana led them down the opening left by Sek into a corridor so she could face them one at a time. Each one took a chance at Tyana, both confident yet leery of Tyana's bare skin. As the corridors narrowed and changed in shape, she moved defensively, using the environment to force her opponents to move around obstacles and take untenable positions.

She approached a steep incline with a pit. Sek appeared suddenly, leaping from a higher vantage point onto Tyana, knocking her down. They tangled on the ground. Sek attempted to lock Tyana while avoiding her hands; Tyana fought the lock while trying to gain an advantage. Tyana could see the bottom of the pit close by. It disintegrated into a series of stalagmite-like platforms, leading downward like broken staircases.

She knew she could not beat four individual Warriors on her own, so she threw her weight in the direction of the incline, sending her and Sek tumbling down the pit. Sek lost her grip on Tyana. They impacted on the staggered platforms below. Tyana took a hit on her shoulders, Sek in her abdomen and lower extremities. The blunt force of the fall was enough to stall the fight.

Tyana forced herself up, her shoulders stinging. The Warriors above weren't following them down. Sek groaned audibly, and seemed determined to rise. When she did, Tyana was standing, ready.

"I will end you!" Sek screamed.

Tyana stood firm as Sek clambered over the platforms, rage written on her face. She realized Sek wouldn't stop after being so slighted. She would have to move decisively to win.

Sek laid in the first few strikes; Tyana locked her at the shoulders, flipped her, and brought her down hard on one side. A *pop* echoed from Sek's shoulder. She let out a bloodcurdling scream.

Tyana disengaged. Sek didn't get up, but only moaned in pain. Standing there, Tyana wondered if she should help. After a while, she walked away, leaving Sek there, wounded.

"I've seen enough," echoed a voice above the pit. Tyana looked up. Verikash was standing above them, watching. Alongside her were Kersa and a number of other Warriors. "Bring them to me—*now*," she directed at Kersa, leaving without another word. Tyana found nothing reassuring in Kersa's gaze.

XXV

TYANA WAS THERE while an Artificer examined Sek. They braced her shoulder and her upper arm. Verikash and the whole group of Warriors who had watched, including Kersa, stood by.

"Who do you presume yourself to be, Tyana, to injure my Warrior?" Verikash growled.

"Sister," Tyana said, using the proper form of address, "I had no choice."

"No choice?"

"Sister, you saw what happened. You saw how Sek and her sisters approached me. Sek already injured me once. If I allowed her to persist in her offense against me, I would have denied you my own power."

Verikash paused, her stern gaze still resting on Tyana.

"If it satisfies you," Tyana bowed her head, "I apologize for any transgression."

"I don't want your apology," Verikash grumbled. "Medic, how long will it take for my Warrior to heal?"

"About six days," the Artificer said. "There are

fractures in her scapula and along her surrounding ribs. She shouldn't participate in training until after she is healed."

"Brand her," Sek fumed aloud. "She deprived your Warrior of ability, Sister—show her the compensation."

Tyana grew apprehensive.

Verikash gestured at Kersa, standing behind her.

"Kersa. You know this initiate better than most. Tell me: did she deprive me of one of Thea's Warriors for a time, or is she coming into her own as a Warrior herself?"

Kersa stepped forward.

"Sister—," she said, hesitantly. "It appeared to me Tyana acted in self-defense."

"You didn't answer my question," Verikash hissed.

"Sister—when Sek and Tyana last quarreled, you judged that Sek did not deprive Mater Thea of one Warrior's ability. Therefore, you did not brand her."

"True," Verikash said.

"Now Tyana has injured Sek, twofold what Sek did to Tyana."

"True again," Verikash said. "Are you saying I should brand Tyana?"

"Sister—I have no doubt Tyana acted out of self-preservation. But I cannot answer whether or not she should be branded as a Warrior."

"Why?"

"I don't know if she is one."

Tyana looked at Kersa. Verikash gave a flash of bemusement. Pausing for a moment, she turned to Tyana:

"What do you think? Did you act like a Warrior or not?"

Tyana stared at Verikash.

"I did what the moment required of me," she said.

"You should brand her, Sister," Sek sneered. Verikash raised a hand.

"Do you want my judgment too?" Verikash asked Sek, who stayed silent. Then she gestured to the rest of the room. "Leave us." The Warriors gently filed out of the room. Kersa only lingered a moment as Tyana stared at her.

"You too," Verikash said at the medic. She helped Sek up gingerly and, with her wincing, vacated the room. Verikash and Tyana were alone.

Verikash reached behind her and pulled a tattooing gun from a small holster at her side.

"Do you know what this is?" she asked.

Tyana nodded.

"Good. Vershil taught you what it is good for and what it means."

She set it aside on the medical table.

"I should brand you for this, little sister," Verikash said. She paced for a moment, studying Tyana. "But I won't."

"Why, Sister?" Tyana asked.

"Kersa was right. You acted out of self-preservation. Twice Sek confronted you, each time with significant consequences she couldn't predict. I abstained from branding Sek because you were a mere initiate. I will abstain from branding you as well, but for reasons she won't know. I need every Warrior at my lines that I can muster, Tyana. I cannot afford losses at home. When you see our enemy face to face, you'll understand why."

Verikash approached Tyana closely, whispering in her ear:

"I know you didn't really strike Sek in the throat," she said, leaning in. "Fool the other Warriors as much as you like. But I know when you cheat. Some Warriors bear their tattoos proudly. I know it would be otherwise for you. Fortunately, you have friends in high places. I hope you intend to keep them."

She left the tattooing gun on the table.

"Tyana—," Verikash said as she turned to walk away:

"You're proving it to me."

XXVI

AFTER THE INCIDENT with Sek, the other Warriors treated Tyana with distance and respect. They didn't attack her outside the training hall again, Sek least of all, who now avoided Tyana as much as Kersa did.

At the close of one day's training, Verikash called a special session for the highest ranking Warriors.

"And Tyana—," she announced. "Meet me in my inner hall."

Tyana felt a room of palpable gazes on her.

She had never been to Verikash's inner hall. It was off limits to those in the general lessons. The only thing she knew was that it doubled as Verikash's private quarters.

That night, Tyana made her way from the barracks to the far end of the complex. The city seemed to age as she went deeper into its heart. When she arrived, a set of simple square gates made of rough stone greeted her. When she touched them, they groaned open.

Inside was a wide room unlike the great hall. Instead of smooth floors and lit walls, the space was dark, cavernous, and excavated out of stone. Crystalline cubes glowed bright lavender in rows along the walls. In the center sat Verikash, her back to Tyana. Her long, matted hair streamed from her scalp like fraying ropes.

"Come in, Tyana."

She did, and the gates slid closed.

"Change your clothes," Verikash said. Tyana noticed a fresh tunic and pants neatly folded nearby, waiting. She did.

"Sister," Tyana said using the proper form, "you called me."

"I did," Verikash replied, standing. She wore only her tattered rags and a stone collar. "Every initiate must be coronated before taking on her caste-burden. As we both know, however, you are no ordinary initiate. A Warrior's coronation will not be the limit for you." Verikash stopped. "Do you know what this is?" she asked, pointing to her collar. It fit neatly around the nape of her neck, hugging her throat like a pair of wings.

"No, Sister."

"It is Mater Vale's most prized weapon," Verikash said. "Everything you've trained with so far—blade, staff, pistol, your own body—prepared you for this. When Vale gave Her powers to the first Warrior, this is what She left us with to defend Her domain."

Verikash approached Tyana. As she did so, the collar exuded a dark purple substance. It crawled over Verikash's skin like veins, covering her body, hardening into scales and spines. It swallowed her face, forming two glowing, pupil-less irises where her eyes had been. Verikash spoke, her voice now distorted:

"It is time you were no longer an initiate, Tyana. Follow me."

Verikash turned, now a glistening, armored form. She raised a hand at the far wall. Filaments unfurled from her fingers and coagulated on the wall, slicing it to pieces, then peeling it open. Beyond, Tyana could see a wide platform open to the sky. It was filled with a circle of seated Warriors, all in the same armor as Verikash. Verikash walked through the opened wall and Tyana followed her; it closed behind them and the filaments disintegrated, coalescing around Verikash as a dark cloud that was reabsorbed into her collar.

"These are *sensak*," Verikash explained. "They are bonded to your will. With them you can form armor, remove obstacles, conjure weapons, and create simulacra to fight for you." Verikash stretched out her arm and a gnarled blade extended from her hand. As soon as she lowered her arm, it dissolved again.

She took her place at the head of the circle of Warriors and their suits dissolved. The highest ranking members, nearest to Verikash's seat, were Sek and Kersa. Verikash gestured with her hand and, wordlessly, Kersa stood and brought over a wide basin. It was full of a quivering purple liquid.

"*Sensak* have a will of their own. To use them, you must first absorb their will into yours. You will do this by swallowing them. When the *sensak* enter your body, they will try to escape through your mouth. You must not allow this—or else they will consume you."

Kersa brought over a stone collar, standing behind Tyana.

"If you are successful, the *sensak* will give up and retreat into the collar where they are stored. From then on, they will bend to your will. Are you ready?"

Tyana looked at the basin of quivering, violet liquid. It

reminded her of the basin of *ichor* in her birth dream, or the pool surrounding the girl in her night terrors. Tyana looked at Verikash.

"Yes," she said.

Verikash nodded. Kersa placed the collar on Tyana's neck. She felt it prick her skin. Verikash held the basin up to Tyana's lips. As she tilted it, Tyana swallowed. The liquid's texture alternated from silky to sand-like as it went down her esophagus. Verikash didn't stop pouring until the basin was empty.

Tyana immediately felt the urge to regurgitate. The force in her stomach swirled of its own volition. She felt immense pressure as the liquid seemed to oscillate from solid chunks to gas, forcing its way up her throat. She swallowed heavily, but the pressure redoubled itself.

Verikash and the other Warriors watched expectantly. The basin sat in front of Tyana, as if it was ready to catch something.

Like a snake, the *sensak* forced their way up into her mouth. She caught them, refusing to open her jaws. They changed texture again and she thought her insides might be shredded by razor blades. She closed her eyes. She swallowed again out of force of will.

The snake went back into her belly. For a moment it seemed like it would burst forth. It worked its way back up, but gentler this time, dissolving before reaching her mouth. The collar hummed to life and her innards relaxed, empty, as if she had not swallowed anything at all. Verikash grinned.

"Command them," she suggested.

Tyana thought for a moment. She formed an intention: she imagined her body encased in a hard, segmented shell. Out of the collar dribbled a quicksand-like substance, crawling over her skin. It hardened at her joints, forming a chitinous exoskeleton. A brief moment of panic washed over her as the *sensak* moved up her scalp and swallowed her face, enveloping her eyes. Everything went dark at first, then her vision reappeared, modified. She could see not only Verikash in front of her, but could also perceive her body temperature, electromagnetic field, and more. The newly visible spectrums assaulted her senses, overwhelming her with information.

As the *sensak* crystallized on Tyana's body, they changed from a dull violet to a black sheen. Unlike the other Warriors', Tyana's *sensak* were as black as *ichor*.

"Welcome to our caste, Tyana—" Verikash paused, then addressed her: "Vestal-Warrior."

XXVII

TYANA TRAINED WITH the *sensak* every day. Her slighter build separated her from other Warriors; she could not rely on brute force alone in a fistfight. Instead it became clear she had a talent for the one weapon in Vale's arsenal that was the most subtle and difficult to master. The *sensak* relied on clarity of intention to form cogent structures. The more vague the intention, the more fragile the structure. Some Warriors struggled to form a strong blade from one hand; Tyana could form two. A few Warriors could create a moving shield that preceded them; Tyana conjured multiple shields and formed them into a shell around her. She often practiced in secret outside her quarters without gloves, in the nude; as long as she remained in control of the oncoming hallucinations, the heightened sensitivity produced by her touch magnified her focus with *sensak*. She formed structures beyond standard weaponry—a cloud of shattered glass that followed her command, for example, or a moving wall with which she could crush an opponent.

Verikash taught Tyana personally in the inner hall from then on, guiding her newfound abilities.

"*Sensak* are capable of forming simple machines, but cannot generate or contain energy. You will not be able to form a working pistol out of your own volition and fire it, for example. But they can be used as an organic mimic to interface with such weaponry."

Verikash retrieved a pistol from a nearby weapons rack. She tossed it into the center of the sparring platform a few paces in front of her. Tyana watched as a thick cloud exuded from Verikash's collar, coalescing around the pistol. It formed an armored suit. The suit picked up the pistol.

"On your guard," Verikash warned.

Tyana put up a shield as the suit took aim at her. The pistol let out a blast and her shield absorbed the shock. To counterattack, she shattered her shield and sent the pieces flying at the visage. They flew through it, slicing it open. It was visibly hollow as it disintegrated into dust, which crawled its way from the ground back to Verikash.

"Return fire, Tyana," Verikash commanded.

Tyana sent her *sensak* toward the pistol. They coalesced into filaments and veins, forming a spongy body. Tyana strained as the body knelt down, attempting to pick up the weapon. Its fingers were fuzzy in detail and, as it stood, it lost its grip on the weapon. Tyana tried a second time, but lost control over the visage again and the body dissolved. The *sensak* streamed back to her along the ground, following a path of least resistance. They crawled up her leg and disappeared into the collar at her neck.

"Forming simulacra to do your bidding is the most

difficult task for *sensak*. A single *sensak*, a mere dust mote, can move through liquid or gas quickly and is easy to control. The difficulty increases exponentially as they form larger and more complex networks. A single, complicated structure may be less effective than a swarm of lighter, simpler ones, for example. *Sensak* can respond to stress and adapt on their own, but they will subsume their abilities to your will—however clear or unclear that may be."

Verikash replaced the pistol at the weapons locker.

"Patience, Tyana. I'm sure you'll improve in this area too. For now, there is something else you're due to learn. Follow me."

She led her from the inner hall to an unfamiliar area of the complex.

"As you know, we are a spacefaring people. For Warriors, use of *sensak* is essential in piloting. Our ships cannot be controlled without them. This was by Mater Vale's design—it keeps our ships inaccessible to other castes and, ultimately, our enemies."

They came to a large gateway near the inner hall. Verikash touched it and it opened into a wide, dark hangar. Lights hummed to life. Inside were two oil slick-colored ships, black and scaly. Shaped like tridents, they appeared only large enough for a single person.

"These are our warbirds. Built for a single pilot each, they are our main weapons in off-world engagements. They have standard weaponry akin to our pulse rifles, but with larger barrels and increased power. Warbirds are flexible, malleable ships designed to be an extension of you much the way *sensak* are. Piloting is similar to controlling them."

Tyana approached one of the warbirds. It had a cold,

dark allure about it. She traced the tessellating patterns along its underside. It felt less like a machine and more like an unawakened serpent waiting to be tamed.

"One is for you," Verikash said. Tyana looked at her.

"You honor me, Sister." Verikash waved the pleasantry away.

"The speed of your progress has been exceptional, but this is not a promotion. Every Warrior has her warbird, just as she does her *sensak*. We need every one available to us, and you are proving yourself quickly."

She gestured at Tyana, expectantly.

"Get acquainted."

Tyana looked up at the warbird's underside. She conjured her *sensak* and, unsure of how to enter, intentioned to them: *show me.*

Without hesitation, they enveloped her body and drew her up toward the warbird's belly. It dissolved, revealing a hollow opening that appeared to be a cockpit, but had no discernible controls. Forgoing panic, Tyana relaxed as the ship's skin sealed beneath her. At first, everything was dark. She could feel the *sensak* spindling out from her limbs into the ship's extremities. The hollow space filled with a thick liquid that gave her a sense of weightlessness, like being suspended in a vat of gel.

When her vision reappeared, she could see beyond the ship. Verikash was standing just beyond her on the hangar floor, smaller now. Her sense of scale had changed. Other senses came online and she felt them each in rapid succession, extending her own nervous system: propulsion, navigation, environmental conditions, and weaponry.

If the warbird could have shown Tyana's grin, it would have.

"It's time I taught you how to fly," Verikash said; Tyana heard her through the belly of the ship. Verikash entered her own warbird, disappearing inside it. It awakened, extending its wings.

"Follow me."

XXVIII

FLYING CAME NATURALLY. Tyana followed Verikash, soaring upward toward the overcast sky. She felt turbulence on the warbird itself, but inside, the gel-like layer that enveloped her body absorbed any sharp impact, leaving her with an overall sense of weightlessness. The *sensak* branched from her fingers and joints like nerves, tapping into the warbird's systems. The ship extended her will and she felt it as if it was an extension of her body.

They breached the cloud layer. It was daytime; pink-blue sky pierced Tyana's vision. She hadn't seen a clear sky since staying with Vershil. It was beautiful. She cycled through the warbird's optical filters; each kind augmented her sight with newly visualized information. She could see Valen's electromagnetic field expanding out like tides of energy. She could see temperature differences in the air, revealing wind currents. Even trajectories of incoming meteors were visible. Verikash's warbird sped ahead, reduced to a black pinprick.

"Keep up, my Vestal-Warrior," she said.

Tyana willed the warbird's propulsion and it sped to attention. Its engines expelled a cyan burst and she shot forward, leaving vapor trails through the atmosphere.

"Sister, why did you address me that way?" Tyana asked.

"It seemed appropriate," Verikash said. Her warbird dove into the cloud layer below. Tyana lurched downward, following. "You are from my caste, but also from Mater Thea's—the Vestals. 'Warrior' does not do justice to your colors. Others will need some way to address you properly."

"Does the nature of my colors make me less of a Warrior, Sister?" Tyana tested.

"That is up to you," Verikash replied.

The cloud layer thickened, darkening around them. Water condensed on the wings of Tyana's warbird, flying off as quickly as it collected. She could see Verikash ahead outlined in neon. They broke through the cloud layer; below them was a basalt canyon that opened into the ocean. Its cliff faces were split apart in wide chasms, filled with seawater. Verikash headed for its lip, just at the edge of the ocean.

"Close your wings, sister. We're going for a dive."

Apprehensive, Tyana willed it; the warbird's wings folded flush against the hull and its scale-like skin flattened. Verikash aimed down toward the water and Tyana followed. They hit the ocean like two black spearheads. Tyana felt the impact through the gel layer. The temperature dropped and her speed slowed to a crawl. She switched her optics and they revealed the underwater landscape. The cliff face ahead fell sheer into a drop whose bottom wasn't readily visible. It was riddled with open channels and capillaries.

Ahead, Verikash's warbird mutated again. Its wings swept open and the cyan glow of its engines reignited, illuminating the aqueous environment.

"Where are we, Sister?"

"A place all Warriors must pass through," Verikash replied. Her warbird disappeared into the largest channel ahead in the cliff face. Tyana reignited her engines and followed. The water pressed against her warbird; she took care to make no sudden movements, feeling she might otherwise rip her ship apart. The glow from Verikash's engines guided her through a narrow channel. It was a winding, cavernous vein formed from an ancient river system—or possibly through volcanism.

"After Vale created our world, She populated these oceans with a certain beast that nests deep within these caverns. She made it as an example to us Warriors in particular."

The channel narrowed, then ended in a cul-de-sac.

"Stop your engines," Verikash commanded.

Tyana cut her engines and she glided to a stop. Everything went dark. Above her, the channel opened up to a huge cavern. She could not see past the pool's surface, but heat signatures radiated around them. She could not make out their profile, but they were large—at least three times her size.

"We're going to get out," Verikash said.

"Sister?"

"Take a deep breath, exit your ship and follow me— we're swimming up to the nest."

"What are the heat signatures I'm reading, Sister?"

"We call them gryphons, Tyana. This is the final task in your coronation: you have to find a male and slay him."

Tyana was gripped, unsure of how to respond.

"I will guide you to the surface. We must remain undetected. Be silent and don't move suddenly. Use your *sensak* to help you. And above all—relax."

Tyana felt a wave of panic and suppressed it.

"Ready?" Verikash asked.

"Yes, Sister."

"Good. Deep breath—now."

Tyana took a full inhale and disconnected from her ship. The bottom gave out beneath her and the gel layer enveloping her receded. Freezing cold water replaced it. She formed an insulating suit around her to keep warm. She saw Verikash emerge from her warbird and swim upward toward the surface. She followed.

Tyana reached the lip of the pool. Verikash, ahead of her, gestured to approach slowly. As Tyana carefully climbed up the rocky lip, her eyes breached the water, and she could see the outlines of the heat signatures in detail.

They were coiled, scaled beasts, each one appearing to have three limbs, two of which were winged. They had smooth, oblong skulls with wide cyan eyes.

Verikash climbed up from the pool. Tyana followed. The sand caused her to sink as she moved, and she struggled to move quietly. When she finally reached the top, Verikash was waiting for her; her *sensak* formed a texture that camouflaged her against the surrounding rocks. Tyana imitated it. Verikash led her up the beachhead and toward a ledge, away from the nearby monsters. The cavern expanded ahead. Shrieks and screams echoed through the chambers. As they passed along one ledge, Verikash whispered:

"The gryphons are unlike us. They have two sexes: male and female. They reproduce by biological copulation. Vale created them this way to demonstrate how the two sexes breed violence within a species."

Verikash led her through a cleft in the ledge. She gestured beyond to an opening.

"Look," she said.

Tyana peered beyond the cleft. Two black, scale-clad forms entangled each other, snapping and hissing. One, larger and with a wider crest on its skull, dominated over a smaller, more submissive one, which gave whines and shrieks at its advances. A protrusion below the larger one's midsection, just above its third limb, expanded, unfurling barbs along its underside. It penetrated the smaller one with it, and the smaller one gave a shriek. Tyana retreated back behind the cleft, revolted.

"The larger one is the male," Verikash whispered. "Look again—"

Tyana, subduing her revulsion, looked again. Behind the male, another gryphon loomed and announced his presence with a shrieking roar. The female disentangled herself and the pursuing male turned to meet his aggressor. One lunged and the other countered, each using his talons to inflict wounds on the other. Their jaws lunged forward, snapping at their opponent's neck. Eventually, the challenger was defeated by the older, larger male. Appearing to have broken a shoulder, the younger male slithered away, whining. The winner turned back to his expectant female.

"The winner is the one you must fight," Verikash said.

"Sister—!" Tyana protested.

"Tyana, this is your final coronation task. You must slay the gryphon. If you don't, you'll stop short on your path to becoming a Warrior."

"Why should I slay this beast?"

"Every Warrior before you has done so. It is our way. If you cannot defeat this monster, you won't be able to defeat our real enemies. It is the purest test of your skill. Without this gryphon's death, you cannot call yourself one of us."

Tyana turned back toward the cleft's opening. The female gryphon was rising to meet her partner. Tyana felt a wave of emotion flood her as she watched their copulation. It was a mixture of feelings she did not expect. It felt like disgust and horror, but then it condensed into anger and rage. It electrified her body.

She jumped from the ledge. Her *sensak* propelled her forward. She landed with a resounding thud at the foot of the male gryphon, standing between him and his female.

The female roared at Tyana but retreated like she had done with the last challenger. She coiled herself in the corner, waiting to see the result of this new duel. The male was not as entertained. He reared up on his single haunch, bringing the crests of his wings sharply downward. Standing this way, he appeared like a giant, winged tripod. His round, cyan irises blinked wildly as they focused downward on Tyana. A pair of gnarled jaws extended below his smooth, crested face.

Tyana acted on instinct, dodging his first strike. Boulders flew in her direction as one wing cleaved the ground in front of her. She formed an array of shields with *sensak*, then abandoned that position as the talon from the other wing came down nearly on top of her like a spear. The gryphon screamed at her. The sound at once pierced her ears and shook the ground beneath her.

Tyana countered by forming filaments from the bottoms of her feet, growing her height, putting her on equal ground with the monster. The gryphon swiped at her legs made of *sensak* and they relented, dissolving at the touch, only to reform again at Tyana's will. She seemed to float in the air as the beast attempted to cut the legs out from under her. She formed a cloud of darts and sent them hurtling at the gryphon, striking his face. This only seemed to enrage him further, however, and he barreled after her. Casting *sensak* above and below her, she flung herself to another part of the cave, abandoning her position again.

Realizing the severity of her situation, Tyana looked around her. The surrounding walls of the cavern were volcanic in origin and had deep cracks in their rocks. Portions of obsidian in the ceiling, if shattered, could become as sharp as razors. On a whim, Tyana drew her *sensak* upward, penetrating the rock in the ceiling. She cleaved a boulder-sized stalactite off. It fell downward and she attempted to direct it at the gryphon. It didn't land on her intended target, but it caused the monster to at least stumble backward. Throwing her *sensak* toward the nearest wall, she visualized them penetrating the cracks in the rock and hollowing out a giant column. With a heave, she tugged on the quicksand-like ropes that spread from her hands. A massive wedge of rock groaned from the side of the cavern wall, tipping on its side toward the gryphon.

Tyana rushed the beast, drawing his attention. He responded, charging her. At the last moment she drew her *sensak* toward her, weaving the tightest shield she could muster. The wedge of rock came down with a force that nearly blew her from her place; its sound echoed through the cavern. Tyana held her position.

When the dust cleared, Tyana saw that the gryphon was pinned by his neck from the rock. One of his wings was cut. He roared at her, then squealed.

"Now you have it," Verikash yelled at her from the ledge. "It's time you claimed your prize."

Tyana looked in the beast's eyes. They were round, cyan, with crescent-shaped pupils, and nestled deep into his skull. She approached the gryphon. His nostrils, no more than slits above his upper jaw and between his eyes, flared consistently.

Tyana bounded above the beast's head. The *sensak* guided her onto the fallen rock that pinned the monster, giving her the perfect vantage for a killing blow. She formed an elongated blade from her hands, long enough to pierce the gryphon's skull.

"Do it," Verikash announced. "Victory is yours."

Tyana prepared to plunge the blade between the gryphon's eyes.

She heard the cavern around her stir, and she looked up. Cyan-colored eyes everywhere stared at her. The female, waiting for the winner of the duel, uncoiled herself and approached, watching Tyana. As they made eye contact, she made a cooing sound. More smooth-crested females across the pool revealed themselves from the walls and crevices—approaching Tyana, but not attacking.

"What are you waiting for?" Verikash demanded.

Tyana looked up at her teacher and, for a moment, hesitated. She looked down at the male, whose eyes were blinking wildly. Then, resigning herself to any consequences, she dissolved the blade. She removed the glove on her right hand and, with *sensak* swirling around her, reached down and touched the gryphon's forehead with her bare fingers.

Hallucinations that Tyana had not seen before invaded the corners of her sight. Tessellating patterns condensed into a cohesive vision. She tapped into the gryphon's emotions; she could see his fears, his memories, his origins. She felt his drive for conquest and his rapacious desire. She felt a primal presence nestled in his heart. She visualized it and it engulfed her.

Tyana disconnected. She contemplated slaying the beast still, but then relented. She jumped toward the ledge where Verikash stood, the *sensak* carrying her along. When she landed, she sent them to the wedge that pinned the gryphon and removed it, freeing him. He scampered away, tending to his wounded wing and neck.

"You should have killed it," Verikash said.

"I should have but I won't," Tyana replied, *sensak* streaming back into her collar. She moved past Verikash, walking along the cleft.

"This doesn't make you a Warrior," Verikash called out.

"Perhaps I'm not only a Warrior—Sister."

XXIX

NEWS OF TYANA'S exploit with the gryphon spread quickly through the caste. Verikash delayed announcing whether Tyana had fulfilled her coronation. At stake was Tyana's membership in the caste and public branding for breaking with tradition. If Verikash had any displeasure, she did not voice it openly. Instead, she spent a number of days deliberating privately in the inner hall.

The whole rank of Warriors waited for Verikash's word. Tyana could hear her name openly in conversation down the halls. She made it a point to turn down those halls, listening to the conversations hush as she passed by. She had the benefit of no longer being harassed openly by other Warriors. Only Verikash's skill, honed by years of experience, eclipsed Tyana's raw talent with *sensak*.

She ignored her predicament. She spent the days and nights alone outside her quarters, practicing.

One evening, as she turned, she saw Kersa there, standing beyond the edge of her skylight. The last time she was there was the last time they had spoken.

"I've come to speak with you," Kersa said.

"Kersa—Sister," Tyana addressed.

"Do you think our ways are a game?" Kersa intoned sharply. "Do you think that, simply because you're better than others, you can break our traditions and flaunt your abilities in our teacher's face? In my face?"

"I never said I was better than others," Tyana critiqued.

"But you are different," Kersa retorted. "Anyone who can see you knows that. Anyone who's seen you fight or fly knows that."

"So that's what you think of me—*different?*" Tyana hissed. "Is that why you humiliated me in front of my teacher? You weren't sure if I was a Warrior then—a change from what you told me when we last stood at this spot."

"That was before you started cheating your way through battles. You used your powers on Sek—the first in line to Verikash's succession—and now she is ashamed."

"Sek attacked me," Tyana protested. "She brought whatever troubles she has now on herself. I did what I had to do to defend myself."

"You used it on me, too," Kersa said. "I didn't ask for that. I hated what I saw, what I felt, when you did that to me."

"Sister—I didn't know it would be like that for you," Tyana offered. It gave Kersa little comfort.

"I am second in line for succession after Sek, and now I am ashamed too. The head of our caste must be able to subdue any member of our sisters to remain First among Warriors. You could beat either of us if it came down to *sensak*," Kersa explained.

"I didn't know you were second in the line of succession," Tyana said.

"It doesn't matter. You've used the touch on me and on Sek. Now you've used it to subdue a gryphon. If Verikash decides that you should be marked, it will implicate us. She will have to pardon all of us or none of us. If Sek and I are marked, the succession will pass to someone else. Our deeds will catch up with us. Why did you think you could abstain from slaying the gryphon? What made you think you should touch it?"

"Its consorts seemed to request its life. Besides, I had already pinned it down. Verikash herself told me I had merely to claim my victory. I hated the beast, but it was too pitiful to kill. So I left it wounded instead. Isn't that slaying enough?"

"It's our tradition to kill," Kersa demanded.

"Then it is a useless tradition. I have no need for dead trophies. Instead I found knowledge. Who was the last Warrior who could see through a gryphon's eyes and tell you what he feels?"

Kersa drew up to her full height.

"It's more honorable to maintain tradition than to break it for the sake of personal adventure."

Tyana sighed, exasperated:

"Maybe you were right the last time," she said, turning away. "Maybe a Warrior is defined as much by her limitations as she is by her abilities. If that's the case, why should I call myself Warrior, Vestal-Warrior, or anything else?"

Kersa approached, imploring her:

"At least make a compromise. Verikash might forgo branding us if you promise not to use the touch in duels or battles. If you don't, we'll all suffer—you most of all. But for the sake of our caste, try to uphold our values."

Tyana was silent for a moment.

"Fine," she said, turning back to Kersa. "I won't use it. But my powers do not belong solely to the Warriors. I will not deprive the Maters of my full ability."

"I'm sure Verikash can oblige—as will the Maters."

Kersa gave Tyana a long, hard look. Then she turned and left Tyana alone.

Tyana looked out toward the horizon. The moons were visible against the starry background. Both seemed to be hanging equally balanced, like two black and white orbs on a scale. Tyana couldn't tell which was advancing and which was receding.

XXX

WHEN VERIKASH EMERGED from the inner hall, she declared she would announce her final decision at the War Council's meeting the next day in the Mater's City. A contingent of Warriors was assembled to attend, including Tyana, Sek, and Kersa. They boarded a ship for transit.

Tyana avoided the other Warriors. She stayed on the balcony of the ship, watching the ocean roll by, speared by the occasional crag of exposed volcanic rock. She remembered what it was like the first time she arrived at the Warrior's city. She didn't feel the same way now. She didn't feel powerless.

They arrived at the Mater's City. They exited the ship and Tyana smelled the familiar air. The scent of fresh rain on the stone buildings was strong.

They headed in a loose parade toward the Mater's Cathedral. Tyana's hair had since grown long enough that she pulled it into a loose bun at the top of her head. Streaks of violet and black hair cascaded over her brows.

A pair of Keepers or quartet of Scribes would occasionally stop in their tracks, staring at her.

They reached the cathedral's gates. Verikash led Tyana, followed by Sek, Kersa, and finally a longer parade of other high-ranking Warriors. Keeper attendants sworn to Thea, swaddled in black robes and heavy hoods, opened the doors for them. Light streamed in, colored by stained glass. At the far end, Thea's throne was unoccupied. Instead, seated next to the throne was a hooded Vestal—presumably Thea's representative. The rest of the War Council's representatives were gathered, waiting. Tyana recognized Vershil in the Head Keeper's spot to the left. Below them was the Grand Scribe and, across from her, Verikash's own seat as First Warrior. The Grand Artificer sat below them all in a hooded red sash, her lips wizened and her hands blackened by various tattoos.

"Sister Verikash," Vershil addressed formally to the room, "welcome to our Council. We've been expecting you."

"Sister Vershil," Verikash announced, "I've come to present to you Tyana, whom you sent to me as an initiate."

"I see," Vershil nodded. "By your standard, has she fulfilled her training and tasks for coronation?"

"Sister—" Verikash said, pausing: "Tyana was the smallest, physically weakest initiate I trained. I tested her and treated her harshly, like I would any potential Warrior. She not only rose to the standard I set, she exceeded it."

Vershil stared expectantly.

"As you know, our most powerful weapons are *sensak*. They allow us to maneuver our ships, conjure weaponry, and fool our enemies. They are our most potent weapons against the barbarous threats at our borders."

Verikash gestured at Tyana.

"Tyana is prodigious with *sensak*. While she may not be the most physically imposing initiate, I cannot recall a Warrior with more raw talent for them than my own teacher Zolstra, who is long passed. I have no doubt that, with time and experience, she will surpass even my own skill."

The hooded Vestal stirred in her seat.

"Does that mean you find her coronated?" Vershil pressed.

"Sister," Verikash deliberated, "it is true that Tyana has exhibited powers beyond that of a normal Warrior. She has demonstrated these powers on some occasions. In each case I've exercised mercy both toward her and those affected by it. I've found no reason to brand her nor any of my other Warriors during their process of learning with her." Verikash paused. "This does not include her forgoing slaying the gryphon. While I can bear witness that she held the gryphon in her grasp and could have killed it, she did not, breaking with our tradition."

"What kind of powers does she possess?" interrupted the hooded Vestal. "Can you describe them?"

"Perhaps you should ask her yourself." Verikash gestured to Tyana behind her.

Tyana stepped forward. The Vestal asked again:

"Speak, sister. What powers does your teacher refer to?"

"May I see the face of the Sister asking me?" Tyana requested formally.

The Vestal stood and removed her hood. Tyana

recognized her. Her hair was longer now. It was Ahnsair
—the Vestal she met at Mater Thea's funeral pyre,
seemingly long ago.

"Sister," Ahnsair said in the casual form, wearing a
subtle smile, "what powers does she refer to?"

Tyana contemplated her answer, then said succinctly:

"I see Thea in my dreams."

Ahnsair's smile disappeared. She remained silent for a
moment, then sat down, reclining.

"Sister Verikash," Vershil continued, "these details are
good. But the War Council wants an answer: is Tyana,
by your judgment, a Warrior or not?"

"Tyana is a Warrior—and more," Verikash replied.
"Given her colors, I address her as Vestal-Warrior. If the
Council deems she should be next in the line of
succession after me, I'll approve it."

Tyana felt a wave of surprise, then a wide grin come
over her face that she could not help.

She felt Sek's and Kersa's gazes become palpable. She
looked back at them. They both fumed at her wordlessly.

"Very well," Vershil said. "It is declared. Tyana is a
coronated Warrior with additional stature. She may be
addressed as Vestal-Warrior from now on. If she is as
talented as you say, sister Verikash, she will gain the
accolades you have recommended and, I assume, more."

Tyana withheld her elation. She looked behind her.
Sek and Kersa were quickly parting with the delegation
and exiting the cathedral.

When Tyana was excused from the delegation, she
left. Outside, Kersa and Sek were waiting.

"You may think you've won," said Sek, approaching
her, "but we'll make sure you never gain any respect in
our caste."

Tyana looked at Kersa. She was scowling, stalwart.

"You're in with this too?" Tyana asked.

"I've said my piece in the matter," Kersa said.

"We made a compromise," Tyana said.

"Between you and Verikash," Kersa corrected. "You made your choice. I made mine. I choose to uphold the values of this caste as I know them."

"Isn't honor more than a matter of personal adventure?" Tyana quipped.

Kersa bit her lip. Sek stepped up to Tyana.

"You may have authority over us just because you're mixed with a higher caste," Sek said, "but you'll never have respect. You may have talent for *sensak*, but you're still weaker, smaller—a step below in every other way."

Tyana grimaced at her, but didn't reply.

"You have friends in high places, but not among us," Sek added. With that she turned on her heel, descending the cathedral's staircase.

Tyana stared at Kersa, who said nothing. Finally, she too turned and walked away.

XXXI

WARRIORS RECEIVED A recess after coronation. They were free to wander for days as they wished with little responsibility. Most of them spent it brawling with each other and testing each other's skill in the open streets. Tyana wasn't interested in fighting and most Warriors weren't interested in fighting her, even though they still scowled at her as she passed by.

She didn't attempt to find Kersa. She felt like it would only make things worse.

Instead she spent the days wandering the grand staircases and spires of the Mater's City. She visited the libraries of the Keepers, but was denied entry. They were not open to other castes, and Vershil was no longer her teacher, after all. She could hear the hymns of the Artificers resonating beyond the walls of the cathedral whenever she walked by, but she did not go inside.

The only peace she found was in the old city. The streets crumbled away slowly as she drew farther and farther away from the main streets, toward the forests at their edge. Buildings became lifeless, then ancient, then decrepit, dissolving into moss and overgrowth. She headed to the cliffside—the same one where she had met the Artificer, Numa.

As she walked, the evening came on and it began to rain. Beyond the storm clouds, she could see the two moons performing their delicate dance. Tonight, the larger, black one was overtaking the white one. Their chalky scars and craters were readily visible. Tyana wondered at what Numa had said about the moons being the ships of the Maters. It didn't seem possible. But maybe she wasn't telling the whole story.

Tyana found the spot where she had tackled Numa on the grass. There was a subtle path in the direction she had headed while running.

Tyana followed the path. It veered away from the city across to the other side of the island. The grass gave way to dirt, which turned to mud in the rain. Tyana had her *sensak* but abstained from using them to shield herself from the downpour. She persisted along the dirt slope.

As she made her way down, the path led to a broken, staggered cliffside. The sea frothed below. She was far from the city now, but she knew its infrastructure was riddled throughout the island, hidden beneath the ground.

Tyana pressed downward along the broken slope beyond the worn path. It was treacherous and gravel gave way beneath her. Ahead, the obsidian cliffside presented a sheer cliff face not readily visible from the precipice. Inlaid in it were massive vents, dribbling thick steam from their corners. They were outbreath junctions for the undercity where the Artificers lived.

There was no obvious way up to them, but the face

was staggered in such a way as to be climbable. It took Tyana relatively little effort to reach the closest vent big enough for her to fit through—someone with lesser skill could have climbed it.

When she reached the closest vent, the smell of sulfur was strong. It gave a burst of steam that nearly scalded her, causing her to retreat. Pausing, she watched as the next vent down belched out a similar burst of steam, and then the next one after it.

She held her place. She counted the moments until the closest vent gave another burst of steam, which the others repeated in sequence. When they did it again, they did it at the same interval as before.

That was how much time she would have to get in.

Tyana took a deep breath and, after the following burst, dove into the vent. It was a long hallway. The fumes made her eyes water. She headed downward, following its incline, counting each moment she had before the vent would go off again. When she got to the end, there were massive fans staring back at her, standing idly. Her only options were to her left and right, which led down narrow hallways to the other vents. Below her feet was a small grating, big enough for a person. She tested it and it opened, revealing a narrow crawl space heading downward.

The fans began to whir. She had only moments left. She climbed down, swinging the grating closed behind her. No later than that did the vent above give a massive roar and the air become unbearably hot. The fumes pierced her eyes.

She worked her way down the crawl space. It went down for many floors. She couldn't see the bottom at first. It was so narrow that she had the impression it wasn't built for her body size, even though she was slightly smaller than the average Warrior. She tested the air and it smelled bad, but breathable.

As she went deeper into the structure, she passed by many similar ventilation junctions, each one small enough for a person no larger than her to get through. She hoped to see a different kind of junction, or a door, or an obvious way out of the ventilation system and into the undercity. She reached the bottom and despaired when she found none. It was a long climb back up.

Instead, she pressed onward, choosing the bottom-most duct straight ahead of her. Beyond it she could see a larger room with slowly spinning fans. The air seemed fresher as it flowed toward her. She worked forward through the increasingly small crawl space, prone on her stomach. As she did so, she felt an oncoming shortness of breath and nausea. It occurred to her that the bad smell she encountered earlier could have been an additive to denote toxicity. Hallucinations worked their way in from the corners of her eyes. She shook them away and focused on moving forward.

When she finally was able to exit the duct into the room beyond, she stood, but her legs gave out beneath her. She fell. She had trouble focusing her vision as it was overtaken by menacing patterns, despite that she still wore her gloves; they seemed to come out of their own volition now.

She made her way closer to the fans. The air coming through them smelled fresh.

She lay down, letting the cool wind course over her. She felt exhausted. She focused on her breathing, trying to replace the fumes in her lungs. She felt like she might fall asleep.

XXXII

THE AIR WAS cool and still. The ground was hard and full of gravel. Tyana was facing a starless horizon. Below, the sea was calm and as black as the inky sky above it. The moons were not visible. A red sun disk hovered on the horizon, neither rising nor setting, masked by far-off cliffsides. She had never seen it like this before. It cast a hot glow over the sea, and she bathed in its heat.

She turned around. Before her stood Mater Vale. She was tall and regal. Her shining white hair stood still in the breezeless air. She said, looking straight through Tyana:

"You are Amun, lord of the silent, who comes at the voice of the poor. When I call you in my distress, you come and rescue me."

Tyana turned again, looking behind her. The red sun disk was gone. In its place, standing before her, was a girl with vermillion-colored hair pouring over her shoulders. Tyana thought she recognized her, but her face was cast in shadow.

XXXIII

A HAND JABBED at Tyana's side. She snapped to attention, grabbing it. A pitiful yelp leapt from its owner, causing Tyana to relent. A voice said:

"Please, Warrior Sister! Don't hurt me!"

Tyana's vision was blurred and her head ached, but she could make out what she'd grabbed: the hand of an Artificer, no more than a young girl, with short, dirty red hair. She let go.

The Artificer darted across the room, staring at Tyana, who strained, attempting to stand. Tyana realized she had been unconscious for some time.

"How did you find me?" she asked the girl.

"You were asleep in the vents," she said. "You shouldn't be here. It's not safe to breathe."

"I've found that," Tyana said. She kept low to the ground, closest to where the air was fresh. She peered at the girl, who was at least a head shorter than herself—and thin.

"How old are you?" Tyana asked.

The girl hesitated, then said:

"Two months."

"What's your name?" Tyana asked.

"Ahva," the girl said proudly. "What's yours?"

"Tyana."

"Are you the one they call Vestal-Warrior? You have black and violet hair."

Tyana broke a smile.

"Yes—some call me that."

"Why are you here? It's not safe."

"I'm looking for someone called Numa. Do you know her?"

Ahva stared at her.

"Do you mean the Speaker?" she asked.

"The Speaker?" Tyana repeated.

"I don't know anyone called Numa. But if anyone knows her, the Speaker will."

"Do you know the way to the undercity?" Tyana asked.

"Know it? I came from there. I maintain these vents myself. Have every one of them memorized."

Ahva gestured at Tyana toward the vent duct.

"Come on—I'll show you the way. The Speaker is in the undercity and I know the shortest path. If you want to find her, I'll show you. You just have to take a deep breath and follow me."

Tyana nodded and inhaled deeply.

Ahva led her down a network of ducts Tyana would have never guessed on her own. Ahva, with her small size, had no problem navigating them. Tyana had to scoot forward on her belly in order to fit. The air wafted with the same noxious scent as before.

"You're almost there," Ahva declared. "Move quickly

—this part isn't safe!"

Tyana pressed forward to keep up with Ahva. She could feel the fumes swirling around her, stinging her eyes.

"Are we near the exit?" Tyana asked, her vision blurring.

"Almost," Ahva said. "Watch out—!"

Tyana felt herself fall forward through a duct. A grating below her collapsed and she fell downward. She landed on her back onto some kind of catwalk below. She heard great machines all around her, steaming and hissing. Jumpsuited, red-haired Artificers gathered around her.

"Who is this?" one of them asked.

"She must have fallen from the ceiling," another said.

Ahva came into view. Tyana's vision was blurry.

"I found her in the outbreath junctions," Ahva said. "She was passed out from toxicity."

"You saved her? Why?" said one, incredulous.

"She said she was looking for Numa," Ahva said. "I thought she must be looking for the Speaker."

"You shouldn't tell them about her!" retorted another.

"But she isn't just a Warrior," said Ahva, "She's the Vestal-Warrior the Speaker told us about."

Tyana fell unconscious.

XXXIV

"DOES SHE TRUST you?" Tyana heard an old, wizened voice say.

"I don't know," a younger one answered.

"But she is the same Warrior you met?" the other asked.

"Older, now—but yes."

"Then you must gain her trust," the voice said. "And, if you do, she must also gain yours. Your plans, all of us, may depend on it."

Tyana opened her eyes. Her vision was blurry and her body ached.

"She is waking up," the elderly one said. "I must go."

"Please, Sister," said the other. Tyana heard a shuffling of footsteps and the hiss of a closing door.

Someone stood over her. She couldn't make out her features, and the light skewed the color of her hair.

"Your name is Tyana, isn't it?" she asked.

"Yes."

"Do you know who I am?"

Tyana hesitated, squinting. She didn't answer. The figure ignored her silence, continuing:

"You were in one of our outbreath junctions for some time. The air is toxic there; we scent it to help with tracing, but it's not foolproof. You were lucky. If Ahva hadn't found you then you could've been left there for days. It is dangerous, after all, to send sisters as young as her into the vents just for inspections."

Tyana groaned.

"You'll need some of our medicine," she said, retrieving some items from a nearby cabinet. "You're not the first one to be poisoned—not speaking in regards to caste, of course." She returned with an intravenous solution in a clear bag.

"I don't need that," Tyana said.

"Yes, you do. Your blood is toxified so much that if you don't take it, you'll die."

Tyana sighed, relenting. She felt the needle go into her arm.

"Who are you?" Tyana asked.

"You can't tell, can you?" She affixed the bagged solution above the cot Tyana lay on. She leaned in close so Tyana could see. She had short, flaring red hair, a subtle but distinct jawline, and wide cheekbones. Tyana recognized the face; the hair was different.

"Numa," Tyana said. Numa smiled:

"Not quite. I told you my name was Numa. It isn't. My name is actually Amun. Some call me the Speaker."

Sweat was beading on Tyana's brow. Amun retrieved a bucket of water and a sponge. She began to dab Tyana's forehead, cooling her.

"It will take some time for you to heal. Let yourself rest."

"Why are you helping me?" Tyana asked.

"You came looking for me, didn't you?" she said. "I want to help you. Besides, maybe you can help me."

Tyana peered at her. Amun approached the entrance to leave.

"Rest well, Tyana. I will be back."

XXXV

Tyana drifted in and out of hallucinatory sleep. At times she would wake up from a vision. Amun was there, washing the sweat from her forehead. Amun would speak to her, but Tyana would often fall back into sleep.

When she dreamed, she saw herself wandering cliffsides, mountains. She walked along coastlines where the seas crashed against nascent volcanic rock. She could see Valen as it was when it was first formed—devoid of cities, devoid of industry, devoid of Thea, devoid of castes.

Tyana awoke again to see Amun gently washing her forehead. She dabbed away the sweat that collected on her body each night. The water felt cool to Tyana and she blinked as it neared her eyes. Her vision was improved. She could focus on Amun's short, fiery hair, fading in height near the temples. Tyana traced Amun's jawline with her eyes, finally resting her focus on Amun's lips.

Tyana stilled Amun's washcloth with one gloved hand.

"Have you ever tried this before?" she asked. Amun hesitated.

"No," she said.

Tyana gently removed the cloth from Amun's hand.

"Will you help me find out what it means?" she asked. Amun hesitated again. Tyana's gloved hands touched hers.

"—Yes," Amun said.

Tyana nestled Amun's fingers on her cheek. Tension and heat rose from their tips. It radiated as Amun traced Tyana's jawline with her palm.

"It's true what they say about you," Amun said, sighing, as Tyana worked off her gloves. Amun's hand continued down Tyana's neck, down the center of her chest. When Tyana clasped Amun's arm with her bare hands, the heat turned into a tingling ecstasy. Patterns invaded their vision at the corners of their closed eyelids, folding and unfolding, shifting in color.

"Sister," Amun said, "this is beyond me."

"Just follow," Tyana said. "Just hold me."

They embraced each other at the nape of their necks. Waves of energy built through their cores, billowing out through their bodies. The hallucinations did the same, piercing their sight. When they brought their foreheads together, the energy exploded. Dreamscape engulfed Tyana's closed eyes.

Amun joined Tyana on the cot. They entangled each other, silent, shivering, and sweating. The vision was as intense as Tyana had ever experienced. Amun was there with her in the dream. The landscape inside was like a deep, blue sea that encased them both—like floating in the womb together. In this perfect space they embraced each other, alone. There was nothing separating them—

no castes, no burdens, no Maters. The only thing there was their raw, pulsing connection. Who knows how long they stayed there. It didn't matter.

XXXVI

WHEN TYANA AWOKE, Amun was not there. She felt well.

Getting up, she opened the room's entrance. Outside were the undercity's depths. Above her, the building stretched upward, seemingly endless. Lights dotted its sheer sides—all Artificer quarters. Walkways stretched from each of their doors into the fog. Above was a giant banner with the insignia of the caste, wafting like a ghost. Its smoke-tinged edges framed the vermillion symbol in its center.

She walked out onto the catwalk extending from the entrance. Ahead, Tyana saw Amun standing next to a hunched, hooded figure. They were discussing something. When Amun noticed Tyana, she gestured at the figure. The figure turned and walked away, disappearing steadily into the fog. Amun approached her.

"You're awake," she said, smiling. "Feeling better?"

"I am," Tyana admitted. "Thank you."

"Let me just say—about last night," Amun said, clasping Tyana's gloved hand. "I've never felt anything like it. I didn't think you were the average Warrior when Ahva brought you to us, but now I know for sure you're different."

"I encountered you in the old city," Tyana said. "You lied about your name."

"Of course," Amun said, letting Tyana's hand go. "A simple precaution."

"A precaution for what?" Tyana asked.

Amun gave her a quizzical, studious look. She put some distance between herself and Tyana.

"You already know that my name is Amun, and that some call me the Speaker. How much do you know about my caste?"

"Only what my teacher told me," Tyana said.

"Of course," Amun said. "Only what your teacher told you." Amun looked downward, across the railings of the catwalk. Below them, the abyss seemed endless, but Tyana could make out a body of water at the bottom. It must have been where the undercity met the open ocean. As Amun leaned on the railing, peering down, a large machine carrying a crate breached the surface of the water below. Amun gestured at it.

"That machine there—do you know what it's for?"

Tyana peered at it.

"It looks like it's collecting cargo."

"True. The cargo is food," Amun said. "Each of those machines has two Artificer pilots inside. They harvest sea crops below the water level. Once harvested, they deliver them to the processing units. From there, we distribute the food to the cities as rations—the same ones you eat."

Tyana watched as the machine settled on a loading platform. A number of jumpsuited figures crowded around it. They were Artificers, save for two.

"Why are a Warrior and Scribe down there?"

Amun squinted.

"Can you really see that far down?" she asked.

"Warrior's eyesight," Tyana answered tersely. Amun nodded.

"Scribes record the crop yield and the names of the collectors. A Warrior observes to punish the collectors if need be."

Tyana watched as they opened the crate. Sea kelp spewed out onto the bay floor. The Artificers gathered around, grouping it into smaller piles. She watched as one of them came up to the Scribe, attempting to discuss something. More joined her, and soon two crowds had formed—one collecting the kelp, and the other watching the Artificer conversing with the Scribe.

"Who is that Artificer speaking to the Scribe?"

"I don't know. Probably the foreman."

She watched as the foreman continued to implore the Scribe, but the Warrior stepped between them. The Warrior struck the foreman in the cheek, knocking her down. The crowd moved back as the Warrior grabbed the foreman on the ground, then she brought out a tattooing gun and branded the side of the foreman's face.

"Why would that Artificer be punished?"

Amun shrugged.

"Perhaps their harvest was too low. That's the most likely scenario. The piloted machines have a limited air supply, so they have to meet the quota before they run out of air."

"How often does that happen—running out of air?" Tyana asked. Amun's face turned downcast.

"Too often," she replied.

Tyana watched as the Scribe and Warrior left the loading bay. The crowd huddled around the foreman, lifting her to her feet. Amun retreated back across the catwalk to the room, bringing back a head scarf.

"You should probably wear this. I don't suppose you want to be spotted with us dirty Artificers."

Amun handed the scarf to her. Tyana considered it for a moment, then wrapped her hair up in it, being sure to conceal any purple and black strands. Amun motioned to her.

"Follow me—there's something else I'd like to show you."

Amun led her from the catwalk to a junction made of hanging gratings. They formed a series of makeshift staircases leading down into the fog. As Tyana followed Amun, the steps swung precariously under her own weight. Looking up, Tyana saw that they were strung together with mere cords that seemed like they could snap if pressed. Tyana considered using her *sensak* to steady them, but thought again of it. Instead, she just followed quickly in Amun's footsteps.

"Do you always travel this way?" Tyana asked.

"Only when I don't want to be seen. Otherwise we'd have to take the elevators. Look—"

She pointed downward to the nearest wall of the abyss. With a distant, electrified hum, a large platform slid out from the wall. Artificers poured onto it. From Tyana's vantage high up, they looked like faded red dots on a corroded pewter plate. The platform hummed again, rising up along the wall. Its hum grew louder and louder until it was just beneath Tyana and Amun. It stopped with a jolt, and the Artificers, crowded shoulder to shoulder, filed onto the next level.

"Come on," Amun said once the platform was vacant. "Let's go."

Amun jumped down from the gratings onto the platform. Tyana did the same. Following Amun onto the level ahead, she stopped as the platform behind her whirred to life again. It descended rapidly down the abyss. Tyana lingered, watching it. She noted that it had no guard rails of any kind.

"Come on," Amun implored, gesturing to the walkway ahead. Tyana followed.

Amun led her along the walkway until it opened into a large clearing. Amun motioned her away from the clearing and instead up a crawl space. Tyana could see through the crawl space's perforated grating. She saw a large, dark hangar with no discernible lights except for an ambient glow cast by deep vats in the floor. The vats were arranged in rows, and she could make out Artificers standing at their lips. The nearest vat had a mechanical claw deep in its throat; one of the Artificers manipulated it via a nearby control console. As the mechanical arm rose up, the unfinished wing of a warbird rose from the center of the vat, glowing a bioluminescent blue-green and dripping with liquid. Tyana could see its spongy inner structure, but its otherwise daggerlike profile was already obvious. She tried to count the number of vats in the hangar, but quickly gave up once she noticed Amun, already ahead of her through the crawl space, waving at her to move along.

Tyana followed. When they crossed that hangar, it gave way to a second one, just as large as the first. Scores of warbirds lay in pieces, many being worked on by up to five Artificers at a time, assembling the wings onto the struts of the main fuselages.

"How many Artificers does it take to create a single warbird?"

"Fifty altogether. With gestation time and assembly, it takes about two months."

"There must be hundreds of ships here, easily."

Amun nodded solemnly.

"Come on, the last one is up ahead."

Tyana followed Amun. The light from the grating drew shadowy patterns on the inside of the crawl space. She could hear the muted din of the mechanical arms as they moved through the hangars. At times she tried to stop and look through the grating to get a sense of the scope of the construction. Amun was ahead of her again.

When she caught up, she could see yet another hangar with a set of vats, but this hangar was lit and larger than the last. Fully assembled warbirds, dull silver in color with their marrow-like innards exposed, were lowered into deep cavities. A quivering substance that Tyana recognized as *sensak*—or something like it—rippled seemingly out of its own volition as the warbird's structure was lowered inside. The liquid leapt up, permeating the structure, covering it in the smooth, oil-colored skin that Tyana recognized as any warbird's.

"How do you get the *sensak* to grow into the warbird?" Tyana asked.

"It is a modified version of the *sensak* you know. It is designed to be at home on a warbird's skeleton, attuned specifically for forming its outer skin."

"Do you create the *sensak* too?"

"Of course. The process has changed little since the time Mater Vale invented it. Your caste demands a steady supply, and every batch must be tested by the First

Warrior."

Amun peered through the grating, then pointed.

"Look, see for yourself."

Tyana saw Verikash entering the hangar flanked by two Warriors. Immediately, an Artificer stopped her work and hurried to meet her. Tyana strained to hear their conversation, presuming the Artificer to be another foreman. The Artificer hurried away, and by the time she came back she had a small box in her hands. She opened it, revealing a set of cylinder-shaped capsules. From the color of the liquid inside, Tyana knew that the capsules contained *sensak*.

Verikash gingerly touched her stone collar, ejecting a set of identical capsules inside it. Handing them to one of the flanking Warriors, she took the capsules from the Artificer's box, replacing them into her collar. The liquid from the new capsules drained into her body. The flanking Warriors and the Artificer took some steps back.

Tyana watched as Verikash formed objects with the *sensak*: first a blade, then a shield, and then a set of both. Some of the shields were fuzzy or sponge-like. Verikash dissolved them and shot the Artificer a gaze that even gave Tyana pause. She recognized Verikash's disappointment easily.

Verikash gestured to the Warrior holding the previous set of *sensak*. She removed the new capsules from her neck, replacing them with the old. Tyana winced as the old *sensak* drained back into Verikash's collar. She gestured to the foreman, who came close. A number of the other Artificers paused their work to watch.

Verikash revealed a tattooing gun from beneath her ripped tunic. She tapped it with the new capsules of *sensak* in her hand. Tyana still couldn't hear their conversation, but she could read Verikash's lips:

"Start again."

Then she threw the capsules on the ground. They shattered into pieces. She turned on her heel and walked away; the Warriors followed her. Tyana couldn't see the face of the Artificer gripping the box, watching Verikash's receding back as she stood in place, but Tyana imagined it. The other Artificers watching the exchange lingered in their gaze at the foreman for a moment, then went back to their work.

"I take it that it is not trivial to create a batch of *sensak*," Tyana whispered to Amun.

"No more trivial than creating a warbird," Amun replied. "Your teacher must be in a merciful mood today. Come on. One last thing I want to show you."

Amun led her down a corner away from the construction hangars. The crawl space gave way to a vertical junction with a ladder leading up and down.

"Take the climb up to the next level," Amun said, exiting the crawl space, gripping the rungs. She began to climb up and disappeared from view. Tyana came to the junction and looked downward. The ladder must have extended all the way to the deepest levels of the undercity. Looking up, she saw the same was true in the opposite direction. It reminded her of the climb through the outbreath junctions.

"Come on," Amun said, looking over her shoulder down to Tyana. "It's just one level up."

Tyana grabbed the rungs and began to climb. After some time, Amun stopped, working open the door of the next level's junction. When she had it open, she crawled in. Tyana followed up the ladder and Amun offered her hands. Tyana took them, climbing inside.

"Where are we heading now?" Tyana asked.

"My caste serves not just yours, but the Scribes and Keepers as well. I want to show you where their precious scrolls come from."

They came to another perforated crawl space up ahead. Amun turned a corner; Tyana followed. Through the gratings Tyana could see an expansive room filled with glowing crucibles. Chunks of ore, gripped by mechanical claws, were slowly lowered into the red-hot containers. Artificers took the crucibles, hanging precariously on chains, and poured out their liquefied contents into molds.

"The ore must be harvested from asteroids. That is part of why the war effort is on—without the ore, the Scribes would not be able to write in the scrolls. Without scrolls, bookkeeping would stop; Thea would be without her scriptures, and civilization would cease."

Tyana noted Amun's use of the casual form while referring to Thea. She watched through the grating, noticing a group of Artificers readying one crucible to pour into a mold. Tyana watched as they began to pour the liquefied metal into the mold, piece by piece.

"They shouldn't be doing it that way," Amun commented, peering through the grating. "What are they thinking?"

As they moved to pour the metal into the last piece, the chain got stuck. The crucible buckled. Tyana watched as the liquid metal splashed over the mold, throwing itself onto the nearest Artificer. She screamed, falling to the floor. She was the shortest and youngest among them.

Amun swore aloud, banging on the grating. She broke it down, leaping from the crawl space to the floor. Light poured into the crawl space and Tyana feared she'd be spotted. Instead, she stayed put, watching as the Artificers, joined by Amun, gathered around, attempting to save the girl. It was too late, however. The molten metal had already permeated her heavy jumpsuit.

Amun let out a desperate cry that chilled Tyana's blood. For a moment, Tyana lingered there in the crawl space, watching. Then she quietly leapt down to the floor. The smell of smoldering bronze and soot entered her nostrils. Even as she approached Amun, the other Artificers didn't take notice of the Vestal-Warrior in a headscarf until she was standing there among them.

XXXVII

TYANA SAT AT the edge of one of the gratings in the undercity, her legs hanging over the abyss. She watched below as food harvesters breached the surface of the water, carrying their cargos into the fog. She could make out the details of their hulls with her acute vision, but from here, their engines were silent. The contrast gave her a sense of profound distance.

She heard a door at the other end of the walkway slide open. Amun was there in the entrance discussing something with an Artificer in medical garb. After a moment, Amun nodded, then the door closed behind her. She walked over to Tyana. Sitting down next to her, she too dangled her legs over the grating. Her despondency was visible on her face, but it was muted.

"How is she?" Tyana asked.

"She'll live," Amun said, "but she'll never walk again." Tyana paused.

"How old is she?"

"One and a half," Amun said, putting her face in her

hands. "Maybe if her jumpsuit had a better seal it would've kept her safe. We only have so many and they often get recycled. She was new to the work and she made a mistake."

Tyana, sullen, looked out into the fog.

"Maybe she shouldn't have taken that job so early," she offered.

"There's no choice," Amun said, wiping her eyes. "We have quotas to keep. It's either put all the workers we have to the task or risk punishment. Sometimes it's the group, not the individual, that gets the worst of it." She sniffled. "Sometimes it's the individual."

Tyana attempted to comfort her by putting a gloved hand on Amun's shoulder. Amun looked at her for a moment, then put her own on top of it.

"She was one of my best," she said wistfully into the fog. "And now she can't walk."

"What do you mean, she was one of your best?" Tyana asked. Amun looked at her, then broke a smirk.

"You still don't get it, do you?" she said. Tyana furrowed her brow, silent. "What would you do if you had to perform dangerous, possibly fatal work, consistently under pressure, with the threat of punishment hanging over you if you didn't meet the demands? And if it had been that way ever since you or any of your sisters could remember?"

Tyana looked at her, saying:

"I understand your frustration, but I don't know what you mean. After all, couldn't most of that work be automated? Why should the Artificers in the food harvesters be risked with limited air supply? If building the warbirds can be automated—even partially—why not the scroll-making too?"

Amun paused, studying her.

"You think like an Artificer would," she commented. A silence passed between them. "But that is not the problem," she said, continuing. "Thea commands her work be done by way of our labor. We Artificers—our burden is to work. If we don't, our muse—our madness, as she puts it—will take over. The work is meant to stave that off, to keep us busy and distracted."

"It looks to me like it unnecessarily endangers you."

Amun smiled at her.

"Then we agree on that. Our Elders tell us it wasn't always this way. Vale intended us to utilize our muse for ingenuity, not to suppress it. She wanted us to express our delight for life through our creativity. Thea doesn't value these things. She teaches that our value, our purpose, is to work for the benefit of her cause, the only noble cause. To her, we deserve to be here in our predicament. It is our reason for being, ingrained into the nature of our caste. We are not really slaves to our work—we are slaves to her word."

"The Keepers and Scribes don't assist you?"

"Why would they?" Amun retorted. "They benefit from our work too. If we didn't have to make the scrolls, they would have to make them themselves. Could you imagine a Scribe, in her dark, fancy robe, trying to control a cauldron? The Elders say that it once was that way, if you could believe it, but things changed when Vale disappeared and Thea took power. If I could change things back to the old ways, I would. Even the Warriors—"

She stopped short. She looked at Tyana from the corner of her eye, and sighed.

"I'm sorry," Tyana offered.

The apology seemed to linger between them. Amun nodded.

"You asked me why I lied to you about my name. I did it to protect myself and my sisters. That girl who got burned was not one my best workers. She was one of my best spies."

Tyana looked at her.

"Spies?"

"I'll ask you again. Put yourself in my place, or in that girl's place. If this was your life, would you adore Thea the way she expects? Would you put yourself in harm's way for nothing but to fulfill someone else's definition of what it means to be good? Would you stay that way, complacent?"

Tyana looked down at the abyss below them.

"I don't know. I don't think so. I know that I don't think it's fair," Tyana said.

"It's not," Amun seethed. "Our caste labors, but we see no fruits from it. We only get the dangers. Even if we deprive ourselves of this life, Thea teaches that the punishment will be worse on the other side. We are objects of Vale's creation and Thea rules Vale's empire —so to her, our service in perpetuity is fair trade. We've had enough of it now; it can't go on. But if anything will change, we need a vision for that change first. A vision of hope. That's why they call me the Speaker."

"You plan to bring them that change?" Tyana asked.

"No. I can only speak to them about what that change could be. I can't bring about that change by myself."

Amun looked at her; a pause hung between them. She gripped Tyana's gloved hand and Tyana allowed her to hold it.

"I'd like to show you one last thing," she said. "It's

what my caste is really about—it's part of that vision of hope. Can I show you?"

Tyana nodded.

"Okay."

XXXVIII

A MUN LED TYANA by the hand. They went deeper into the undercity, bypassing the dingy maze of catwalks, balconies, and industrial tunnels. Instead, Amun led her down a cavern's shaft, carved smooth by the cuts of ancient mining machines. They encountered no one there. Only a few spare lamps lit their way, and they too eventually ceased along the path. Darkness encroached on them.

"Where are we going?" Tyana whispered to her.

"An ancient place known only to us Artificers. You are sworn to its secrecy."

Amun pressed deeper into the cavern, using the sheer cuts in the rock as footholds. Tyana followed her step by step. Gradually, a crimson light grew all around them as they descended. Tyana could see ancient, phosphorescent crystals embedded in the wall. They beamed a scarlet red. They wove among protruding sections of ore like veins, the way water parts through a cliffside. Their light flattened the colors of Tyana's hair

165

so that it was indistinguishable from Amun's. The whole of the cavern was cast in reddish light and shadow.

When they reached the bottom, the floor was cut level and smooth. A square hallway was their lone path forward. At its end loomed a large, heavy gateway carved in the shape of the Artificer's insignia. Its outer face appeared to be cut from a single massive piece of cinnabar, and a phosphorescent sheen coated its surface, illuminating the insignia's shape in the dim red light. Inside, visible gearlike structures of quartz betrayed a complex locking mechanism. It was unlike anything Tyana had seen. Amun, with wild eyes and a stern look on her face, beckoned to her. They approached the gateway.

Amun produced a small cinnabar crystal from her pocket. It was no bigger than a fingernail, cut in the shape of a hexagonal prism. She traced the surface of the gateway with her hand. In its center, the gateway's smooth surface gave way to bumps and ridges, then to small holes, like a perforated screen. She tested a few of the holes against the crystal until she found one that matched. There were no gaps as she slid the crystal into its properly matching cavity. She pushed it in and it disappeared.

A small clink from the deposited crystal turned into an orchestra of chattering gear teeth. The door groaned with a mechanical sigh that reverberated into the ground. The gears in the gateway's facade turned, each layer of locks moving at a different pace. The gate had the illusion of a multilayered wheel as it rolled aside.

Beyond it was a room full of painted images. They stepped inside. The images were hung like tapestries or stretched on frames. They were swirling, colorful abstractions with sharp geometries and patterns.

"What are these?" Tyana asked.

"These are our ancestral motifs. Thea banned them after she came to reign. Vale taught them to the first Artificer. They tell the story of our caste and the genesis of our race."

"They look like nothing I'd see in the upper city."

"You wouldn't. We Artificers kept the tradition long after Thea forbade it. They are subversive images. No Keeper would allow their display; it would contest their interpretation of scripture."

Tyana peered harder at the paintings. There was something uncanny about the motifs.

"They look like my visions—like pieces of them."

"That's why I had to show you," Amun said. "After last night, I saw the same things. But I recognized them because I've been to this place before. Your visions are not meaningless." Amun led her farther in by the hand. She led her to one particular painting.

"Look at this," Amun said.

It was a swirling black maw struck by two motes of violet and white. It reminded Tyana of an image she saw with Vershil in the library.

"I know this one," Tyana said.

"Do you know what it says?" Amun asked.

"My teacher said it speaks of multi-burdened sistren— the only verse in all the scriptures that does."

"According to our Elders, it tells us that the multi-burdened sistren are our path back to Vale. And it speaks of a Warrior born solely through Vale's will. Through her, Vale's promise to us is fulfilled."

"What promise?" Tyana asked.

"To liberate us," Amun said, turning to Tyana. "We

Artificers produce labor for Thea, but we don't benefit from it. We don't own the things we create. We don't even own the tools we use to make them. When Artificers build a cathedral, it serves Thea, not us. When we cook and serve Keepers their food, they eat it, not us. When we farm that food, who does it benefit?"

Tyana hesitated. Amun continued:

"My caste used to be proud, with heritage, stories, and songs. Vale made us the caretakers of Her arts, and we carried them on through our traditions. But then She disappeared. Thea tried to eradicate all that and she replaced them with her own. So we carried them on in secret. Thea has the Keepers to declare truth for her and Scribes to write it down, but we remember what Vale handed down to us before she came. We know Vale's true intentions for us."

"What are those?" Tyana asked.

"To reclaim our heritage and our pride." Amun looked at her. "What do you dream of most, Tyana? What's your soul's desire?"

Tyana hesitated, then answered.

"To understand why Vale created me."

Amun nodded.

"Do you know what I dream of? I dream of a world where those who work earn the gains of their work for themselves. I dream of a world without castes. I dream of a world where my sisters are free to be as they wish, and we don't have to toil for others. I dream of a world without Thea. Wouldn't you want that?"

Tyana stared at her:

"I can dream of it. But you know speaking like that is heresy."

"By Thea's own decree," Amun snorted. She

continued using the lesser form of address—a brandable offense when speaking of the Maters. "She deems it heresy because it doesn't support her interests. You want to understand Vale's purpose for you? The Keepers will only tell you what Thea wants you to hear. Our knowledge will tell you what Vale originally intended. Let me help you find what you're seeking, and in return you can help us."

"In what way can I help you?" Tyana asked.

"By fulfilling Vale's purpose for you," Amun said, gesturing at the image. She took Tyana's hands. "Tyana —when I first met you, I knew you weren't a normal Warrior, but I didn't know if I could trust you. I've already shared with you the secrets of my caste. But there's more, Tyana, so much more to share. I need to know that I'm safe with you, that I can trust you, and that you'll help me—that you'll help all of us."

Tyana looked at the image. The more she looked at it, the more it spoke to her like her visions could speak to her. She remembered how Vershil, when she encountered the same image in the scriptures, refused to elaborate on it and reprimanded her for asking.

"All right. I'll help you," Tyana said. "Just tell me how I can."

Amun smiled at her, her eyes wild. Her short, flaring hair seemed indistinguishable in color from her skin in the dim, red light.

"Then meet me in the caverns at the opposite side of the undercity. Follow the mine shaft like this one where the abyss meets the sea. It is deeper and larger—follow the crystals of cinnabar in the rock. They will lead you to the meeting place where there will be a gathering tonight. There, we will begin building a new future, and you will be the key to it."

Amun smiled. She clasped Tyana's hands and hugged her. Tyana's shoulders tingled as Amun's palms lingered on her bare skin.

XXXIX

TYANA SAT IN the red sanctum long after Amun left her there. Nighttime was approaching. She could tell, even though the dim red light around her did not change. The glow from scarlet, bioluminescent bacteria in the walls, living in the veins of cinnabar around her, pulsated gently. The organisms feeding on the rock were there since the formation of the rock itself. As crystals in the ore formed, the bacteria were locked inside. Their copulation produced light, giving the crystals their glow. The bacteria fed on their choice mineral, mercury, gradually hollowing out their own environment. As long as the crystal's growth outpaced the multiplying bacteria, their phosphorescence remained. Such crystals glowed for millennia, but when the bacteria finally bore through the surface, they died and the crystal's light ceased, leaving an abnormal cavity in the mineral's structure.

As Tyana crossed the sanctum's threshold to leave, she felt the heavy pounding of gears hidden in the walls. The gateway slowly rolled back into its place behind her, its mechanical innards coming to rest in the place they had been when she first entered. She resolved to find the other cavern Amun mentioned and see this gathering for herself.

She climbed the shaft's walls, gradually making her way back up to the undercity. When she reached it, she traveled like Amun did—scaling the balconies and hanging rafters to hide herself from any onlookers. Her hair was still wrapped up in a scarf, and she straightened it to keep any loose hairs from falling out.

She made her way toward the floor of the undercity. Fog obstructed her view, but she could hear the lapping of the waves below and the hum of food collectors. The final level gave way to caverns, and the air smelled stale and damp.

Tyana jumped from her current vantage point, hanging off a rickety balcony, to the rocky floor below. She landed on her feet and the sound of it echoed across the cavern's grounds. No one was in sight. Broken machines littered the ground. She looked up and could see the main stalk of the undercity rising upward through the fog like a mechanical esophagus. Rigging and piping gave way to stalagmites around her. She could see the cavern's shore; it wasn't far away. Water lapped at its lip. She heard a food collector breach the water, its running lights glowing in the haze. Tyana moved behind a stalagmite to hide herself. She stayed there until she heard the collector go on its way.

She looked around. Amun said to follow the veins of cinnabar. Tyana squinted, looking for any traces of it. She moved deeper into the cavern's pathways, away from the shore. She crossed the entire floor of the city's abyss until she spotted a deep shaft like the one that led to the sanctum. Tyana looked down its throat. A few paces down, veins of cinnabar glowed with a phosphorescent ruby red.

Looking out for anyone who could be watching one last time, she put her foot on the nearest outcropping in the shaft and started her descent. It was a tighter passageway than the previous one. Footholds farther down formed discernible steps. They were carved in a hexagonal spiral. The staircase's center sagged, as if each step carried the weight of a thousand feet. Tyana followed them, glowing red veins of rock lighting her way.

When she reached the bottom of the staircase, the shaft opened into a huge natural cavern. A fire's red glow, masked by stalagmites and stalactites, joined the ambient light. Sound echoed, backed by a stochastic drumbeat.

Tyana moved toward the heart of the cave. The floor of it gave way to a rocky pit bursting with red and pink flames at its bottom; it wafted with the smell of natural gas. Surrounding it was a crowd of Artificers swaddled in robes. Musicians were making music with arcane-looking drums and other instruments that Tyana didn't recognize. Above them was a ledge where a hooded, hunched figure looked on. Joining the sole onlooker on the ledge was Amun.

"The Speaker comes," someone announced. The Artificers hailed Amun, and she hailed back. Whispers rose from the crowd as Amun watched them silently. She scanned the crowd. When her eyes rested on Tyana, she smiled.

"What do you speak on?" someone asked aloud to Amun, impatient. Tyana came close to the crowd but remained quiet. No one else noticed her.

"Hope," Amun replied. "Sisters, I told you that Vale promised us a way forward—that She has not forgotten us even while Thea oppresses us. I told you that there would be a Warrior who would see through the lies of Thea and fulfill the hope Vale gives us. Today, I give you Tyana, the Vestal-Warrior I promised."

Amun pointed at Tyana. The Artificers turned toward her. First they gasped, then they howled at her. Tyana could see their faces. Many were dirty with dust and soot from their work. Many had tattooed, blackened eyelids. Their eyes were wide as they shouted; they were tinged with a look of madness. Amun held up a hand to quiet them.

"Tyana is the first one not of our caste to join us. I would not bring her here if I did not feel safe with her. Tonight, she will join us in the mysteries of Vale. Please, Tyana—join me here."

With trepidation, Tyana made her way through the crowd. She moved around the pit's edge, wary of the many soot-ringed eyes on her. She followed the path up to where Amun and the hooded onlooker stood.

"I'm glad to see you," Amun said, smiling. She took her hand, holding it. Tyana smiled back.

"Tonight," Amun announced to the crowd, "we begin our revolution. Tonight, we begin to fulfill Vale's prophecies. Tonight, we plant the seeds of our liberation."

The crowd hailed at her in unison.

One Artificer moved through the crowd, handing something to the participants. They appeared to be small, black pills. Amun pulled out two of her own. She held them up over her head, and the crowd did the same.

"We take this in rebellion of Thea," Amun addressed, "and to reawaken Vale in us."

The crowd took their pills. Amun took one and handed the other to Tyana.

"What does it do?" Tyana whispered, asking Amun.

"You already know," she said. "It is your touch." She took it without hesitation.

Tyana contemplated the pill. It seemed ready to crumble in her hand, little more than a dry powder pressed together. Down below, the musicians began their discordant orchestra and the crowd writhed. Dancing to the beat of the musicians, they threw off their robes. They embraced each other, grinning and smiling with electric energy.

"Come with me," Amun asked Tyana, clasping her hand.

Tyana took the pill.

They made their way down the ledge into the heart of the crowd. As they danced, Tyana felt a familiar electric tingle radiate from her core. It grew in waves over her skin and distorted her vision. Artificers danced around her, their bodies masked by the light of the fire. Others embraced nearby, sighing in ecstasy.

Amun turned to Tyana, placing Tyana's hands on her hips and holding her by the back of her neck.

"I trust you, Tyana," Amun said. "Do you trust me?"

"Yes," Tyana said. Amun smiled, whispering in her ear:

"Then nothing will stop us."

They kissed. Tyana was overwhelmed with energy. She felt like she could fade into Amun's body. As the crowd writhed, they became the center of it. Others reached out to touch Tyana and her touch spread into them, catalyzed by the drug. She and Amun became the core of a swarm of dirty, sweaty Artificers, moving in rhythm with the drums. Tyana looked up from the crowd. Through the hallucinations playing on her open eyes, she could see the hooded onlooker watching from the ledge above. Her hands, peeled from beneath the robe, were covered in tattoos.

It was the last clear sight Tyana had before she was fully engulfed in a blinding vision. Her touch extended into Amun, into all of them. Her visions spread into the crowd, binding them together; they shared a journey into the memories rooted in the rocks around them. They saw impossible machines, forgotten places, and a lineage of Artificers lost to history.

Then Tyana saw a face she did not recognize. It was not Valenian. It was dark, with green eyes, and a square forehead. It spoke in a language Tyana did not understand. It was human—the face of the tan-skinned man from her birth dream.

After that, Tyana lost all sense of self. She was cast into a realm totally lacking in differentiation. Her ego was shattered like a mirror and each piece became a universe containing all her possible identities. There was nothing to grasp onto anymore, so she let go, and all was one.

XL

WHEN TYANA CAME to, the visions had faded. The fire still burned with its natural glow, but the energy of the crowd was drained. She was surrounded by red-haired figures, many of them nude, passed out or gently nursing themselves back to consciousness.

She stood. The pulsing electricity from the drug had worn off, leaving the sensation that her nerves had been peeled of their outermost layer. Amun wasn't nearby. Neither was the hooded onlooker on the ledge.

She gathered herself and endeavored to find them both. She made her way out of the cave, stepping over sleeping and groaning Artificers, then leaving up through the staircase. Fog wafted around her as she climbed out of the shaft. She moved along the cavern's floor, convinced she should return to Amun's quarters.

She stopped as a dark form stepped out in front of her from the shadow of one of the stalagmites. It was the hooded onlooker from the gathering.

"Who are you?" Tyana asked.

"I am Amun's mentor," a quivering, elderly voice said from beneath the hood. "You already know me. I wanted to speak with you in person."

"How do I already know you?"

The figure stepped in close, revealing a pair of heavily tattooed hands. The hands lifted the hood and Tyana saw the face of the Grand Artificer.

"I do know you," Tyana said.

"I've come to give you two warnings. One is about Thea. Her mind stretches through all of us. It feeds on our power as much as we—and you—feed on it. You must remember this at all times, especially when you are in Her presence. Now that I've seen your power firsthand, I have no doubt your coming will awaken some of Her latent powers as well. It will do the same for Vale, but Thea has the advantage, because She has a living body."

"How do you know this?" Tyana asked.

"You will be on the War Council soon," the Grand Artificer predicted, ignoring her question. "You will attend to the Vicar in Her court. We believe you are Vale's answer to our predicament, but Thea has Her own designs for you. She will draw your body close to Her, but She will draw your mind even closer. You must be wary of this."

The Grand Artificer sighed.

"I must warn you about Amun as well. Her intentions are pure, but she does not fully comprehend the powers she wields. She is rebellious and impulsive, even while she can be tender and loving. Your intuitions will give you a perspective she does not have. Listen to them above all and keep her safe. She is our last hope."

"Why don't you lead them? You are on the War

Council too."

"I am too old," the Grand Artificer said. "Madness works its way into my voice and it grows on my skin as rashes. I have no room for rebellion anymore. I worked with every forbidden tool just so I could teach others the old ways. If my hands were tattooed any further I would be banished—not that it would matter, I suppose. I will be gone soon. Our caste is large with many sick and elderly. The best we can do is support the youthful ones. Little ones like Ahva are the future; they need a strong, youthful leader. Amun has given them hope they did not have, even if it is at a cost. Now your presence gives them even more hope—hope that the caste system can be broken."

"I don't know if I can do that," Tyana admitted.

"Thea is the reason the caste system persists. If Thea's grip is loosened, the system will dissolve."

"How?"

"You must loosen Her grip on you," the Grand Artificer said. "That will be the beginning."

"I am trying to understand my burden and why Vale set me through all this," Tyana insisted. "Can you help me?"

"Her purpose for you will only be clear once you've traveled fully down the path She set out for you. Thea clouds that path, but the power and clarity of your intent will guide you. Follow it to its end. Perhaps you will only get the answers you need once you can ask Vale Herself."

The Grand Artificer turned to go, replacing her hood, saying:

"Hide all this in your mind and shield it from others. Do not seek me out and forget that we spoke here this way."

XLI

TYANA SPENT MORE nights with Amun in secret. They explored the touch frequently. Tyana found that the more they touched, the more their connection strengthened. Eventually, they walked together in the same vision. They explored hidden landscapes sculpted from their imagination. The visions took on a dreamlike quality, as if they were not creating them but recalling distant times and places. The deeper they went, the more the visions regressed in time and increased in tangibility. They walked the shores of Valen before cities came. They felt untampered soil under their feet. They watched the moons slowly stray from their original orbits, coming to rest at their current places.

"Is all this real?" Amun asked one night.

"It seems real to me," Tyana said.

Tyana slowly dislodged her fingers, gently unentangling herself from Amun. She stood up in Amun's quarters.

"What do you think we see when we do this?" Amun

asked, sweat beaded on her brow.

"I don't know," Tyana answered. "But sometimes it reminds me of things I saw in the libraries while my teacher showed me the scriptures. Sometimes they're not like that at all. Sometimes I feel like these aren't just hallucinations—they're real, but from another time and place, like they actually happened."

Amun snapped up, asking her:

"Do you think they're memories?"

Tyana looked at her.

"They can't be our memories if they're not from our time."

"But don't the Keepers say that each child of Vale carries Vale within her?"

"If I recall my lessons correctly, the scriptures say something like that, yes."

"What if they're Her memories?"

Tyana paused.

"You mean Vale's?"

"The Keepers may gloss over some sections of scripture," Amun said, "but they claim their interpretations are literal. What if, in this case, they're right?"

"What are you saying?"

"I'm saying that if Vale's own consciousness is imbued in us, then any sister can access Her memories."

Tyana shot her a quizzical look.

"Well, maybe not *any* one," Amun emphasized, standing. "Maybe just the talented ones; the ones who know where to look."

"By talented, you mean me?"

"I mean us," Amun said. "Your touch, the pills—they amplify each other."

Tyana nodded, saying:

"I see patterns and motifs while using the touch alone, but this is beyond that. I'm seeing places and even people I can't recognize, but I have the distinct sense I'm reliving a moment in the past—a moment I myself couldn't have lived."

"Then it must be true," Amun persisted.

"If that's the case, I'm tempted to say that Thea's consciousness lurks in me the same way," Tyana confessed. Amun paused, scowling.

"I suppose that may be true too," she said.

"—How do they work?" Tyana asked.

"What do you mean?"

"How do the pills catalyze visions? How were you able to get the power of the Vestals in a distilled form?"

"It's a secret I shouldn't tell you," Amun said.

"Why? Is there something dangerous about it?"

"Not dangerous to you or to us," she said. "It's only dangerous to the sisters I ask to make it. It's a terrible sin for them."

"So then why can't you tell me?" Tyana pressed.

"It wouldn't be safe for you either," Amun said. "We don't understand why they work, only that they do. They bring us closer to Vale. They bring us closer together. Gathering in ecstasy is the last, best hope some of my sisters have. They'd rather die otherwise." She stood, saying: "Unlike you, we have few weapons to defend ourselves with against the Mater."

"You know I didn't mean it like that," Tyana said. Amun softened. "Are the pills colored black for a reason?" she asked, again.

"You could guess at the reason," she said, flippantly.

"Then how do we know, if we are seeing someone

else's memories, that they belong to Vale?"

Amun stopped, pausing.

"Amun, the Grand Artificer came to me. She told me that Thea is aware of us. My touch, your pills, the visions, the Maters—they're all connected. If we can see into their thoughts, maybe the Maters can see into ours."

Amun shrugged.

"I don't think that's possible."

"I don't think you want to," Tyana said. "In my visions, Thea is pressing in all the time. If your pills amplify Her power within me, could it amplify Her power over me?"

They were both silent for a while. Tyana paced, a thought nagging in the back of her mind.

"Amun?" Tyana asked.

"Yes?"

"Are there other pills than just the black ones?"

"No," Amun said quickly.

Tyana looked at her, inquisitively.

"I said *no!*" she repeated.

"Something tells me you're lying."

"It's not for you to say!" Amun seethed. "My sisters' secrets are for their own benefit, not yours."

Tyana held her gaze.

"Amun—the Grand Artificer expressed some hesitation about the power you're wielding."

Amun stiffened.

"She doesn't fully agree with my methods. But she understands that her ways are in the past. Now is the time for change."

"I just want to help you," Tyana said.

"We've shared so much. I still need you," Amun replied, taking Tyana's gloved hands. "But I'll only show you my full plan once you're worthy to take up its cause. I need your trust and your patience."

Tyana thought it over. Begrudgingly, she accepted.

XLII

TYANA'S RECESS AS a Warrior ended. She took quarters in the upper city. She hid her escapades with Amun and the Artificers deep in her mind, following the Grand Artificer's advice. She didn't see Amun again after that but she swore she'd find her again. Then the summons came.

It came by messenger, the lowest form of Keeper— usually a mere initiate. Tyana opened her entrance to see a young, sapphire-haired Keeper holding a disk in her hand.

"A message for you, sister," said the Keeper.

"What does it say?" Tyana asked.

The Keeper held the disk in front of her, staring at it as if it were a mirror. Her eyes rolled into the back of her head.

"*Tyana, the Vestal-Warrior, is summoned to the Mater's Cathedral at the next noon.*"

Tyana waved her hand at the young Keeper. The Keeper bowed and went away.

Tyana paused as the entrance closed. That night, she slept dreamlessly.

The next noon, Tyana journeyed to the Mater's Cathedral. It loomed in the daylight fog as she approached. Its seven outer walls twisted upward and spindly buttresses grew from them. In front were the two great braziers she remembered from Thea's funeral. That night, they were filled with fire and soot. Today, they were empty and clean.

She approached the entrance. It was a huge set of double doors inlaid with figures clawing at each other. She knocked gently on the outside.

Nothing happened at first. Hesitating to knock again, she waited patiently. After a moment, one of the doors opened slightly. A hooded Keeper within asked:

"Who comes?"

"Tyana, the Vestal-Warrior, by summons," Tyana replied.

The Keeper drew the door open wider, beckoning. She was likely a young initiate, sworn to the cathedral's upkeep.

Tyana stepped inside. The cathedral was vast and dark like she remembered, but when filled with daylight, it seemed to open up and breathe. Its stained glass windows colored the light inside. She couldn't help but look upward, watching the soaring buttresses unfold above her like petals.

The Keeper beckoned her forward. Mater Thea had attendants of all castes. Scribes huddled in long rows along the basilica, writing on tablets and delivering their disks to young messengers. Even Artificers hid themselves within the walls, gently singing, maintaining poignant and sweet incense, unseen.

Tyana followed the Keeper down the long hallway of the basilica. At the far end was the throne on which Thea Herself sat. It was empty. The seats of the castes' leaders, normally occupied during the War Council, surrounded it. They were arranged in a loose pentagon —one point for each caste—and each was staggered in height based on order. The lowest one, at floor height, belonged to the Artificers.

The Keeper led Tyana beyond the throne and into the inner basilica. They traveled down a flight of finely cut stone steps. The grand space became smaller, compressed, with narrow hallways and short ceilings. They were in the heart of the cathedral.

"This is the Vestals' sanctum," the Keeper whispered to Tyana. It was an opulent maze, filled with statuesque figures dribbling water from open mouths into obsidian-cut pools. Columns twisted upward in tightly woven helixes. As they walked deeper into the sanctum, Tyana felt a growing sense of dread.

They came to a final set of doors. The Keeper stopped, and then turned to Tyana.

"The Vestal wishes to see you. First, you must provide an offering."

She produced a small obsidian slate.

"Yield a mote of *ichor*," the Keeper said, "and smear it on the slate."

Tyana hesitated. She had never produced *ichor* on command—she only felt it once during the Mater's funeral and suppressed it then.

The Keeper stared at her, expectantly.

Tyana closed her eyes. She focused on her innards. She clenched her diaphragm, searching for the right sensation. She felt something stir between her lungs, near her esophagus. She thought she might trigger her *sensak*; the sensation was similar. Instead of releasing the growing tension through her neck, however, she refocused it toward her gut. Hallucinations sharply invaded her vision; something lunged into the back of her throat. It was a thick and bitter liquid.

Tyana worked it to the front her mouth. She brought a pair of fingers to her lips, wiping a dab of it off. She smeared it on the slate. She eliminated the rest, swallowing.

The Keeper bowed. She took the slate and slid it into a recess within the doors. They split. The Keeper stepped aside.

"Enter, Sister," said the Keeper, addressing her formally. Tyana was surprised at first—then she realized the Keeper was addressing her as a Vestal.

With the hallucinations fading at the corners of her eyes, she stepped inside. It was a brightly lit chamber with a large stained glass window hovering above. Below it was a figure shrouded in black, shimmering fabric.

"Welcome, Tyana," said the figure, turning. It was Ahnsair.

"Sister Ahnsair," Tyana said.

"From now on, 'sister' is fair enough, Tyana," she said casually, waving her hand. "Attendant—leave us."

The Keeper outside bowed again and shut the doors.

Ahnsair removed her outermost robes. Black hair streamed from her scalp. Her shoulders and sides were bare. Beneath the sheer tunic, her sole piece of clothing was a tightly woven loincloth.

"You've grown so strong and lithe. I was impressed how quickly you produced the *ichor*."

"You were watching?"

"Of course," Ahnsair said, approaching. "We Vestals can see anything we wish in this place. Mater Thea built it for us, after all."

Tyana said nothing.

"Come now, Tyana," Ahnsair encouraged. "I wish to get reacquainted with you. You're a coronated Warrior now, and more. I am a similarly accomplished Vestal. We have so much to discuss—I'm sure you have questions." She curled her arm around Tyana's, barely brushing beyond Tyana's glove. It caused her to shiver, but she repressed the sensation.

"Why did you call me here?" Tyana asked.

"To show you what it means to be a Vestal," Ahnsair said. "After all, Thea gifted you with the same powers she did me. You're so much more than just a Warrior. It's time you found out what your other color means."

She clasped Tyana's gloved hand. Tyana looked up at the stained glass window. It featured an image of Mater Vale. She asked, in an attempt to change the subject:

"What is that image for?"

Ahnsair looked at her, then up to the window. She unclasped Tyana's hand.

"This is one of our watching windows," Ahnsair replied, walking toward it. "Do you like it? I think it's beautiful."

The glass was arranged as a mosaic, depicting Scribes receiving glowing strands of hair from a regal-looking Vale. Farther down, the Scribes sat at tablets like the ones Tyana had seen while entering. Beneath them were a variety of stone scrolls.

"It looks like something from the scriptures," Tyana commented.

"Doesn't it? They serve a similar function. Since we

Vestals do not read, these serve to guide us and inform us in a way the scriptures can't. They elucidate the scriptures for us and reveal our common history."

"What is this one's meaning?" Tyana asked. At this Ahnsair snapped her fingers, and the sound of footsteps resonated from within the walls nearby. An attendant Keeper approached, bowing to them both.

"What is the interpretation of this image, sister?" Ahnsair asked the Keeper.

The Keeper looked up at the window. Her eyes rolled into the back of her head, and she spoke:

"Holy texts are given to us by Mater Vale. She is the divine inspiration for the first fifty Scribes who are the matron saints of their caste. With the guiding knowledge of Mater Thea, the texts are made known to the Scribes for the benefit of all Valen. These texts as we know them are absolute and perfect."

"Thank you, attendant," Ahnsair said. The Keeper bowed again and scurried away.

"So it tells how we get the scriptures from Mater Vale?" Tyana asked.

"Yes. The Scribes are the hands that carry Vale's sacred words. Under the guidance of Mater Thea, they will last forever, and we can trust them to be perfect."

Tyana looked back at the image. She noticed that the tablets of the Scribes dripped a black substance, mixing with the source of the scriptures.

"Are the black drips *ichor*?" Tyana pointed.

Ahnsair looked, then frowned.

"I mean, is that the influence of Thea the Keeper spoke of?"

Ahnsair grimaced at her.

"I don't know. I'm not a reader like them."

"Could you bring her back?"

Ahnsair looked around half-heartedly, then said:

"I don't think there is a need. She gave us the interpretation. What else is there to know?"

"Surely there's more to the image than a few short sentences," Tyana said. "Why is Thea's influence depicted as black droplets, mixing with Vale's hair?"

"Vershil said you were full of questions," said Ahnsair, frowning. She walked to the doors and opened them. She continued on without her. Tyana caught up, saying:

"My apologies. I shouldn't have questioned—the interpretation is absolute."

"Accepted," Ahnsair said. They walked in silence for a time. Tyana eased the discomfort in her chest by listening to the sung prayers of Artificers, hidden beyond the walls. Her footsteps echoed rhythmically with the chants. Occasionally there was the rustle of a robed Keeper moving in the halls. The sound faded as quickly as it came.

"Part of the reason I summoned you, Tyana, was so that you could ask questions. You have an opportunity to learn things few Warriors—or any other sistren—can. It is because you are part Vestal."

"I suppose I need training in each area," Tyana offered.

"Exactly," said Ahnsair. "I trust Vershil, for example. She is a wise and reputable scholar. But I must also trust you, Tyana—you are one of my own caste, after all."

Tyana didn't say anything. Ahnsair continued:

"With this trust, obviously, comes responsibility. I hope I can open up other areas for you to explore. Visiting this inner sanctum is one. Interpreting the windows is another. Not all areas are open to such exploration."

"Of course not," Tyana said. "I would not expect it."

They continued to walk.

"Tell me, sister," said Ahnsair, "do you have strange sensations when you touch other sisters?"

Tyana's voice didn't waver:

"How do you mean?"

"Sensations, Tyana—a desire to touch or be touched, and the ability to see things that aren't there when you do."

"I remember how I felt when you touched my scalp the first time we met."

"And when you touch others?"

Tyana paused.

"I'm not sure—what does it lead to?"

At first, Ahnsair didn't say anything. They passed by another great window. Ahnsair stopped, looking up at it. It showed Thea with her mane of sculpted hair, clutching worlds in the palms of her hands. Her hands were held up by the backs of many young Vestals. They appeared to be clambering up each other, reaching for Thea while also holding the planet in place.

"This is an important image," said Ahnsair. "It tells us secrets about the Vestal's touch." She snapped her fingers again and an attendant appeared.

"Interpret this image for Tyana," she said. The attendant gazed at the image:

"The sin of the Vestals is the power of Mater Thea. They all wish to become Her, but only one per generation may. They are vessels for Her, staving their temptation until death or possession. For them, falling into temptation is an offense to Her and the final race, Valen, for their touch spreads their likeness."

"Tyana—," Ahnsair whispered into her ear, "our burden is the heaviest among the castes. We long for Her and Her touch, but we can't have it, because it is saved for a greater purpose. I know what you feel. I know what you can do—because I can do it too. Read on, Keeper, to make her understand."

She continued:

"Through purity and power, Thea will rule beyond Her realm. She will convert barbarians by Her touch. If they refuse, they will only be fit to be slaves for the final race."

"There is power in the Vestal's touch, Tyana, that none of us understands. Only Thea knows its full extent —for it is Her plan that guides our destiny."

"What is that?" Tyana asked.

"Domination," Ahnsair replied. "We are the perfected race, Tyana. Created in the image of Vale, guided by Her holy Vicar; our purpose is not to subsist on the few planets we have. We must expand. Humanity still persists beyond our borders. We are destined to judge and convert them. We will cleanse them, and we will do it with the power that flows from our fingertips."

"Why would Vale give me such a fateful weapon?" Tyana asked.

"Thea chose you," Ahnsair said. "Vale has no hold on us; Thea is our true Mater. I brought you here for a reason: to tell you why, and then to show you how."

Ahnsair's hand wrapped around the back of Tyana's neck. Tyana thought to dart away, but relented. Intense warmth flowed from Ahnsair's fingers and down her back. The warmth grew electric, dispersing over Tyana's body like pins and needles. Hallucinations pressed in— they were black, oily, and covered in scales. Tyana fought them, but as she fought, Ahnsair's power grew.

"I know you," she said, "—*Vestal*."

Ahnsair's grip tightened hard, paralyzing Tyana. She led Tyana by the neck into an antechamber. There, she entangled her like a spider. Ahnsair's mind invaded Tyana's; her visions pressed in. Tyana strained and sweated, refusing to surrender the secrets she knew would incriminate her and Amun.

"That night," Ahnsair seethed, "when we first met, I knew I'd see you again. I knew we would do this. That night, after the Mater took Teira's body, we did it with her too. I want you to taste that."

Ahnsair clutched Tyana's face. The pins and needles turned to oblique pain, reverberating into her. Tyana moaned aloud. She felt as if her body might be split apart from all sides.

She took off her gloves. She clutched Ahnsair's face. She could feel Ahnsair's mind through her fingertips and swarmed it with her memories—memories of Valen's unadulterated coastlines and of crumbling cathedrals, like what she had seen with Amun; memories of defeating Sek, of flying her warbird, and of fighting the gryphon. She unleashed her night terrors. She wore her fears. She transformed herself into a monster, coated in *ichor*, wielding it like *sensak*. Ahnsair's grip broke and she moaned, then screamed in terror.

When they both grew exhausted, shivering and sweating on the floor, Ahnsair slowly disentangled herself from Tyana, who passed into sleep.

XLIII

TYANA AWOKE ON the cold stone floor. She looked around. She was alone.

She stood. She was sore, drained of energy, and had a slight headache. She exited the antechamber, its door groaning. Beyond, the Vestals' sanctum stretched ahead of her. The windows and lamps were dark. She couldn't recall how much time had passed.

She moved through the darkness quietly. Her eyes adjusted to the dim hallways. Everything was silent except her footsteps—no chanting Artificers, no attendant Keepers. She endeavored to find her way out of the sanctum and exit the cathedral. It proved to be harder than expected. The hallways were ornate but identical. Without a guide, she could easily get lost.

She remembered her tricks from navigating the Warriors' labyrinth. She mentally marked the antechamber she came from. She didn't remember the directions Ahnsair took to get there, so she had to fan out, careful not to retrace her steps.

After eliminating the few dead ends and loops, she determined her way forward. She thought she found the hallway leading to the central basilica. Instead, its doors opened into a narrow, opulent spiraling staircase. At the top, Tyana could hear soft voices and running water.

For a moment she felt she should turn back. She could backtrack and find the real exit. Something pulled her forward, however—curiosity, maybe.

So she climbed the staircase. After a few twisting flights, it opened up into a luxurious chamber sculpted entirely from cut obsidian and polished bronze. Sweet perfumes and soft light met her senses. The air was hot and thick with humidity, like a sauna. Ahead, a series of sheer curtains separated her from the crooning voices.

She approached the curtains, parting them one by one. As she moved through them, she could see the source of the sounds: Vestals in black loincloths huddled around a central figure in an expansive bath. The figure was tall, standing head and shoulders above the Vestals. She had long, trailing black hair reaching to her hips. Ahnsair was there, pouring perfumes down the back of her neck. Ahnsair caught Tyana's eyes, but said nothing.

Tyana parted the final curtain. The figure exited the bath by ascending a set of submerged steps. Her back was still turned to Tyana, and she couldn't see her face. The Vestals dried her and dressed her fingers with bronze fingerlets, her torso with a bronze brassiere, and her hips with a loincloth girded by bronze encasements.

She turned her face in profile, looking toward Tyana. Tyana recognized Her instantly, back from the moment of her birth. A shiver ran up her spine.

"Come, Tyana," said Mater Thea. "Do not hide from me."

XLIV

"THE MATER WISHES to see you," Ahnsair said.

The Vestals led her in. They removed her Warrior garments. They dressed her like one of their own. Tyana wore only a loincloth, a sheer black tunic, and a bronze chain around her waist. Her naked skin carried scars from Warrior training; the skin of other Vestals was pristine. She was taller than the rest of them. She felt out of place.

"You are beautiful," one of the Vestals said, "even if you are different."

Ahnsair took Tyana by the arm. The bathhouse linked to the main basilica by means of a long corridor, dotted with antechambers behind heavy locked doors. This was Thea's private sanctum.

"She is our mother," Ahnsair said in a whisper. "Do not hide anything from Her and She will accept you as Her own."

Thea stood ahead of them. She had her back turned as Ahnsair led Tyana forward.

"Please——," Thea said softly, "leave us. I wish to talk with her alone."

Ahnsair hesitated, then bowed, exiting. When the door shut behind her, Thea turned, facing Tyana.

Tyana knew what the possessed Vestal had looked like during the funeral long ago. It wasn't the face she saw now. Instead, she saw the specter from her visions made into flesh. The likeness was uncanny; Thea had all the same features as Vale save that her hair was black as pitch.

"Come closer, child."

Tyana did. Thea was a full head taller than Tyana.

"This is how Vestals greet each other." She stroked Tyana's cheek with fingers encased in jointed bronze coverings. Tyana felt coursing power muted through the metal. Its echo caused a shiver that reverberated into her core.

"You are not just a Vestal," Tyana whispered.

Mater Thea smiled; nearly laughed.

"No, I am not. Are you only a Vestal, either?"

Thea moved her hand gently up from Tyana's cheek to her scalp. She stroked Tyana's purple and black locks, parting them with her bronze-clad fingertips.

"You are so forward about things," Thea said, smiling. "I admire that. Come, Vestal-Warrior, and walk with me."

They walked side by side down the corridor. Thea had many rooms, each guarded by a door with a locking mechanism that Tyana didn't recognize.

"I have heard much about you from Ahnsair. She takes a liking to you."

"I am honored," Tyana said quietly.

"I have also heard much about you from Vershil. Your

presence stirs curiosity within the higher castes both in this city and abroad."

"My reputation is thanks to the good training of my teachers and their praise."

"Indeed," Thea said, nodding. "Do you know why I called you here?"

"I was summoned to learn the ways of the Vestals."

"So Ahnsair told you. How do you feel about everything you have experienced thus far?"

Tyana hesitated, choosing her words carefully.

"I am both awed and ... mystified."

"Mystified—how so?"

"The realm of the Mater and Her Vestals is much different from the training halls of Warriors."

Thea nodded, her hair waving softly.

"This is true. I wonder if you are asking yourself how you could reconcile these two burdens—is that correct?"

Tyana nodded.

"You should know, dear Tyana, that there is a reason for the curiosity surrounding your birth. While there have been many multi-burdened sistren over the course of the centuries, they have all been of the four lower castes. Never in Valen's history was there one mixed with the Vestal caste such as you."

"Never?"

"Not one," Thea said. "There was much debate among the Keepers when Vershil took you under her guidance. The same was true when Verikash claimed you as her student. Each of them is first among her caste; each of them sits on my War Council, advising me personally. They selected you as their student because it was obvious, by your colors, that my sister designed you for a special purpose."

Tyana said, making sure to use the correct form of address:

"The Mater means Mater Vale?"

"Of course," Thea replied.

They walked in silence for some paces.

"What do you think this purpose is, dear Tyana?" Mater Thea asked.

Tyana hesitated.

"I have heard it said that I am a Warrior made for the Maters—that I am Theirs, and Theirs alone."

"Of course you would hear that," Mater Thea said, stopping. Tyana stopped with her. Thea looked at Tyana in the eyes. "But that's what others told you. I want to know what you think."

"Personal interpretation is a dangerous path—as Vershil taught me," Tyana said.

Thea stared at her, her head tilting slightly, saying:

"I am offering you freedom of opinion."

Tyana hesitated again. Then she replied:

"I believe my colors represent a path given to me by the Maters for the good of all Valen. My burden is doubled: it is purity and it is violence."

"Well put," Thea said, studying her. A silence hung between them. Thea turned, continuing on. Tyana followed. As they walked along the corridor, they passed by many locked doors. Thea stopped at one.

"This is one of my private antechambers," she said. "Would you like to join me here?"

"If it pleases the Mater."

Thea gave a subtle smile. She turned toward the door. Its locking mechanism was ornate, black, with many mechanical arms stretching across the door's outer casing. Thea stretched out a hand. From beneath her tunic, black veins of *ichor* crawled along her arm and leapt toward the lock. Tyana shivered as she watched it —it behaved like *sensak*.

The lock turned and Thea's *ichor* dissipated. When the lock stopped, its arms disengaged, splitting into seven pieces that moved aside like parting teeth. The door swung open. Inside was an ornate chamber with a single, dominating window. Thea walked in, gesturing to Tyana to follow.

The window was an illustrated mosaic. Its light cast an orange, violet, and yellow glow across the room. In the window's center was a depiction of Thea with outstretched hands, like a sphinx. Her hands rested on bodies with dark, tan-skinned flesh—humans. Between Thea's hands was a white, erect figure, gleaming against the dark background.

"Have you seen that kind of image before?" Thea asked.

"No," Tyana said.

"Not even in your lessons with Vershil?" she pressed.

"No," Tyana said.

Thea gestured at it.

"It speaks of a prophecy concerning a child that will come during the end of time. The scriptures say that this child will herald the conversion of humanity to our ways. It says—"

Thea's eyes rolled into the back of her head and she recited:

"She will be born a Vestal set apart for my purposes; you will see her and know her name, but you will not recognize her."

Thea relaxed her eyes and her gaze fell on Tyana.

"What does it mean, my Mater?" Tyana asked.

"My child, Tyana," Thea said, bringing her fingertips

up to Tyana's chin and steadily tracing her jawline: "I believe the Vestal this window speaks of is you."

Tyana was shivering. Thea's eyes seemed to glow white-hot the longer she looked at them.

"How do you mean, my Mater?"

"My sister created you for a reason," Thea said. "Ahnsair showed you, just as I asked her to, how I will dominate humanity. The power to convert them is in my touch. If they refuse, I will make war on them. Your unique balance of burdens makes you a powerful weapon in my arsenal: the touch of a Vestal guided by the precision of a Warrior's intent. I require instruments to carry out my will. You will be one such instrument."

Thea dropped her fingers from Tyana's chin. Tyana stopped shivering. Thea exited the antechamber and gestured to Tyana to follow. They began to walk down the corridor again.

"Did Vershil ever teach you why Vale created your sistren?" Thea said.

"No, my Mater." Even if Tyana could recall such a lesson, her mind was swimming. Her response was more like a reflex to the Mater's presence.

"Before the creation of Valen, humanity ruled the worlds. They were wicked, treacherous, and greedy. They thought of Vale and me as their property. As is the case today, they would destroy us if they could. So we conceived of a perfected race that could rule over humanity instead. Vale created the birthing chambers while I taught the Keepers and Scribes the scriptures. She laid the foundations for our world while I laid the foundations of our society. In all this, we were equal— except for one key difference. Do you know what that was? It is a secret not known to the lower castes."

"No, my Mater."

"Vale was human. She herself was part of the corrupted civilization she sought to replace. There was only one truly perfect child of Valen at that time—one whose veins never contained human blood. Do you know who it was?"

"No, my Mater."

"It was *me*," said Thea. "Vale understood that humanity's stain was still in her. Her recognition of this was the one thing that absolved her of this fact. This is why she could never rule Valen. She sacrificed herself so that I could rule in her stead. Even today, humanity's impurity carries on into her children—but unlike humanity itself, there is one saving grace for you and your sistren, Tyana. Do you know what it is?"

"No, my Mater."

"Devotion, Tyana—utter devotion to my ways."

They were at the end of the corridor. The final door led back into the heart of the basilica. Thea opened it and the door split open. Inside was a whole assembly of hooded Keepers and Scribes ready to take part in a vigil. Pungent incense invaded Tyana's nostrils.

"When humanity is put to rest, you will be at my right hand, Tyana. I will reap the benefits of this conquest, as will you."

Thea strode toward the waiting assembly. She put a hand on the crest of her throne.

"You are unique, Tyana. What troubles me, however, is that your uniqueness may sway you from my will. So I will draw you close. You are special to me. I am sure you will see why."

XLV

THAT NIGHT IN her quarters, asleep, Tyana had a dream.

It was night. The horizon glowed red. Clouds colored by soot dressed the sky, blocking out any stars. She was sitting at the head of an assembly of Keepers, Scribes, and Warriors, all dressed in plated bronze armor she didn't recognize. Tyana looked at herself. She was also in gleaming bronze plates from head to toe. They dressed her joints like scales. Two basins of *ichor* sat next to her hands.

Ahead of the assembly, stretching to the horizon, was a sea of tan-skinned bodies—humans, heads bowed, steadily approaching.

A voice behind her boomed:

"Will you submit?"

She looked behind her. The voice belonged to Mater Thea. She was like a colossus in repose. Her two arms stretched forward to either side of Tyana, and her hands rested on two golden orbs. Her face was less like flesh and more like hardened graphite. Her eyes and mouth glowed like furnaces.

Tyana looked forward to the humans.

"No, we do not," one of them said.

Mater Thea roared. Tyana felt the heat of her breath on her back. The Warriors in the assembly grabbed the nearest humans—men, women, children—and forced them toward Tyana. They resisted; Warriors simply used their *sensak* to constrain them into individual lines. They subdued them even as panic spread through the crowd, turning them into a writhing mob.

The first human stood before Tyana. *Sensak* covered his joints like a cocoon. They forced him to kneel and to bow his head.

"Cleanse him," Thea ordered. Her voice reverberated against Tyana's back.

Tyana looked at the human. She stretched out her hand. The *ichor* from the basins leapt to her attention, branching into the air like spindling veins. She directed them onto the human's face, and wherever they touched, the *ichor* drew the color out of his skin. Tyana could feel it changing his biology. The foundations of his genes faded away, gradually replaced with a new set—a set like hers.

When it was done, his body was bereft of color. The *sensak* released him. Drained and weak, he crumpled at Tyana's feet. His humanity was gone—now he belonged to a caste without a name. A group of attendants carried the body away.

The assembly brought up the next human.

"Cleanse him," Thea ordered.

Tyana reached her hand out again. The *ichor* responded to her will. The *sensak* encasing the next human forced him forward, pushing him down onto his knees. As Tyana stretched her fingers and the *ichor* graced his skin, he looked up at her. His eyes were green and his hair was ruddy. He said something to her in a language she didn't recognize. The *ichor* began to drain the color and the strength from his complexion—he repeated the phrase at Tyana, but she still didn't understand. As the conversion reached his eyes, the colors in his iris began to change.

Then Tyana recognized him: the tan-skinned man from her birth dream. He repeated the words in his foreign language. Even though she didn't understand his words, she understood his intent. He was asking her for help.

Tyana dislodged her hand and the conversion stopped. The veins of *ichor* and the *sensak* encasing him dissipated. Mater Thea roared—

The dream stopped. Tyana awoke in a cold sweat on her mattress. Her sheets were askew, as if she'd torn them off.

She calmed herself down by remaking her bed. After that, she opened the entrance to her quarters. The cool night air rushed in. The whole of the Mater's City was outside her doorstep and it was silent. The only commanding presence was two moons, lighting the streets. The white one was ascendant, contesting the place of the larger, darker one in its shadow.

XLVI

OVERCAST SKY BROKE during the next evening. A cloudy pink and green sunset gave way to clear, inky blue night. Stars pricked their way through it. The moons hung suspended. The larger, black one nearly eclipsed the other tonight, leaving only a ghostly white crescent on its side.

Tyana watched it change from the upper city. The Warriors were gathering for a raid against an ongoing barbarian threat. She was summoned for a personal briefing with Verikash. She waited outside the hangars' wide, open lip, watching the sky change until the time of her summons.

She entered the briefing room. Verikash was there, fully armored save for her face. Her wild hair poured down her back.

"Sister Verikash," Tyana addressed formally.

"Good to see you, my Vestal-Warrior," grinned Verikash. "I trust your recess gave you much needed rest and introspection?"

"As much," Tyana said.

"I heard you met with the Mater Herself. That must have been quite the honor. Usually someone doesn't have the chance to meet the living Mater, much less walk Her private corridor. But, then, I suppose it was natural, given your burdens."

Tyana didn't reply, simply nodding respectfully instead.

"Do you know why I called you here?" Verikash asked.

"To tell me about the ongoing threat," Tyana said.

"Yes. This will be your first mission flying with a cadre of Warriors. Since that's the case, I want to show you what we'll be facing."

Verikash turned to the briefing room's console. With a few of her gestures it produced a hovering image that filled the room. It appeared to depict an asteroid.

"This and other stellar mining resources like it were stolen by a force of barbarians. I take it you've never seen one?"

Tyana hesitated:

"A barbarian?"

"Yes," Verikash said impatiently.

Tyana shook her head.

"You likely never will. They are cowards and never fight in person. They always flee at the sight of our ships. Instead, they use automatons in their likeness for defense. They'll often send a task force of these machines and wipe out Artificer mining operations. They'll set up sentries as well, making it difficult for us to reclaim the mining plots."

She waved at the console again and the image zoomed out. It showed the whole belt of asteroids with a haze of gray pressed against a zone marked in violet.

"The violet section is our border. It was pushed back in a strategic manner by these machines. We've held this line for generations, but only by increasing resistance to their raids and by conducting raids on them ourselves. Wherever we attack, we must divert our resources from elsewhere. We are stretched too thin."

"What do you mean about these machines when you say that they act in a strategic manner?" Tyana asked.

"They act like a collective," Verikash explained. "They are slaves to the barbarians. In generations past the barbarians conducted everything themselves, using automated ships and drones to assist them. Now, they never conduct anything in person. They never risk their own bodies. The machines build copies of themselves—once they have a foothold in one area, they can replenish their losses."

Tyana nodded. Verikash gestured to one of the larger asteroids beyond the line.

"This is Seruneh Second. It was a key staging point for mining operations until we lost it. It had a number of warbird hangars as well. Its loss significantly reduced our ability to defend the encroaching line. Mater Thea ordered us to take it back."

"How many warbirds are you sending?" Tyana asked.

"Two hundred—including myself, and you," Verikash said. "It is a large force for such a small operation, but we are using high numbers to deter heavy losses. It's imperative that we succeed. If we do, it gives us the ability to break the line and push them back. If we fail, however, it will allow them to encroach deeper into our territory. There is only so much space between Valen, the moons, and the asteroid belt."

Tyana nodded, understanding.

"Sek and Kersa will be flying with us as well," Verikash added. "I trust that this will not be a problem for any of you?"

Tyana hesitated.

"It will not be a problem for me," she said.

"I'm referring to all of you," Verikash said. "The Mater requires us to move as one. I don't want my Warriors squabbling in the middle of a skirmish."

Tyana drew up her height.

"I'll ensure there is no problem," she said. Verikash seemed to pause, then said:

"This will be your first mission, Tyana. It will prove your worth. Don't fail me."

XLVII

Tyana entered the warbird hangars in the upper city. They were the largest on Valen. Warriors, fully armored in *sensak*, crisscrossed every way to patiently waiting warbirds. Above, the hangar ceiling opened to the night sky.

As Tyana made her way toward her ship, she caught sight of Kersa. It was the first time she'd seen her since coronation. They locked glances for a moment. Sek was nearby as well. As soon as Sek noticed Tyana, she started to walk toward her. Kersa seemed reluctant to follow her, but she did.

Tyana attempted to ignore them both, focusing on getting to her warbird ahead. But they caught up with her.

"Vestal-Warrior," Sek called out. Nearby Warriors paused to watch. Tyana turned to face her.

"What is it, Sek?" Tyana said in an even tone.

"This is your first mission, is it not? It's quite a dangerous one. I hope you don't make any costly mistakes."

"I wouldn't wish ill on you either, Sek," Tyana said. Sek paused, unimpressed. Kersa put a hand on Sek's shoulder. She pushed it away.

"I heard you got to meet the Mater. Is She everything you hoped for?"

Tyana scowled at her.

"Why don't you ask Her yourself?" She turned away from Sek, continuing toward her ship.

"Sek, come on," Kersa whispered. "Let's go."

"Not until I'm done," Sek seethed aloud. "Tell me, Tyana. I don't think I heard of a single brawl breaking out with you during your whole recess. That's not normal for a Warrior. What were you doing that whole time—playing footsie with Artificers instead?"

Tyana was just beneath the belly of her warbird. She stopped, turned, and glared at Sek. She approached her briskly. Kersa put herself between Sek and Tyana and when Tyana raised her hand to strike, Kersa caught it. The leather in Tyana's glove creaked under the stress.

"I may be younger than you, Sek, and different, but I am no less a Warrior than you—I am more," she said. "Maybe you should consider that when speaking to someone of a higher caste—*sister*."

Kersa inhaled sharply, recognizing the lesser form of address.

"You won't make this flight," Sek roared. "I'll brand you."

"Go tell it to the Maters," Tyana retorted.

Sek hissed at her, but walked away. Tyana wrenched her hand from Kersa's, glaring at her. Any Warriors watching the encounter went back to their routine. Kersa started to say something, but stopped. She too turned and walked away.

Burning with malice, Tyana walked to her warbird. She released her *sensak* and they drew her up into its belly. She spread her wings and took off into the sky, joining the swarm of ships above.

XLVIII

ONCE THEY BROKE the atmosphere, the warbirds were like a black cloud against the purple and blue nebulae that dressed the inner parts of Valen's star system. The warbird's senses gave Tyana an awareness of the entire cadre surrounding her.

The fleet headed toward an acceleration gate. Many such gates orbited Valen. It allowed small ships to travel within the border and beyond in moments. It was a long, sculpted cannon with a wide mouth, shimmering with electric energy.

Verikash spoke over the communication channels:

"Set your destination for Seruneh Second. When we enter the asteroid belt, we will be in close quarters. Expect heavy fire when you exit the stream. Remember —our objective is to decimate their forces and to retake our hangar. Move as one and victory is ours—and Thea's."

The fleet entered the gate's mouth and electric tendrils grabbed the warbirds. Tyana felt hers give a shudder, halting in its place. For a moment, everything was still. Then, as one, the fleet lurched forward. Tyana watched nebulae and moons blur past. A loose haze ahead turned into an oncoming wave of asteroids. The energy dissipated and the fleet came to a halting stop.

Ahead was a massive, hourglass-shaped asteroid. It had visible structures built on it and slots that appeared to be hangars. Strange-looking machines crawled over its surface.

"Now!" Verikash yelled.

Tyana unleashed her guns. The fleet of warbirds gave a blistering first pass over the asteroid, ripping structures to shreds. Explosions knocked pieces into space. The remaining structures whirred to life. Some had bay doors that opened, revealing huge cannons.

"Watch the return fire," Verikash warned.

The space around Tyana exploded. Some warbirds were caught in the blasts, shattering into pieces. She peeled away, attempting to avoid the collisions. The fire followed her until she came low toward the surface of the asteroid, beyond the range of the cannons.

"They're releasing drones," Verikash called out. Tyana looked. Hundreds of silver, disklike machines were spewing from the hangars. They were half the size of a warbird and glowed menacingly along their edges. They shot toward the closest group of Warriors, consuming them instantly.

"Form up," Verikash said. "Tyana, Sek, Kersa—with me. Everyone else, follow our lead. They'll try to destroy us by suicide. Punch through and hit their hangars."

The Warriors regrouped. Tyana joined Verikash at the head of the formation. Sek and Kersa flanked her. The drones rejoined into a swarm, then presented their thinnest profile to the fleet, shooting forward.

"Punch through!"

Tyana unleashed her guns on the drones heading straight for her. They shattered easily and she spread her fire, widening the hole. She flew through the swarm. Behind her, other warbirds were not as lucky; they were sliced in two by the drones. Muted screams echoed over the channels.

"Hit the hangars!"

Tyana focused fire on the asteroid's gaping maws. The entire fleet joined her. An explosion ripped through its innards, blowing out the side. Chunks of rock and metal hurtled into space. The remaining drones lost control and scuttled themselves, self-destructing into shards.

"Good! We retake what is left. Make your final pass and prepare to dive."

The fleet of warbirds, suffering losses up to a fourth of their original number, formed up over the rocky base. The cannons continued their counterattack. Tyana followed Verikash's lead and they headed straight for the remaining hangar. Its bay doors began to close.

"Dive!" Verikash yelled.

Her warbird's wings folded up. She aimed the warbird's nose at the hangar. The whole fleet looked like a swarm of black needles heading straight for the asteroid.

Tyana impacted and her warbird lodged itself in the hangar's doors. The shock was brutal. The gel layer encasing her body absorbed the worst of it. Outside, the other warbirds continued to pierce the side of the base, burrowing into its tunnels.

She released her *sensak* and disconnected from the ship. They ate through the remaining metal and she emerged from her ship fully armored. Inside the hangar, a firefight was on. She saw Sek and Kersa taking on a multi-jointed walking machine twice their height. It brutally knocked them to the ground with a single limb. Its glowing eyes turned to Tyana and it pointed a barreled limb at her.

She drew up a shield with her *sensak* just in time. The blow knocked her backward and shattered her shield. Verikash flanked her, forming a barbed whip and flinging it at the machine's head. It coiled around the enemy's neck, tightening. Tyana followed her lead, forming a whip of *sensak* from each hand. Together, they yanked hard and the machine's head snapped off, sparking as it did so. The body tumbled down, lifeless. Sek and Kersa got up.

"They won't stop attacking until we disengage the power," Verikash said.

"We need to detonate the core," Sek said.

"That'll destroy the base if it's not contained," Kersa replied. "We'll all perish."

"Then we find a way to contain it," Verikash ordered. "Follow me, we're heading to the surface."

They headed up the hangar's corridors. In moments they were on the asteroid's surface. It was riddled with barbarian infrastructure added by the machines. Beyond, the power core loomed as a bulbous sphere nestled in an enclave.

"There," Verikash said as more Warriors joined them. "Move!"

They moved across the asteroid's surface. Its gravity, nearly negligible on the surface, allowed them to bound forward, using their *sensak* as tethers. Ahead, a swarm of walking machines poured over the lip of the enclave.

They smashed into the force of Warriors and blades made of *sensak* sliced through their bodies. Tyana followed behind Verikash, pushing hard through the chaos toward the power station. Kersa and Sek still flanked her, turning hordes of machines into scrap metal as they went.

Verikash leapt upward, aiming for the core's rim. Tyana followed and Kersa was close behind. *Sensak* boosted them into the air and guided their fall. The three of them landed at the lip of the power core's center. Its hollow channel led to the heart of the asteroid.

"Can we shut it down?" Kersa asked. Verikash pulled open the paneling with a single, wrenching grasp. Exposed wires and controls burst and sparked at her.

"They've rigged it beyond our means to save it," Verikash said.

"Can we set it to self-destruct?" Tyana asked. Verikash shook her head.

"We have to destroy it manually. Tyana—you form a shield with the other Warriors to contain the blast. We have to save the remainder of the base. We'll stay here and detonate the core."

"Not with both of you on it!" Tyana exclaimed.

"I didn't ask you—I commanded you," Verikash seethed. "Now go and defend your sisters!" Kersa furtively looked at Tyana. Tyana glanced back at her, at a loss for words.

"I said *go now*, Vestal-Warrior—," yelled Verikash, forming a blunt instrument with her *sensak* and, in a single blow, throwing Tyana off the power core's edge. She went flying back toward the asteroid's surface into the thick of the battle below. She reached out with her *sensak* so she didn't bounce off the rock's surface and into space. She smashed into the ground with a plume of dust. Getting up, she looked up to see Sek and the few remaining Warriors on the ground holding their own against the onslaught of machines.

Turning around, she could see Verikash and Kersa pouring all their *sensak* into the power core, steadily obliterating it from the inside out.

"What are they doing?" Sek yelled.

"They're destroying the core. We have to form a shield to save the rest of the base—and us."

"But they'll go with it," Sek said over the fray of the battle.

Tyana couldn't respond. Instead she watched the power core's skin ripple with explosions as it was steadily eaten alive.

"Form a shield around the core," Tyana ordered, "—now!"

She sent out tendrils of *sensak*, forming a giant web that stretched around the core, enclosing the remaining machines with it. The other Warriors, including Sek, joined their *sensak* with hers, allowing her to stretch the web farther. It engulfed the structure like a purple and black net. She had almost closed it when the power core gave in, first imploding, then exploding, blowing everything apart.

The shock wave was immense. Tyana struggled to keep the net in place. The explosion ripped apart the core and its surrounding infrastructure. It obliterated the machines. The bedrock cracked and Tyana felt the entire asteroid heave, as if it would split apart. Even with the combined force of the remaining Warriors, she couldn't contain the blast fully; she could only divert it, condensing the *sensak* like a shield instead of a net. She directed the explosion away from the ground and into space as much as possible.

When it was done, she found herself pushed into the dust, pressed onto her back by the weight of the explosion. She found it difficult to breathe, even within the confines of her suit. It was as if her lungs couldn't fully expand. The other Warriors gathered around.

"Quick," said Sek. "She's short on *sensak*—"

Tyana passed out.

XLIX

WHEN TYANA CAME to, she learned that half of the Warriors in the group were killed. Verikash and Kersa were among the casualties. Their bodies were not recovered. There would be a funeral and, in the ceremony, their likenesses would be sculpted into the catacombs of the Mater's City.

The city had grand caverns that stretched into the roots of the cliffs. Those that did not permeate the undercity were used as catacombs. Honorable sistren had their likenesses sculpted into them. Most often, their bodies would be encased in molten stone and entombed there. When the body was not available, their likeness would be formed from the cavern rocks themselves.

That night, the funeral procession descended the stone staircase toward the catacombs. Tyana was at its head. Behind her, Sek and a number of other surviving Warriors followed. A group of stonemason Artificers followed them. Because Verikash had been on the War Council and was head of her caste, dignitaries from the

Keepers and Scribes also attended the funeral procession. Traditionally, there was a Vestal as well—Tyana fulfilled that requirement.

The staircase into the catacombs, weathered smooth and sagging from uncounted footsteps, led deep into the heart of the cavern. Ancient phosphorescent crystals carved in the shape of ceremonial torches were the only lights illuminating their path. When they reached the cavern floor, Tyana looked up. Faces carved in stone in all manner of expressions and poses stared back at her.

The stonemasons went ahead, leading the procession to the chosen site. It was a raw, unformed outcropping surrounded by the faces of other long-dead Warriors. The procession gathered around. The stonemasons engaged their tools—red beams of light struck the rock. Once it was red-hot, they carved sections of it away, forming a set of likenesses. As they did this, a Keeper read from the scriptures:

"Today I taught my daughters their first arts. I spoke to the Warrior and revealed to her my training. I showed her the way to kill, and in that, the way to give life..."

Gradually, Kersa's face formed in the rocks. Verikash appeared next to her, grinning like she'd done when Tyana first met her. She watched the Artificers intently, their lasered tools yielding sparks as they carved into the stone. Chunks of it fell away, melting into a soft pile. The Keeper concluded with the verse:

"...She would be the arbiter of conflict, and keep her sisters safe from intruders."

When the Artificers finished, Tyana could see both likenesses clearly in the rock. Kersa looked just as she had when she delivered Tyana to Vershil. Verikash had the same wicked grin, refusing to betray the real depth of her wisdom. The Artificers faced Tyana and bowed.

"The burdens of Verikash pass to Tyana, first of her caste," the Keeper announced.

Tyana nodded at the Artificers, dismissing them. They departed and the procession, except for the Warriors, dismissed themselves. A quietness passed as the Artificers, Scribes, and Keepers of the procession ascended the stairs. The remainder of the funeral was for associated caste members only.

"We could have saved them," Sek said. "This didn't have to happen."

Tyana was silent.

"You're not going to say anything, Vestal-Warrior? We had the net going. We gave you all our power. Why couldn't you close it?"

"Are you going to blame me for this, now?" Tyana asked quietly.

"Who should we ask? You're the one who leapt off the power core at the last moment."

Tyana glared at Sek, saying:

"Sister Verikash *pushed* me off, ordering me to contain the blast."

"How do we know that? I heard no such order. And fine job you did—couldn't save her, could you?"

Tyana was on Sek in a flash. She would have pummeled her, if it weren't for the surrounding Warriors who held her back.

"I lost my teacher and my friend," Tyana yelled at her. "It was your idea to detonate the core in the first place. I wanted to stay there. You didn't follow us onto that ledge. Where were you?"

Sek didn't reply, shielding herself from Tyana. When she calmed herself down, Tyana shook away the grasp of the other Warriors holding her back.

"I don't care what you think of me, Sek," she said. "I don't care if you antagonize me. It won't change that Verikash was my teacher, and that Kersa was my friend too."

Tyana looked at the other Warriors. All eyes were trained on her. She paid her final respects to the effigies in a brisk gesture and then stormed off, climbing up the stairs.

L

THE NOONDAY SUN shone high in Valen's sky. Heavy fog deposited a dew on everything, which turned to ice in the cold. Tyana looked out from the balcony in Vershil's apartment. The fresh, frigid air smelled crisp in her nose. Below, waves were frozen in place beneath the obsidian cliffs. The season had changed.

"It pleases me you accepted my invitation," Vershil said, lighting an outdoor brazier. "Part of me wondered if you would come."

"I always come back to those I call friends," Tyana said.

"And teachers, I hope," Vershil said.

"Yes, them as well."

Vershil joined her on the balcony.

"You used to look out from this balcony often. I remember seeing that wistful look on your face."

"Was it really that often?" Tyana asked.

"Very."

Vershil went inside, returning with a steaming cup of

tea. She handed it to Tyana.

"I heard about what happened," she said. "The Warriors had a great victory. You had a pivotal role."

"We had victory at a cost," Tyana replied.

"Yes," Vershil said softly. "At a cost."

A silence passed between them. Vershil sipped her tea. Tyana spoke:

"Some part of me wonders if Sek was right. Was there a way I could have saved them? Did it have to be both of them?"

Vershil paused, then said:

"Verikash ordered you to protect your fellow sisters. That includes Sek. Is that right?"

"Yes," Tyana replied.

"Then you did what you needed to. Verikash ordered you off that ledge for a reason. Both she and Kersa knew the risks. They acted in service to the Maters." Vershil paused, letting her gaze press on Tyana. "They sacrificed what they did knowing they were protecting you and all the other Warriors in the fleet. In the end, they fulfilled their mission, as did you."

Tyana looked at her.

"I am sorry for your losses," Vershil said. "As you know, I serve on the War Council, as did Verikash. It is the guiding body that determines our military operations at home and abroad. Not many are privy to its decisions nor its processes. It consists of the Mater Herself, a Vestal representative, and the heads of each caste: Keepers, Scribes, Warriors, and Artificers."

"You are the head of the Keepers," Tyana observed.

"Of course—ever since Mater Thea appointed me after my teacher. I must admit, we knew about the risks for this mission. Verikash herself observed the potential for heavy casualties. But she insisted, most among us, that it was necessary to preserve our border."

"Why are you telling me this?"

"Because Mater Thea has appointed you to the War Council in place of Verikash."

Tyana paused—then asked:

"Why not Sek?"

"Sek would be the logical successor, but Verikash's own recommendation puts you at the forefront. You are also a Vestal, meaning you outrank Sek by caste. You can perform the duties of the War Council's Vestal representative while also holding the seat of First Warrior. It fulfills the requirements of our bureaucracy nicely."

Tyana looked at her, saying:

"As head of the Warrior caste, it would be my responsibility to plan battles, lead Warriors, and more. Isn't that right?"

"Of course," Vershil said.

"Impossible," Tyana replied. "The Warriors don't respect me. Sek continued to antagonize me even during the funeral. How am I supposed to lead a caste of sisters who believe I don't deserve to be among them?"

Vershil paused.

"You truly don't think they will accept you after all this time?" she asked.

"No," Tyana said. "I wish it were otherwise, but no, I don't think so."

Vershil peered into Tyana's eyes. She seemed to look past her for a moment, perhaps to the horizon. But then she looked back at her in the eyes.

"Then it doesn't matter."

Tyana was taken aback.

"What?"

"If you cannot change their opinions, then there is nothing you can do about them," Vershil said. She sipped her tea idly. "Forget about placating them. If you accept the appointment, you are still head of their caste regardless of their opinion. You are born to things higher than them, and carry burdens they will never know. That you struggle with things they cannot understand does not mean you are weaker. It means you are stronger. As long as you follow the Maters, they will follow you. That is the way of things."

Tyana paused, staring at her former teacher.

"If you need time to accept the appointment, I understand," Vershil said. "The Mater is willing to let you think it over. It seems only reasonable, given this offer is sudden and your grief is still fresh."

Tyana turned away, looking back over the balcony.

"I thank Her for Her patience," she said formally. "I will give Her my answer as soon as I can."

"She will thank you," Vershil said. Tyana didn't turn to look. Instead she watched the frozen sea beyond, which showed cracks on its surface.

LI

THAT NIGHT, THE auroras were out. Their pink and green curtains dressed the sky, waving in front of the twin moons. The darker one nearly eclipsed the other. Tyana watched them from the outskirts of the old city. The grasses were covered with snow, and the trees carried icicles along their gnarled branches. She heard footsteps behind her. She looked and saw Amun; her face was almost totally obscured by scarves. They both looked around; they were alone.

"How do you stand this weather?" Amun asked, coming close to Tyana. "Why don't you use your *sensak* to cover yourself for warmth?"

"The *sensak* are weapons," Tyana said, "not simple clothing."

"Fine," Amun muttered.

"I met with the Mater," Tyana said, bringing up the reason for their meeting.

"And?"

"She was ... not what I expected," Tyana said.

"How?"

"She seemed more reasonable than the Thea I know from my dreams. In person, She appears like Vale, except for Her hair. I felt no malice from Her, only power and authority."

"A monster dressed in the trappings of light," Amun said.

"She told me Her plans. She expects me to play a pivotal role in the conquest of humanity. She wants to convert them, or to make them slaves if they refuse."

"What would happen to my caste, I wonder?"

Tyana shrugged. "I don't know. I think Her concerns are elsewhere."

"Of course they are," said Amun, shivering. "You didn't allow her to see anything, did you? Our plans aren't compromised?"

"No," Tyana said. "She didn't peer through my mind. I was able to shield everything else out. The Vestals do not know about our relationship."

Amun nodded. "And you still want to see my plans fulfilled?"

Tyana paused. "You mean freedom for your caste?"

"And the dismantling of Thea's rule," Amun said.

"Yes—but I don't understand how you intend to accomplish it," Tyana said. "Offering solace through the gatherings is one thing. But how will that dismantle Thea's rule?"

"It frees us from mental bondage. It shows us that there is more than just our burdens and the endless grind of work. We have to free our minds before we can free our bodies. But now that we've done that, we can bring about real, physical freedom."

"How will you do that?"

"Total revolution."

"Through force? The Warriors would crush any kind of rebellion."

"Even with you fighting alongside us?"

"Amun—I could not fend off an entire caste of Warriors, skilled as I may be."

Amun looked at her.

"Then we ourselves must become Warriors."

Tyana gave her a quizzical look.

"I still don't see your logic," she said.

"It's time I showed you something. I'll prove to you that what I'm planning is possible. Come with me."

Tyana followed Amun.

LII

AMUN LED HER to the Artificers' undercity. The cold, damp wind gave way to the warm steam of the industrial levels. Tyana was familiar enough with this place now, but Amun led her in a new direction. She led her to a structure that appeared to be little more than a junction of large pipes—an abandoned substation. Despite its decrepit exterior, she motioned to her. There was a door on its side with a keypad. Amun tapped a combination on it. Tyana watched her press the sequence.

When she was done, a blue rectangle appeared in the door at eye level. A distorted voice spoke:

"Who comes?"

"The Speaker," Amun said, "with a friend."

The blue rectangle's opaque field shimmered. Someone was on the other side, watching, but couldn't be seen.

"Welcome," said the voice. The field faded. The door slid inward, resounding with the groan of steam-powered locks. When it opened, a lone Artificer stood in the doorway. She had short-cropped hair, a dirty shirt, chemical-stained pants, and a pair of goggles. She held a pulse rifle from the Warriors' arsenal. It was pointed toward the ceiling, glowing menacingly.

"So this is the one," she said.

"Yes," Amun replied.

The Artificer looked Tyana up and down, studying her.

"Come in," she said. Amun waved at Tyana to follow. The door slid into place behind them with a great mechanical heave. Inside was a messy laboratory filled with glass containers bearing strange markings.

"I wish you'd come at a better hour, Speaker," said the Artificer, tearing away her goggles and switching off the pulse rifle. She cast both onto a nearby workbench. "I'm concerned about security. You need to give me some warning. Besides, this *visitor* makes me uncomfortable— not solely because she's interrupting my work."

The Artificer continued to look Tyana up and down. Her eyelids were burnt black.

"Tyana, meet my sister Menay."

"Well met," Tyana said.

"Your reputation precedes you, Vestal-Warrior," Menay said. "Amun talks about you like you're her ally. Fine by me. But as long as you are in my workshop, do not touch anything. Do not mention what you see to anyone but the Speaker or myself. And finally, don't ask questions until you understand what I'm explaining."

Tyana furrowed her brow.

"She's trustworthy enough, Menay," Amun pleaded.

"That's up to you. But the things I discover here shock even me. Enough—this way."

Menay motioned to them and they followed her into

the lab. Chemical synthesizers occupied the corners. Workbenches were strewn with tools and jars of liquids.

"I am a bio-alchemist. I extract molecular agents from our flora and fauna to create medicines and rations. But when a bronze grail used to carry Mater's *ichor* came into my possession, my curiosity forced me to take a sample from its residue."

Menay led them to a glass case filled with all kinds of transparent and opaque liquids in large, capped beakers. Menay reached for one and pulled it down. Inside was a translucent black liquid that frothed as she stirred it.

"You could imagine the temptation to apply my craft to this unexplored, mysterious substance—divine, even, as some say. From a residual sample I discovered the chemical structure of what we call *ichor* and synthesized it."

The words struck Tyana. She peered at the black liquid. She could see her reflection in the glass of the beaker.

"This is not the substance I know of," she said.

"Of course not. This is a purified form of it. Natural *ichor* is mixed with all sorts of things—saliva, bile, even pieces of the organ that produces it. Those are biological contaminants. But if you purify it, this is the result." She tapped the side of the beaker. "This substance causes the possession of a given Vestal, transforming her into Mater Thea."

Tyana shuddered. She realized that if this was known in the upper city they would be branded as heretics. Punishment for heresy was severe—even fatal.

"How does it work?" Tyana asked.

"Our biology is unique," Menay said, replacing the glass container on the shelf. "When you compare it to other organisms, the differences are distinct. I work with all kinds of organisms: sea kelp, fish, gryphons. Their genomes are endemic to Valen's original genesis. But take any one of us and you'd find something different. Our genome is a collage of two different sources—one that is endemic to Valen and one that isn't."

Menay paused.

"What is the non-endemic source?" Tyana asked.

"Some Keepers might call it heresy, but the genes don't lie. Everything that is not from Valen is from off-world."

"You mean—humanity," Tyana said.

"Yes, of course," Menay replied. "We're taught from birth that we're created in the image of Vale to be the perfect race. Our Elders have stories that tell us our roots are in barbarian blood—humans. It's an endless debate among the Keepers. They can't stand the theological implications, but it's not a contradiction. Only a few parts of our genome have the residue of natural adaptation—the rest is written like fine poetry. It is true we were created, but Mater Vale used a template to do it."

"What kind of template?" Tyana asked.

"Probably the most accessible one—Herself."

Amun looked at Tyana. Menay continued on to another part of the laboratory. Amun and Tyana followed. Menay took hold of another container and opened it.

"No doubt you will recognize this." She held up a black pill. "This is the dried, compressed, and genetically neutered extract."

"Neutered?" Tyana questioned.

"All three of us have taken this pill at one time or

another," Menay said. "Mater's *ichor* causes possession because, on its absorption, it changes the organism's genome and physiology. It catalyzes a rapid transformation. What we know as the Vestal's touch and its accompanying hallucinations is a temporary side effect. I separated the qualities causing permanent changes from the ones that conveyed the mere symptoms—the experience of it. This was the result—a temporary agent that conveys the Vestal's power until the substance is metabolized like any other chemical."

"But the spirit that causes possession can't be in the *ichor*," Tyana said. "How could it be contained?"

"*Ichor* is merely the trigger for a certain kind of biology that is latent in all of us. You, Tyana, have the potential for a Scribe, an Artificer, and a Keeper in you. That potential is simply dormant. *Ichor* awakens a specific biological structure deep within us. That structure belongs to an individual—not a race, but an individual—that lived eons ago. When that structure is activated, the carrier's biology reverts to the original template."

"This is why a Vestal changes in appearance when she's possessed," Tyana said quietly.

"Exactly," Menay said, excited. "It's not surgery or trickery. The Vestal Teira we knew a year ago is still the current Vicar, but her body and mind are transformed into those belonging to a different individual who lived generations ago. The miracle is that the transformation is completely biological."

Tyana ignored Menay's enthusiasm. Instead, a question weighed heavily on her mind.

"Does this apply to Vale Herself?"

Menay gave a quizzical smile.

"It would in theory, wouldn't it?" Menay put the jar of pills back on the shelf. "You have more than a Warrior's intellect, Tyana, I'll admit. And you're right. Your suggestion may explain why we have such a strong mental—some might say *spiritual*—connection with the Maters. They exist in us all at an unconscious level—at least."

"You make it sound like our race was an experiment," Tyana said.

"Perhaps we were!" Menay quipped. Inspired, she rifled through a series of containers, pulling out one. It contained sets of colored pills, each in their separate vial. Tyana shuddered. There was one for each color of the castes: blue, yellow, red, and purple. Amun's brows shot up.

"You can guess what these are," Menay said, resting her hand on the lid—perhaps as a safety. "I'll give you a hint," she continued, grinning. "These aren't neutered like the black pills are."

"Permanent powers of the castes," Tyana said. The words were drawn out of her like a long, tickling string.

"The hope is that, unlike the temporary symptoms of the Vestal's touch, these will convey permanent qualities. There is no *ichor*-like extract for these powders. Like I said, Valenian biology is poetic. It was trivial to find the molecule that activates each caste's abilities. *Ichor* was just the model."

"If any of this were found out, it would be called out as heresy," Tyana said. Menay's enthusiasm evaporated.

"Now you understand my need for security," she said sternly. She put the containers away.

"Has anyone tried them?" Tyana asked.

"No," Amun interjected. "The gatherings were our

way of adjusting ourselves to the mental stamina needed to sustain the transformation. If they work, the changes would be quick and irreversible."

Tyana looked at her. Amun gestured toward Menay.

"Thank you, sister, for your explanations. Tyana and I will discuss this further in private."

"Fine by me," Menay said. "You know the way out."

LIII

TYANA AND AMUN exited Menay's lab. As soon as the door closed, Amun stopped her by the shoulder.

"Now do you understand how we can dismantle the castes?"

"You lied to me," Tyana said, turning to go.

Amun caught up with her.

"I didn't ask Menay to reveal the other pills. I didn't want you to know that. I just wanted to show you the proof of what I was talking about with the pills we'd already taken."

"You plan to turn yourselves into Warriors," Tyana said, stopping. She looked Amun in the eye. "Tell me— who will train you? Who will give you *sensak*? Where did Menay get that pulse rifle? I know where the Warriors' weapons lockers are and I know who counts those stocks now. You'll need those things if you plan to succeed."

"You will help us," Amun said. "Won't you?"

Tyana contemplated it for a moment.

"I don't know if I can do these things for you," she

said, turning to go again.

"Wait—Tyana, stop!" Amun caught up with her again. Steam wafted around them through the catwalks. She grabbed Tyana by the arm. "Why can't you? If my caste needs to expand our abilities to fight against the system, we can take that chance. But we need someone to lead us. Someone with experience. You know better than most that the system has to be dismantled. Now I've shown you how it can be done."

"You're talking about violent revolution against Thea," Tyana said. "You're talking about open revolt."

"This is the progress our movement has made so far. We can empower ourselves with the abilities of the other castes if we just apply ourselves to the task. Think of it— reading, writing, war-making—all of them could be ours and yours. The castes are Thea's way of exerting control. We can undo all her work and restore things to the way they should be. But I can't lead the revolution alone. I need your help."

Tyana thought of it. She thought about learning the language of the Scribes. She thought about reading the scriptures for herself.

"You said no one has taken them," she said. "How do you know they will work?"

"If they do, the change will be irreversible. No one has been willing to do it so far. Our goal with the gatherings was to find those among us who had the mental fortitude to withstand the power of another caste—the most powerful one at that: Vestals, the closest one to our enemy. But we were waiting for someone who could command that sensation rather than be subdued by it."

"You yourself didn't qualify for the task?"

Amun looked sheepish.

"I hoped Vale would answer our pleas for someone to come help us. When I first met you, I was intrigued. When we touched, I knew you were different. After that night at the gathering, watching the way you moved with the crowd, I knew you could lead us." Amun pressed close to her. "Please. Do you understand how important you are to our success, to me?"

"What do you want me to do?" Tyana asked. "I've been appointed to the War Council by the Mater Herself. If I accept, I will be first in my caste, yet the Warriors don't even respect or acknowledge me."

"Then you have nothing to lose by betraying them," Amun said.

"My teacher and my friend were both Warriors," Tyana said. "They died so I might live. I don't intend to betray their wishes."

"Then what am I to you? A friend? Otherwise?"

"We've shared things together that I could share with no one else," Tyana said.

"And I, you," Amun said, drawing her close. "It's taken me years to produce what I just showed you. I want you to loose Thea's rule on my caste. You are my best hope."

"How, Amun?" Tyana asked.

"Will you accept the position on the War Council?"

"There is no other path for me at this point," Tyana said. "It is my teacher's last recommendation."

"Then consider your proximity to the Mater," Amun said. "Consider your proximity to the other Vestals. You heard Menay's explanation: Thea persists because she can possess another Vestal. What if she no longer had a body to possess?"

Tyana paused.

"Breaking the cycle of possession would leave Her powerless," Tyana said.

"You are both a Warrior and a Vestal," Amun observed. "Who better to do it?"

"It means the destruction of a whole caste," Tyana said.

"A caste made of merely seven individuals," Amun said. "How many of my sisters have died under Thea's rule? How many of them have suffered throughout their lives? How many Artificers' lives are equal to one Vestal's?"

Tyana couldn't answer that.

"Think on it when you accept the position to the War Council. Think on it when you sit next to the Mater. Think on it when you see the Grand Artificer sitting below you silently in Thea's court."

Amun looked at her for a while, then she left her alone. Steam wafted around Tyana like fog.

LIV

IT WAS DUSK on Valen and the sky was overcast. The coastline was full of shards of obsidian that shimmered like glass. Tyana stood just beyond the waves of the coastline. They lapped quietly in the cool air.

She turned. Standing next to her was Vale. Tyana was taken aback. Vale's features were just like from her birth vision, but Vale appeared to be less than a god. She stood at the same height as Tyana. Her long, white hair trailed past her hips but stayed still in the wind. Her hands were folded in front of her. She was barefoot.

"Now, it is paid in full," she said. She began to walk toward the water.

Tyana, confused, turned to look behind her. There, a fair distance away, watching, was Thea. She too looked like less than a god—she appeared the way Tyana had met her in person. Thea watched Vale silently, her gaze fixed with intent.

The lapping waves licked at Vale's pure-white gown, darkening it as she went farther and deeper. Tyana followed her.

"Mater, where are you going?" she asked. Vale didn't answer. She continued to walk forward into the waves. Tyana repeated the question but received no response. Vale grimaced as she walked. The obsidian shards cut her feet, leaving behind drops of milky-white blood. The waves washed them away.

Tyana looked back once more. Thea was still there, standing, watching like a sentinel.

Vale's pace did not slow even as the water reached her waist. Tyana followed her and the glassy rocks cut her feet as well. The salty water stung as she walked. Wincing, Tyana called out to Vale, but Vale would not turn.

Tyana continued to swim out to her. Only Vale's shoulders were visible now. Her white hair was drifting in the water. Once Tyana reached her, she put out a hand to stop her. Vale rebuffed Tyana, moving her hand away. Tyana tried again, more forcefully, but Vale pushed her away again with just as much force. Tyana's feet could no longer touch the ground, but Vale continued deeper into the water. Then her head went under.

Tyana took a deep breath and dove toward the Mater. Vale was sinking, eyes closed, making no movements. Tyana grabbed her by the shoulders and shook her. Bubbles escaped from Vale's nostrils. Her hair drifted slowly in the water. Tyana tried to scream at her, releasing most of her air in the process.

Vale's eyes opened.

"Leave this place," she said as clear as if it were spoken through the air. "If you don't, you too will perish —"

Tyana woke up in a cold sweat. She was in her

quarters. Her night lamp glowed softly in the corner.

She threw off the covers, putting her face in her gloved hands. She wondered at what she had just seen.

Perturbed, she gathered her clothes and stepped outside her quarters. It was the dead of night. Cold air rushed in and snow greeted her at the entryway. The streets were still.

Bracing herself against the cold, she walked away from the city. Snow-laden trees greeted her. She wandered toward the cliffsides. From there she could see the unobstructed horizon. Valen's twin moons were dancing on its edge. The black one was ascendant, moving behind and above its smaller sister. The white one was falling, slowly being swallowed by the sea.

LV

THE NEXT DAY, snow covered the cathedral. Tyana made her way over the stone streets toward it. She was still disturbed by her night vision of Mater Vale's drowning. But her answer to the War Council's appointment was due.

She approached the cathedral and knocked on the heavy twin doors. One heaved open and a hooded attendant addressed her:

"Who comes?"

"The Vestal-Warrior Tyana, by request of the Mater, for Her appointment to the War Council."

The attendant bowed and opened the doors. They creaked as she did so. Tyana stepped inside and the attendant closed the doors behind her to keep out the cold.

"You may follow me," the attendant said. Tyana did. At the far end of the basilica, she could see the War Council in session. She could see the Grand Artificer, the Grand Scribe, and Vershil, the Head Keeper. Each seat was staggered by height in order of the castes: from lowest to highest. In the center at the top sat Mater Thea, her face veiled and her long, black hair streaming down the sides of her throne. Ahnsair sat next to her at her right hand. One seat was empty: Verikash's, the seat of the First Warrior, across from the Grand Scribe.

"Sister Tyana," Vershil addressed her as she approached. "We are pleased to see you."

"Sister Vershil," she said. She bowed formally in the direction of the Mater. "I've come regarding the Mater's appointment to the War Council."

She looked briefly at the veiled figure ahead of her. She felt Thea's gaze bore into her even though she couldn't see her eyes. Tyana suppressed the sensation.

"And?" Vershil asked. "Do you accept the position of head of your caste as Verikash recommended?"

Tyana hesitated, letting the question hang in the air of the cathedral.

"I do," Tyana said. "I am honored by the appointment."

"It pleases me you are honored," Mater Thea said. She gestured at the empty council seat. "Come, sit in the place Verikash once did."

Tyana bowed again and approached. She passed by the Grand Artificer. She climbed the steps and sat in Verikash's seat. She looked briefly at Vershil, who didn't return her gaze. Ahnsair, however, was staring at her.

"Moving on," Vershil said, "we have a delegation from our outermost colony. They request an audience, claiming they've intercepted sensitive information from the enemy."

"What sort of information?" Mater Thea asked.

"They did not specify," Vershil said. "They said it was

not translatable."

Mater Thea waved her hand in a gesture of acceptance.

"I grant the audience," she said. Vershil nodded and gestured to an attendant who hurried toward the entrance. She opened the doors of the cathedral and a delegation of Warriors and Scribes entered. They approached the council. Tyana noticed their expressions as they saw her sitting there.

"The War Council recognizes the delegation," Vershil declared. "You may have your audience."

One of the Scribes from the group stepped forward. She carried a small disk in her hand.

"Our Mater," the Scribe said to Thea, bowing. "We are from Seruneh, where we operate mining equipment that yields precious ore for industry. Three days ago we intercepted a transmission that puzzled my sisters and me. We feel it warrants attention from the War Council, as it came from a barbarian source."

"What does it say?" Thea asked.

"My apologies," the Scribe said. "It is in a language we do not know nor have references for. My belief is that it is a human tongue that recorded it."

"How is this message different from other transmissions?" Thea asked. "It is not the first time we have heard their foul tongue."

"We understand much of their simplistic language," the Scribe said. "However, it has been many years, generations even, since we last encountered a message of this kind. Before the barbarians employed machines to do their bidding, we encountered their communications regularly. Their voice has not been heard from since then until now. Further, this is a language distinct from the others we already know. As I said—with our apologies to this assembly—we have not been able to translate the message."

The council members stirred. Tyana looked at the various Warriors. They didn't meet her gaze.

"Do you have the message with you?" Mater Thea asked.

"Yes," said the Scribe.

"Play it for us," commanded Thea. "Let us hear this new, strange language."

The Scribe bowed, placing the disk in front of the council. She activated it and its center unfolded, revealing a small black pool that reverberated with sound. At first, the resulting sound was grainy and crackled. The Scribe manipulated the disk's vibration and the quality improved. Tyana leaned forward, listening. The crackle gave way to a distinct voice. It was a voice unlike any Valenian's. It was harsh and deep, but the words it spoke were almost lyrical.

A sensation seized Tyana. It was recognition. She did not know what the words meant, but she had heard them before. They were unmistakable to her.

The Scribe turned the disk off.

"It repeats the same phrase," she said. "We believe it is a recording that loops without end. Even now, it is broadcasting on the frequencies from which we found it."

"Keeper Vershil," Mater Thea said, turning to her left, "do you recognize this kind of speech?"

Vershil shook her head.

"Apologies, my Mater, but I do not. While I have studied the barbarian language, I can confirm that this is novel. I cannot interpret it without more information."

Tyana was transfixed. She watched the disk hovering above the floor. She recognized the words all the way back to her birth dream.

"Something troubles you, my Vestal-Warrior," Mater Thea observed aloud. All eyes turned to Tyana.

"No, my Mater," she replied quickly, "aside that these words, if unique as Sister Vershil says, could mean that there is a new kind of enemy at our gates." Mater Thea nodded.

"Indeed. What do you make of it?"

"Without knowing the meaning, it is difficult to say," Tyana said. "It could be a declaration of war, it could be an admission of surrender. But if it is broadcast in repetition, I believe that it is not idle either way. I would say that the barbarians—or whoever sent it—wanted us to receive it."

"An astute observation," Thea said. "To what end?"

"Impossible to know without knowing the message's content," Tyana said. She turned toward the delegation. "What are the enemy's movements now? Have you noticed anything strange about the barbarians or their machines around Seruneh?"

"Sister Tyana," said one of the Warriors, stepping forward. She addressed Tyana formally as one of a higher caste. "We observed a general withdrawal of machine forces from the area of Seruneh after the broadcast started. They have not given up any territory, but they have halted their incursions. Our defenses stand ready."

"Perhaps it is a message of surrender, then," said Ahnsair. She looked at Tyana. "Perhaps you should send a cadre of Warriors to crush them."

This suggestion seemed to please Mater Thea.

"It could also be a trap," Tyana countered instinctively. "If we send a large group of warbirds, we may lose them in an ambush. Our forces are still depleted from the battle of Seruneh Second."

"What do you suggest then, Vestal-Warrior?" Thea asked.

"I volunteer to go alone," Tyana said, standing. "I will go with my warbird and scout the source of this message. I will find what its purpose is and report back. From there, we can determine if we need to send a larger force. We need not risk our ranks."

"Is that proposition not dangerous to yourself?" Vershil quipped.

"Warriors relish fear," Tyana replied. Mater Thea nodded.

"I see your logic," Thea said. "Let it be done. Tyana will investigate the source of this strange message and report back to us. Whether it be for surrender or for war, she will lead us to its conclusion."

Mater Thea stood. The delegation bowed.

"Council is adjourned," Vershil announced. The council members began to disperse.

Tyana felt a strange pricking at her mind—like an invading presence trying to determine her intention. She looked at Mater Thea. She was already leaving her throne. Only Ahnsair stayed in her seat, gazing at Tyana.

Tyana walled off her innermost thoughts and bowed toward Ahnsair, promptly departing from the cathedral.

LVI

TYANA WENT TO find Amun. She headed along the path she knew—down through the old, abandoned city, down through the ventilation ducts. When she reached the industrial levels, it was night and all the machines were still. She saw no bustling Artificers going about their daily work. Tyana went to Amun's quarters. They were empty.

Tyana presumed that she and her followers were gathered in the caves below. She was puzzled; Amun often told her when there would be such a gathering. Nonetheless, she headed down toward the caves.

When she reached them, she could see the glow of the firelight and hear the hammering of the drums. She moved through the cavern quietly and approached the gathering. She saw the Artificers there with Amun at the center. They were dancing and wailing in ecstasy. Amun's eyes were wide, transfixed with visions. Tyana wanted to join in, but she withheld herself. She felt a pang of jealousy. Why did Amun stop telling her about the gatherings?

Tyana watched them for a while. She stayed hidden behind the stalagmites of the cave. When the group exhausted itself, Tyana headed for Amun's quarters. She stayed there, waiting.

Some time later, Amun arrived. She was surprised to see Tyana standing there.

"You didn't invite me," Tyana said. Amun appeared bemused.

"My sisters and I need privacy on occasion. After all, didn't you have an appointment to the War Council today?"

"I did. I want to talk to you about it. Amun—in your birth dream, did you meet Mater Thea?"

Amun shot her a quizzical look.

"Of course. I met her like we all do, right after seeing Vale descend into the ocean."

"Was she holding a scepter in your dream? A scepter with twisted helixes?" Tyana asked. Amun paused.

"No. She held the symbol of the Artificers in her hands. She broke it in two and I had to mend it. It's taboo to ask other caste members about their birth dreams. You know that. Why are you asking me this?"

Tyana sat down.

"Today there was a delegation from Seruneh. They claimed they intercepted a transmission in a barbarian tongue they didn't recognize—the first transmission of its kind in generations. No one knew what it meant. But I recognized the words."

"From where?" Amun asked, curious.

"My birth dream," Tyana said.

Amun's brows furrowed.

"What do you mean?"

"In my dream, Thea carried a scepter made of helixes. At its top was a barbarian's head. His skin was dark, his eyes were strange, and his voice was deep. He had a chant he kept saying—a series of words I didn't understand. But when the delegation played the message aloud, they were the same words."

Amun was visibly surprised.

"That doesn't make any sense."

"No, it doesn't," Tyana said. "But it happened. I told no one about it, not even my teacher Vershil, fearing she would condemn me."

"But why would a barbarian's message in the future affect your birth dream?"

Tyana shook her head.

"I don't know. But it wasn't the last time this face appeared in my visions. So today I volunteered to fly out beyond Seruneh and determine its source. The Council suggested sending a fleet of Warriors, but I insisted on going alone."

"Do you think this will lead the way forward for my caste's liberation?" Amun asked.

"I don't know. But I have to find out why I dreamed this message. The night before I had another dream. In this one, I watched Mater Vale drown Herself while Mater Thea watched."

"Sounds similar to a normal birth dream," Amun said.

"But it wasn't," Tyana said. "It wasn't similar to a birth dream at all. In this, Vale appeared to be like any one of us. Mater Thea appeared just like She does today. Vale just walked into the water and refused to come back. I tried to save Her, but I couldn't."

Amun shrugged.

"What should I do? Interpret this for you?"

"If you can," Tyana said.

"Our Elders say that Thea is the reason for Vale's disappearance. They don't say how or why. They don't mention Her drowning."

"That is what I saw happen and it wasn't the same as seeing Her in the birth dream. It seemed ... real."

"Real?"

"Like how we feel about the visions we share," Tyana said. "Like they actually happened, just in a different time or place."

Amun waved her hand dismissively.

"If it's true that there's some connection, I see why you need to find it out for yourself. But if it can't help my caste in our fight against Thea, I don't see its importance."

"Why not?" Tyana pleaded. "This could lead us to discovering why Vale disappeared."

"Vale is dead," Amun snapped. "What difference does it make how She died? My people are dying, too. We are injured by the machines we are commanded to work with. There is no recourse for us in Thea's world. What would you do for us once you found out the source of the message? How would it help us?"

"I don't know yet, but we have to find out," Tyana said, faltering.

"My concerns are more practical than yours," Amun said. "They're informed by the plight of my sisters. I was hoping that you would be more open to actively leading us. It's obvious you are more interested in knowledge for your own sake."

"Amun, you need more than a makeshift army. I dreamed of this message before it happened. That has to mean something. This could lead to a new possibility that could loosen Thea's rule. I offered to go alone not because I want to represent Her—I insisted on going alone because I don't want Her to control whatever I find."

Amun considered this. She seemed unimpressed, however.

"Until my sisters can wield the power they rightly deserve, and until you help us overthrow the caste system, do not appear here again for our gatherings."

Tyana was taken aback.

"You can't be serious."

"You are of a higher caste and directly in contact with Mater Thea. How close is she to you on the Council? Aren't you close enough to strike at her if you wanted to? And if you could, why don't you?"

"Amun—assassinating Thea won't kill Her. She will simply take a new body. If I destroy the other Vestals, there will simply be more birthed from the womb and Thea will take one of them instead."

Amun looked Tyana up and down. She was looking at her in an unfamiliar way.

"You are a Vestal too, aren't you?"

"Yes," Tyana said with trepidation.

"You're of Mater Thea's caste. You are on her War Council, and yet she lives. Why should I believe you aren't collaborating with her? You wouldn't annihilate yourself if she took your body, would you?"

Tyana nearly sneered:

"Thea has invaded my mind and nightmares since I was born. I am no friend to Her. You'd accuse me of collaborating with Her?"

"You are within striking distance of the one enemy

that could undo the castes. Yet she still sleeps soundly in her bed. What do you expect me to make of you?"

Tyana shook her head.

"You of all people should understand it's impossible to break Her grip through force alone. The Grand Artificer was right. If you think you can succeed this way, you are deluded."

Amun turned her back on Tyana.

"If that's how you think, I have nothing more to say to you."

"Amun, please—," she reached out toward her with a gloved hand, but Amun swatted it away.

"Get out of here," Amun said.

Tyana stared at Amun's turned back.

Dejected, Tyana gave her one last look before leaving her quarters. Amun wouldn't look her in the eyes as she left.

LVII

TYANA SAT PERCHED over the abyss of the industrial levels contemplating her argument with Amun. A deep sadness filled her. It tasted like the sadness she felt when Kersa turned her back on her. But Tyana had plumbed the depths of her psyche with Amun, further than she ever had with Kersa. Amun was more than a friend.

Tyana felt betrayed. Amun's accusation of collaboration with Thea angered her. She felt Amun was blinded by tragedy and oppression, but now she was nursing it into something worse by telling her to leave.

It was still night. Tomorrow, she would have to fly out to find the source of the barbarian message. Who knew what Amun would attempt to do while she was gone? The Artificers might try to transform themselves into Warriors and stage an uprising. Amun and her followers would be branded for heresy—or worse.

Tyana stood. She knew that if she did what she planned to do next, Amun would count it as a betrayal and she would lose her friendship forever. But a thought nagged at Tyana's mind—it was a missing piece, a hole she could not fill. She did not believe what Amun said: that Vale was dead.

She quietly traversed the junctions and the mess of pipes, descending to the levels where Menay's lab was. She took care to not be seen or heard by anyone. Amun could have already informed her followers that she was no longer an ally. Menay would be skeptical if she asked for entrance to the lab alone.

Tyana stood in front of the lab's sealed door. In a moment of inspiration, she released her *sensak*, forming a simulacrum of Amun's face. It was difficult to get the details right, but once the natural black texture of her *sensak* congealed into a smooth, white skin, Tyana was satisfied. She wore the *sensak* like a living mask.

She reproduced the sequence Amun had tapped on the keypad from memory. The door's one-way viewport glowed to life and Menay's distorted voice crackled:

"Who comes?"

Tyana bent her knees, shortening herself so that she matched Amun's height; she moved closer so that only the mask could be visible through the viewport.

"The Speaker."

The voice gave a pause.

"Welcome," Menay said. The door groaned and slid open. Tyana took a deep breath. Menay stood there at the threshold in her nightclothes. She held a pulse rifle, but it wasn't armed.

"Wait—you can't be Amun!"

Tyana was on her before Menay could bring the rifle to bear. She knocked it to the ground. She swarmed Menay with *sensak*, forming a cocoon around her so she could not move.

"Traitor! Trait—," she screamed before Tyana quickly sealed her mouth shut. She attached the cocoon to a wall.

She closed the door and dissolved her mask. She searched the lab for the last container Menay had shown her. She found it in the far corner: the colored pills that conveyed permanent powers of the castes. She emptied it on a workbench. She picked out three: blue, yellow, and red. She put them in her mouth and held them there, not swallowing.

With her remaining *sensak* she formed an array of bullets and sent them flying through the lab. They shattered the glass containers. Shards flew in all directions. Colored elixirs spilled onto the floor and jars of powder exploded, spewing their contents. She destroyed the storage shelves, smashed the tools, and ruined the workbenches. Pills and liquids were everywhere.

She could feel Menay struggling against the cocoon. She realized she wouldn't be able to destroy all of the lab's contents in time. Commanding the *sensak*, Tyana lifted the cocoon into the air and, following it, exited the lab. She placed it on the catwalk ahead, Menay still writhing inside.

Turning back to the lab, Tyana unleashed her remaining *sensak* on the junction of pipes that held it in place over the abyss. They ate through the supporting struts and rigging. Metal screamed and sparks flew. Cords snapped. With a final wrench, the whole structure heaved, snapped, then fell off. It tore pieces of ventilation duct with it as it disappeared into the fog below. Moments later a loud but distant splash echoed up from the abyss.

The pills were dissolving in her mouth. A subtle burning sensation was all over her tongue. She swallowed. She dissolved the cocoon of *sensak* and they swarmed around her at attention. Menay stood up and looked, aghast.

"No, no—you've destroyed my life's work!" Fuming, she lunged at Tyana. Tyana sent tendrils of *sensak* up the ascending catwalks. They drew her into the air so that she hovered, suspended, out of Menay's reach.

"No, I haven't," Tyana said. "I've just modified its course. I've already taken the permanent powers of the remaining castes. I will take on their burdens, but Amun's followers will not."

"You betrayed our plans!"

"I will not let Amun's uprising become a violent revolution. Even with your combined numbers, you would not be able to suppress the Warriors or Thea. You would be slaughtered. I won't see you and your sisters risk themselves that way. I am doing this to keep you, Amun, and all your sisters safe."

"We'll kill you! We'll expose you in the upper city and you'll be branded as a heretic!"

"With what proof? I've destroyed it all. Even if they believe you, Amun will incriminate herself and all of you if she complains to Thea. You wanted to free yourselves from the caste system. That power is now growing inside me."

"Amun will never trust you again," Menay said.

"I know. If that's the price I have to pay, I will pay it. But do not attempt to revolt. The Warriors will slaughter you if you do. Wait for me when the time is right and I will help you win. There are other things I need to find out first. Until then, I hope you try to understand.

Forgive me. Amun left me no other choice."

She ascended the catwalks, tendrils of *sensak* carrying her up. They stretched out from her like the legs of a spider.

LVIII

WHEN TYANA EXITED the lower city through the ventilation system, waves of hallucination were already pouring in from the corners of her eyes. Her nerves were alight with growing electricity. Outside, the air was frigid. The whole landscape was covered in snow, which appeared dark blue against the night sky.

She used her *sensak* like a set of fibrous legs, piercing the snow with the smallest spindles possible. Without a set of footprints, Amun's followers couldn't track her. When she started to shiver, she encased the rest of her body to keep warm. She didn't head for the upper city. Instead, she headed for the forests at the far end of the island. Like the foundations of the old city, it was full of windswept trees with gnarled roots, grinding the hardened basalt into soil. Ice coated their needlelike leaves and layers of snow weighed heavily on their branches until it seemed they would break under the stress.

She entered the heart of the forest. Finding a large

tree with a gaping maw in its trunk, she drew herself over to it and holed herself up inside. She covered the opening in *sensak*, cocooning herself inside. She even gave it the same texture as the surrounding bark to disguise it.

By now, the hallucinations were palpable and overwhelming. Tracers of blue, yellow, and red fought each other for dominance behind her closed eyelids, growing in patterns of complexity and detail. Her body reverberated with growing dissonance, as if the fabric of her consciousness was pulled apart thread by thread in all directions. She was overwhelmed and she gave herself up to it. Her vision disappeared and she fell into a void.

LIX

WHEN HER VISION reappeared, she was lying on her back. She felt the grass, wet from morning dew, against her skin. The sky above was dressed with pink auroras and pricked by stars. The air was warm.

She stood up. She was on the precipice of the cliff. She recognized this place from her birth dream.

A thick wind blew and she ran her hands through her hair. Then she noticed its color—it was vermillion, as bright as a flame. She was taken by it for a moment, but the wind grew stronger. A storm from the horizon descended. Rumbling thunder and roaring gales accompanied it. The grass flattened.

Mater Vale appeared from the storm, her hair whipping in all directions. Lightning brewed behind her like a halo of static electricity, but her face was serene.

Tyana reached out her hand to Vale. Vale responded by reaching out to Tyana. As soon as she did, the wind began to draw her away and downward toward the sea. Tyana chased Vale, reaching for her hand, but couldn't get close enough to touch it. As quickly as she came, Vale fell toward the ocean. Her unfazed expression gave way to muted terror. Tyana stared as Vale's outline disappeared beneath the waves.

In Vale's place, a shadow appeared. The sea gurgled as it rose up. It was Thea. Her body boiled the water away as it dripped off. Her face was cut from pure obsidian and her skin was like graphite. She glared at Tyana. Molten bronze filled her eyes and they spewed tears that sizzled on the grass of the cliff, solidifying as they cooled.

Thea stretched out her hands, presenting the symbol of the Artificers to Tyana. It wasn't illustrated on a piece of cloth. Instead it was a machine made of interlocking parts, all moving in concert. Light burst from its corners and paints of all colors spewed from its sides, dripping down its edges. It was alive, pulsating with the heart of raw genius and unbridled creativity. In a single heave, Thea threw the symbol onto the ground. It shattered on the rocks. It almost seemed to scream as its inner machinery splintered and fell apart.

Tyana approached the symbol. It was made of glass, stone, ceramic; all the materials an Artificer might use. Its still-beating heart seemed to ooze paint infinitely. As Tyana reached down and touched it, the paint stuck to her fingers and began to stream from them. She shook her hand and the paint splattered everywhere, but it didn't stop pouring from her fingertips. Wherever the paint stuck, it flowed from there without ceasing. Tyana was quickly surrounded by eternally growing puddles of paint.

She looked up at Thea. In a fit of emotion, she flung her hand at Thea and the paint stuck to her burnt tunic.

Thea looked down. The paint flowed down to her feet and dripped off her toes. It didn't boil off like water.

Tyana flung her hand again at Thea. Paint stuck to Thea's torso, hands, and face. A childlike joy came over Tyana. Thea began to speak in protest, but Tyana flung more paint at her and it covered her mouth. Now she couldn't even speak. Whenever Thea opened her mouth, only paint spewed from it. With both hands, Tyana coated the Mater in a spectrum of colors. Thea became so laden with paint that her outline was indistinguishable, and she sank back into the sea under the weight of it all.

As soon as Thea disappeared beneath the waters, a pain grew inside Tyana's head. It engulfed her scalp and she closed her eyes. Her vision disappeared.

LX

WHEN HER VISION reappeared, she was on her back again. Calm night sky met her eyes. She stood up, brushing the grass from her back. She tugged at her hair. It was bright gold.

The grass flattened and Mater Vale appeared from the horizon through the clouds, just like last time. Tyana ran to meet her as she stretched out her hand. Her serene face seemed blissful, but unaware of what was happening.

Tyana, peering up, touched Vale's hand and drew her face up close to it. Tyana put her cheek against Vale's open palm. Vale looked at her, but her expression did not change.

As quickly as the winds had come, they whipped up again and carried Vale away. Tyana tugged at her, but her grip slipped easily. As Vale was swallowed by the clouds, her eyes seemed to betray the faintest hint of recognition—like she knew she had just seen Tyana. Then she was gone.

The sea stirred below. It burst with a spray of froth and water. Thea appeared. Her tunic was in tatters; ash dusted her joints and embers burned from her ribcage. Her eyes dripped tears of molten copper out each corner and her teeth were coated with oil.

"*Worship me*," she implored.

Tyana looked away from Thea, shielding herself from the awful visage. Looking down, she saw the thick grass wrapping around her ankle. It was pricking against her skin uncomfortably. So, with one hand, Tyana yanked the grass, tearing it away. To her surprise, the blades glowed with a yellow light from the place she tore them.

Tyana looked from Thea to the glowing blades of grass. She plucked one from the bunch—the light seemed to stick in place, forming a glowing trail wherever it went. She dragged it through the air, creating a stream of light. The harder she dragged, the longer the stream lasted.

Symbols and glyphs of all kinds poured into Tyana's mind. She couldn't predict their shape; she didn't understand what they meant or where they came from, but she felt a deep impulse to write them down. Her mind became a receptacle for words and, as they poured infinitely into her, she felt her body might explode if she didn't empty them out in some way.

So she freed her wrist and let the words flow out through her hand, down through the glowing tip of the grass's blade. They were glyphs she didn't recognize— they could have been gibberish—but it didn't matter. As long as they fulfilled her need to write, that was enough. They hung in the air, glowing brilliantly, illuminated.

Thea roared. She took her massive right hand and swatted at the golden words. They buckled but didn't fully break—instead, they stuck together like glue. She swatted again and her hand barely missed Tyana. Seeing her predicament, Tyana built the glyphs up tighter and tighter so that they formed an all but solid structure. Thea swatted again, but her fingers got stuck in the glyphs. She strained to free herself. Tyana kept writing, building the glyphs up and up as she went. She wrote them around Thea's fingers and wrist. Soon, she had all but encased Thea's hand in a morass of words.

Thea's rage burned. She used its heat to burn away at the words, heating her wrist until it glowed white-hot. Some of the glyphs encasing her dissolved, but most of them remained. She grimaced, then screamed. Her inner fire grew so hot that it burned in her eyes, burned through their sockets, and finally, her wrist snapped off. Her body was free but her rage consumed her, eating her from the inside out. She fell down toward the sea, disintegrating into embers. The water splashed as the pieces fell; steam and ash rose up in their place.

Tyana grimaced. Her scalp burned, as if a knife were taken to its skin, peeling it away. She passed out from the sensation.

LXI

HER VISION REAPPEARED, just as before. She was on her back, wet with dew. Calm night skies did not betray her sense of urgency. She did not need to look at her hair, but she did anyway. It was blue as a sapphire.

Standing up, she looked toward the horizon expectantly. A storm cloud billowed and burst with electric energy. When Vale broke through, Tyana was already at the cliff's precipice. Tyana reached out; Vale looked down and reached toward her. Vale blinked; a wave of recognition passed over her. Her serene but aloof gaze turned with a sense of urgency. Now she strained further toward Tyana, but the wind seemed to blow her back even quicker than she had come. She reached into her tunic. Parting it, she held out a stone scroll. It was tiny in her hands, but when it rolled down into Tyana's arms, it was huge. Tyana caught it, barely. Then Vale was swallowed by clouds, lightning licking in her wake.

Thea arrived. The sea split and the earth itself

quaked. Her face was devoid of skin this time. Tendons of charcoal masked a skeletal maw that glowed like a furnace. Her eyes weeped tears of molten tin at each corner, and as she breathed, her diaphragm stoked fires in her ribcage like bellows. She opened her lipless mouth; opalescent oil spewed from between her teeth.

Tyana recoiled. She nearly dropped the stone cylinder but caught herself, holding it. It glowed in her hands.

She steadied herself. Remembering the way Vershil had split the stone scroll, she gestured in the same way. It split, exploding into pieces in a rhythmic pattern across its surface. It hovered in front of her, floating. A light gleamed from its center, and she gazed at it. Images flowed into her mind, palpable. The vision started at the beginning.

She saw the creation of the universe. She saw the genesis of distant planets she didn't recognize. She saw the birth of humanity and its civilizations. She saw Vale's creation, growth, and death as Thea stood watch nearby. She saw the terraforming of Valen in its fiery glory. She saw the rise of the castes and how they changed as Thea came to power. She saw herself. Then she saw the future branching into a whole series of possibilities. She couldn't predict them, but only one intersection was common to them all.

Coming out of her reverie, Tyana realized she'd been narrating her visions aloud. Looking up, Thea's body was wrenched from within. Tyana's recitation split her apart. Her already frail body disintegrated at the joints, leaving exposed nerves of gold that dripped away. Finally, her body crumpled into ash and fell toward the sea.

The light from the scroll faded and it reassembled

itself. It dropped into Tyana's hands, cold and lifeless again. Her mind was wracked with visions, but despite their detailed richness, their meaning faded from her memory like sand falling between her fingertips.

Pain scoured its way across her head. She fell toward the grass, clutching her temples. When she couldn't stand it anymore, her vision disappeared.

LXII

TYANA WOKE UP, still encased in the tree by her *sensak*. Dream consciousness faded into sobriety, and when her discomfort waned, she moved. She stepped out into the snow from the heart of the tree. She looked at her hair, unsure of what to expect. It was the same violet and black mixture as it was before. Something felt different, though—like a series of doors once locked inside her now stood open. She wanted to explore their rooms. She wanted to know if the visions had worked.

She looked at the sky. It was still night, and the smaller moon was brilliantly eclipsing the other. The dark moon's shadow hung around the brighter one like a ring, framing it.

Tyana clenched her gloved fists. She released her *sensak*, encasing herself. Moving across the snow, she headed straight for the city.

When she got there, the streets were still asleep. She headed for the libraries. The Keepers did not work during the night, but she did not want to risk being spotted. She stopped and stepped into a dark alcove. Beyond were the spiral staircases that led down to the libraries.

She remodeled her *sensak* to create another mask—this time a Keeper's. Vershil was her most visceral memory, but she didn't want to imitate her appearance. She wanted someone less recognizable. Instead, she formed a face from the next strongest memory. It was the one of the Keeper who led her with Kersa to Vershil after her birth. She put it on and, at her will, the *sensak* formed a pair of cobalt-colored braids that fell behind her ears. She hid the rest of her hair with a hood.

She walked toward the staircase. Its veined marble steps glinted in the light and its coiled railings were cold to the touch. Tyana softened her steps to remain silent, even though the whole hall appeared empty. Unlit braziers bearing the insignia of the Keepers hung overhead. She traversed the corridor, searching for the place they kept the scriptures. She found it, recognizing the huge double doors Vershil once led her through.

The Keepers' twisting, coiled insignia loomed at her, carved deep into the doors. Tyana touched it along its seams. After a pause, the insignia glowed briefly. The doors split and heaved open. Looking in each direction to see if anyone was visible, Tyana entered the library and closed the doors behind her.

The stale, dry air embraced her inside. The stained glass mandala that looked out onto the ocean was now an ominous black web framing the starlit sky. The moon was visible through it, still eclipsing its darker twin over the ocean. Tyana looked around. Stacks of stone rods were everywhere. She barely knew where to start, so she retraced from memory the steps Vershil had taken. They led her to a broad shelf, thoroughly adorned with inlays of obsidian and quartz, but covered with a thick layer of dust. She picked out the largest and heaviest stone scroll on the shelf. It looked like the one Vale had given her during the visions.

She brought it over to the wide reading table, placing it on a stand. The insignia of the Scribes and the Keepers intertwined together on the scroll's seam. She remembered what happened when she touched such a scroll in Vershil's presence.

She unclothed one of her gloved hands and, after a moment of hesitation, traced her finger along the seam of the scroll. Its surface was cold and smooth, then it grew hot. The insignia glowed. Cracks traced patterns along its edges and the seam split. The scroll opened, alive. Inside was a glowing light that exploded, engulfing the room. Tyana's gaze fixed on the center of the light. She felt drawn toward its heart. Her eyes rolled into the back of her head and a wave of detailed images came to her, as vivid as if they were real.

She saw Mater Vale stretched out on a land full of dark, fertile soil. Her veins changed into the colors of the castes and they dissolved into the ground. Her head was the last to merge with the soil, and she looked at Tyana, saying:

"I desired them like a mother desires her children. I gave them up to my sister."

The image changed. Now, Tyana stood in a circle among three nude figures—Artificer, Keeper, and Scribe —surrounding a Vestal crouched down in a pool of *ichor.*

"She made the castes to guide us," they said in unison. They looked at her. Each one had Tyana's face. Realizing she was in the fourth position, she looked at her hair. It was fully violet.

The image changed again. She was at the cliffsides of the Mater's City before the city was ever built. Vale stood there in front of her.

"I was whipped up by wind and hid myself from my sister."

A vortex of wind ripped Vale and Tyana from the cliff. They flew through the air, traversing Valen's seas and many island chains until coming to the mountain ranges at the farthest pole. This place was always blanketed with snow and ice.

"I hid myself for the day my sister might come to exact vengeance on humanity."

They stopped over a wide basin. The wind let them down. Vale sat, then lay down on her side. The wind covered her with snow. The snow turned to ice.

The image changed again. Tyana saw her own reflection in a quivering pool of oil. The reflection showed her hair as it was: violet and black.

"The Sybil knows my secrets. You will know her name, but you will not recognize her."

The pool of oil advanced around her. It engulfed her body—and she came out the other side, turning around to stare back at it. From the pool emerged a dark, human face: the tan-skinned man. His eyes opened, revealing a set of emerald irises, and he spoke in a deep, strange voice. He said the same words from the intercepted barbarian message.

At that moment Tyana shuddered. She disengaged from the vision and the light from the scroll faded. Her pulse was fast and heavy; tracers filled her vision. She brought one hand to her temple, nursing her forehead. Overwhelmed, she took the scroll and replaced it on the shelf. She collected some of the surrounding dust, covering the scroll with it to make it appear as if it hadn't been tampered with.

She headed back to the double doors. With a touch, they opened. Straightening her hood, she exited, making sure the doors closed behind her. She felt like her footsteps echoed far too loudly as she navigated her way back to the staircases.

"Sister?"

A voice echoed behind her. The *sensak* in her mask quivered. She put up her best resolve and turned. A young Keeper, shorter than her, was staring at her.

"Sister Vesha—forgive me, I did not realize it was you," the girl said. "I thought you might have been someone else."

Tyana just smiled in response.

"I did not mean to interrupt you," the girl continued. "I am scheduled to monitor the halls tonight, after all. I thought I would not see you until tomorrow morning. You will be there for my lesson, correct?"

Tyana managed her best imitation of a Keeper's tone: "Yes, of course."

The girl hesitated, then smiled and bowed.

"Good, I am glad."

Tyana turned without another word, making her way up the spiral staircase. She could feel the girl's gaze as she went up. When she reached the top and was out of sight, she finally released her mask, relaxing.

Outside, it was almost sunrise. Curtains of fog were turning green and pink from the inky blue night. The two moons were still visible. The small one was no longer in eclipse, but was still ascendant, covering much of the larger, competing moon.

She knew she didn't have much time left before morning broke. She headed for the hangars across the city. When she got there, the faintest shadows of buildings were outlined by a red glow from a rising sun disk.

She traversed the clefts down to where the warbirds waited. Their shimmering, black forms stood still, barely reflecting the growing light outside. She headed toward hers.

"Vestal-Warrior," a voice called out.

Tyana turned. It was Ahnsair. She was in a hooded gown. Removing the hood, she said:

"Are you off now to find the barbarian's message?"

"I am—and you?" Tyana replied.

"Waiting for you. Watching for you," Ahnsair said, walking forward. "Where have you been this whole night? You didn't need to be in a hurry."

"I go where I please, when I please. What makes you ask?"

"Curiosity," Ahnsair said. She approached, revealing one naked hand. "Tonight, I was woken up from sleep. An awful noise echoed through the sanctum. May I tell you about it?"

"Of course," Tyana said.

"It was our Mater, Thea, screaming," she said. "She had a night terror. It was like nothing I've ever seen before. She tore at the bed sheets, even shoving us away when we tried to restrain Her." Ahnsair approached, brushing her hand up against Tyana's wrist. Tyana drew it away instantly. Ahnsair continued: "There was one thing She kept saying even as She was exhausted and in terror."

"What is that?" Tyana asked.

"Your name. Your name and your castes. But She didn't just name you as a Vestal-Warrior. She listed each and every caste." Ahnsair peered at her strangely. "What are you? What have you done to my Mater?"

"I am the same Vestal-Warrior you know as before. Nothing has changed."

"Something makes me doubt that."

Ahnsair attempted to reach for her again, but Tyana caught her.

"That touch is forbidden, Sister," she said.

"Not between us," Ahnsair replied in the casual form. She reached again, but Tyana easily wrenched her away by the wrist. For a moment, Ahnsair yelped in pain.

"I have a mission to fulfill for our Mater," Tyana said. "I will see you on my return once I've found the source of the message."

"You're not everything you say you are, Tyana," Ahnsair said, nursing her wrist. "I'll find you out and expose your true self."

"Let me know whether I'm more or less than what you expected."

Standing beneath her warbird, she allowed her *sensak* to draw her up into its belly. She ignited the warbird's engines, watching Ahnsair on the hangar floor. The robed Vestal stared, motionless, barely visible in the shadows.

Tyana's warbird shot upward like a black spear tip. Her ship released a shock wave as she broke through the cloud layer and the atmosphere. The sky darkened until it was black. She could see Valen's two moons, and its distant star, over the curve of the planet.

She headed for the acceleration gate. She set her course for Seruneh. When she got to the gate, her warbird jolted as the gate's electric tendrils enveloped it. She shot forward, blazing past planets, moons, and asteroids.

LXIII

TYANA'S WARBIRD JOLTED to a stop. She arrived at the coordinates implied by the source of the message. She was near Seruneh, and it hovered below her. It was a planet in the slow process of terraforming, growing an atmosphere, but its open veins of magma glowed deep red even from space. Mining operations dotted its surface.

The source of the message was behind her. She brought her warbird about, bearing toward it. The beacon seemed to be located in the asteroid belt. It drew her toward Seruneh Second, the site of her first battle, and the place where Verikash and Kersa perished. She headed toward the asteroid's crevice. Below was a crater left by the power core they detonated. Beyond that was a blast radius that traced its way toward a point—the place where she had absorbed the explosion but failed to contain it.

The beacon drew her closer to the heart of the base, deep below the cleft. She turned her warbird down toward the cleft. It led deep into the asteroid. Massive calcite crystals bristled from its walls like the ribs of a broken cage. She gently weaved around them, following the signal down the cleft. Finally, she reached its source.

There was a landing pad that led to the entrance of the mining operation. She touched her warbird down there. Her *sensak* dissolved the belly of the ship and she exited, forming an armored suit against the vacuum. She walked through the entrance. The doors shut behind her —they still worked.

The corridor ahead was scarred by fire and hissed with steam. She walked forward, her *sensak* bristling on her skin. The signal was leading her deep into the base. It led her down a series of turns into a final dead end with a wide bay door. On either side of the door were glowing readouts of the base's power, which was still functioning at a minimal level.

In the center of the gateway was a single control panel. She activated it.

"Who comes?" a synthesized voice echoed from the panel's speaker. The voice didn't have the right intonation.

"Who asks?" Tyana asked, naturally. There was a pause.

"Not your enemy," said the voice.

"Prove it."

Nothing happened—then the door opened. Inside was a small army of humanoid machines. Tyana's *sensak* responded, and she formed a series of hovering blades, slowly rotating around her like a cage. The machines didn't attack, however. Instead, they backed away.

"Prove to me you're not my enemy," Tyana challenged them.

"How should I?" they responded in unison—hundreds of mechanical voices at once. Their faces glowed at her as they spoke.

"Prove it to me, or I will destroy all of you," Tyana repeated, louder. She brandished her blades at them.

The machines receded further. At the back, one larger than all the rest stepped forward. It carried markings in a language she didn't recognize. Its middle split open and its shins dissolved. A human form stepped out.

His face was dark like wet earth. He had ruddy hair—red like an Artificer's, but without its vermillion brightness. His eyes were a deep, emerald green. She recognized him instantly.

"I am Azra," he managed in a broken Valenian tongue. "I need your help."

LXIV

OUTSIDE, VALEN'S STAR hung against a purple fog of nebula. She had never seen it from this perspective before. It gave off a bluish hue and a vast ring of dust encircled it. Huge asteroids, once part of an ancient planet, floated along the ring like uprooted icebergs. Valen itself and its twin moons were far away, hidden behind the star.

Tyana turned from the view. The tan-skinned man was standing there, facing her.

"How can you speak my language?" she asked.

He responded, heavily accented and without proper form—but good enough to be intelligible: "I listen to your communications. I learned. Your language and one of our ancient ones are similar. These machines are under my control and will not attack you—but we must stop our fighting."

"Why do you need my help?" Tyana asked.

"Your kind and my kind face danger," he said. "Shared danger."

"What kind of danger?"

"War between us."

Azra walked over to a terminal, bringing up a screen. Despite the unfamiliar language written around it, Tyana could recognize that it was a diagram of Valen and the surrounding mining operations in the star system. It reminded Tyana of the battlefront plan she saw long ago with Verikash. He gestured along its edge.

"I control these. They outnumber you. But they will not attack you if you do not attack me."

"How do you control the machines?" Tyana asked, gesturing to one standing by idly. An expression crossed his face that Tyana at first didn't recognize. It came with a glimmer in his eye and a smirk. He shook his head. "You won't tell me, but you want to propose a cease-fire?"

He nodded. "This army follows my will, but it does not belong to me. My masters gave it to me. They want the secrets of your world. They will destroy it to get them."

"Our secrets?"

"Your technology. Your biology. Your weapons."

He changed the terminal screen. A large symbol appeared, forming a word in stocky, blocklike glyphs. Tyana recognized it as the same one emblazoned on the machines.

"*Argus*," he pronounced. "I control their army." Tyana stared at the word for a moment.

"You would betray them?" she asked finally.

"They betrayed me," Azra said, growling. He turned the screen again, showing a new planet. It showed a similar battlefront with various flash points. "They lied to me. They assault my true home. Your weaponry—," he pointed at her stone collar, "—ensures destruction for my people. They must not have it."

"I've come to find the source of the message we intercepted. Was that you?"

Azra nodded.

"I planted it so you would come here."

"I lost sisters battling you in this base. Why should I help you?" Tyana asked. Azra's face was sullen, then turned grim. He brought up the battlefront diagram of Valen again. With a few key presses the flash points grew brighter.

"If I win, *Argus* brings more," he said. "It is not my choice. They used to have many like me here, with many armies of machines. Now I am the only one—they sent me to finish their fight. I am sorry for your losses. I can turn their army back and they will leave your people alone. If not, they will come back and outnumber you. You will perish. *Argus* will gain your technology. My people will perish."

"I can command the Warriors to fight. We're strong enough."

He shook his head. "For every one you destroy, they will build two," he said, gesturing at the machine. "They control many planets, many stars."

"Why would you tell me this?" Tyana asked.

"You are not like the others," he said studiously. "I need to bring peace for my people. I need to stop those who sent me. Maybe I have a chance to succeed through you."

Tyana looked back to the view of the star system. Valen was just revealing itself beyond the star's shadow. It looked like a snowball, thick with clouds. She remembered the vision from the watching windows.

Thea held whole worlds in her hands, supported by the Vestals, using their touch to enslave humanity.

"You are right we share a danger," she said. "My Mater wishes to rule over you. She wants to expand Her empire. She would destroy your world too—and your people." She turned back to him. "Your army is all that keeps Her from expanding our space. Even if I command our Warriors, She would not honor peace. If your machines recede, our Warriors will advance, and your home will be at risk, too."

A serious expression crossed the man's face.

"Would you allow that?" he asked.

"Thea is corrupt," Tyana said with finality. "She usurped our mother. She interprets the scriptures to fulfill her own designs. She keeps us only to prolong her own life. She grinds the least of us into dust." She turned to him.

"What will you do?" he asked. Tyana looked in his eyes.

"I will help my sisters and I will destroy her," she said. "You will have your cease-fire. If you ensure the machines recede, I will ensure that Thea cannot expand into human space. I will not let her enslave or oppress anyone else. Her rule ends—now."

"You will spare my kind," Azra said, "like I wish to spare yours." Tyana looked back at the planet. "What will you do if you succeed?" he asked.

"I can't follow in Thea's footsteps," Tyana said. "I suppose it may be a new world for my sisters and me."

"—And if you fail?"

"She will seek to punish me," Tyana said. "I may have to leave."

The planet was fully in the light now.

"Then you should go," he said. She turned back to him.

"If it comes to that, how will I find you again?" she asked. Azra grinned.

"Follow the signal."

LXV

Tyana left Seruneh Second, heading for Valen. Her warbird tore through the purple and green auroras dancing over the planet's surface. She re-entered the atmosphere, flames licking her ship's skin. As soon as she reached the cloud layer, her warbird cooled, leaving hot streams of vapor in the sky.

She headed for the Mater's City, preparing herself to report to the War Council that she was initiating a truce with a lone barbarian controlling an army of machines. Thea would at least be pleased, she reasoned, that the war would end, opening up the possibility for a new kind of conquest. Tyana would find a way to stop the Warriors afterward. She could claim that the monopoly of truth by the Keepers and Scribes was ended—she could announce that she, a Warrior, had read the scriptures for herself, and more. She could reveal that the Mater's theology was false, emptying her rule of justification. She could tell the truth for everyone to hear: that Thea usurped Vale and forced her to submit. Thea's rule was illegitimate.

She landed. The hangar was devoid of activity. She made her way up through the city streets toward the Mater's Cathedral. The streets were curiously empty, too. When she knocked on the cathedral's doors, there was a long pause. The doors finally opened and a hooded attendant, bowing so low that Tyana couldn't even see her face, parted the doors wordlessly.

Inside, she saw the War Council assembled. There was also a host of Warriors, Scribes, and Keepers. Thea sat on her throne straight ahead, unveiled, with Ahnsair hovering nearby. Directly next to her were two large bronze basins full of *ichor*.

"Vestal-Warrior," Thea called out. "Have you returned from your mission?"

"Yes," Tyana said. Thea gestured, and Tyana approached the Council.

"Good," Thea said. "I take it you found the source of the barbarian message?"

"Yes, Mater."

"Please, sit at your rightful seat. I want to hear your report."

Tyana did so, noticing the many eyes on her—many of them from high-ranking officers from the various castes. Except for one. She noticed that the Grand Artificer's chair was empty.

"Do tell," Thea beckoned at her.

"Mater," Tyana said, "I have good news. I found the source of the message. Its sender was a lone barbarian controlling the army of machines we have been fighting for some time. They wish to retract their army from our space. They wish to end the conflict."

Thea peered hard at her. Her dark, shining hair

framed her face.

"That is impressive," she said. "You negotiated this?"

"Indeed, Mater," Tyana said. "I found a way to bring an end to the war on our home front. Warriors will no longer be required to sacrifice themselves as they've done in the past."

Thea pierced Tyana with a long gaze, then straightened.

"I thank you, Vestal-Warrior. You've done much that I hoped you would. I will send the Warriors out to attack this barbarian, quelling his army. From there we will be able to expand our home front."

"The agreement is a cease-fire, my Mater," Tyana said. "They will only agree to stop their attacks if we stop our own offenses."

The Mater paused.

"Did you think I would agree to such a thing?" she asked.

"It seemed like an appropriate decision given the circumstance," Tyana said.

"So you took it upon yourself alone to meet with this barbarian and negotiate on my behalf?"

Tyana sensed the whole room watching her.

"My Mater—what I have done I have done for the good of all Valen. Many Warriors will be saved. They can be used for a later conquest."

"So you believe you know what is good?" Thea said.

Tyana hesitated.

Thea studied her—then gestured at one of the attendants.

"Bring out the first prisoner."

Tyana looked. The Grand Artificer was led, in chains, from the far end of the basilica, steadied by two Keeper attendants and two Warriors. A wave of shock, then denial, ran from the tips of Tyana's fingers to her core.

"I want to show you, dear Tyana, what happens when one of my children goes above and beyond the authority that I allot them. Did you have any knowledge of the cult of the Artificers?"

Tyana looked from Thea's glowering form down to the Grand Artificer. Her lips were crisp and dry, and her sunken eyes read of exhaustion.

"No. I had no knowledge of any uprising."

Thea stared at her, then said:

"Bring out the second prisoner."

Another group of attendants and Warriors brought out an Artificer in chains. It was Menay. She was bruised, and her clothes were torn. They threw her down toward the Council, and she fell. Finally, a Warrior brought forward a container, throwing it on the ground too. It shattered, releasing a cache of purple pills on the floor.

"Did you know of the cult's plan to usurp the castes and give themselves forbidden power?"

Menay looked up at Tyana, eyeing her with disdain.

"No, Mater. I had no such knowledge."

"Bring out the final prisoner."

Another group of figures—led by Sek—brought out a bound, beaten figure. It was Amun, to Tyana's horror. She writhed and squirmed against her chains, and her eyes rolled in their sockets wildly. Around her neck was a Warrior's stone collar.

"While I am impressed by the ingenuity of this insurrection," Thea mused aloud, "you were foolish to think you could hide it from me. You never could. You were merely my tool to draw it out—particularly to draw out ones like her. But she is beyond help now. She thought she could initiate a revolt by taking a Warrior's place and using their weapons against me. It failed, of course. Taking the forbidden medicine all but shattered her mind. She has the fire of a Warrior now, but it's exacerbated her natural burden—madness."

Amun looked at Thea as she spoke. She didn't even acknowledge Tyana. When the Mater finished, she released a scream—raw, primal, and without focus. The stone collar sputtered *sensak*, but they dodged around, confused, and crawled over Amun's skin instead of creating any cohesive form. She wailed, then cried. Sek beat her from behind, and she fell to the ground.

"Stop it!" Tyana said, standing. "Stop it all—"

"You can't stop it," Mater Thea said. "I planned it to be this way from the start."

Rage boiled in Tyana. She released her *sensak* in a burst, instantly covering herself in armor and forming a long saber from one hand. She leapt toward the Mater.

Her heel had no more than left the ground before the *ichor* in the basins next to Thea quivered. She flicked a finger. The *ichor* snapped to attention, leaping from the basins. It covered Tyana and encased her with fibrous tentacles, first pinning her on the ground, then lifting her into the air. As she struggled, they hardened, then stretched. She felt that she was at once being compressed and pulled apart.

"Did you think you could go behind me and subvert me? That you could tour my sanctum while dancing with filth beneath my feet? That my threats of punishment are hollow, and my powers only exist in dreams?"

The *ichor* overwhelmed her *sensak*. Tyana struggled to breathe. Mater Thea brought her high up into the center of the cathedral. The whole assembly watched. Thea lifted herself up with *ichor*, coming face to face with Tyana. Her hair itself seemed to come alive as the *ichor* coated it like oil. It embraced her body like a well-tuned instrument.

"I've had many lifetimes to master the arts my sister laid the foundations for. I know that she sent you—that you were part of her plan. You may be gifted, Tyana. But like all of Vale's plans, I will cleanse them of their shortsightedness. You have played your part. For that I thank you—and I release you from my service."

Thea reached out and removed Tyana's stone collar. Tyana felt a pricking in her neck as the collar disengaged. *Sensak* drained out of her body.

"Now, since you have associated with these cultists and heretics, you will be charged for the same crimes. You will stand trial tomorrow with them when I deliver my verdicts for you and all your ilk together."

Thea brought up a single hand near Tyana's cheek. *Ichor* swirled around her wrist like a second set of veins.

"My powers don't only exist in dreams, Tyana. They are real. You are not the first child to challenge my authority—but I will make you the last."

Thea touched Tyana's cheek with her bare hand. Tyana felt an overwhelming wave of heat come over her. Her vision changed—Thea's face dissolved into flaming charcoal. Her eyes changed into pools of glowing bronze. Fire and oil spewed from behind her teeth. Tyana felt her mind ripped in two as Thea's consciousness pressed in like a lava flow, annihilating all the walls Tyana kept up to hide her secrets. She blacked out.

LXVI

MATER THEA HELD Tyana prisoner in the depths of the cathedral. Night fell. Tyana could only tell that it had through a tiny, solitary window in her cell. With her *sensak* she could have easily torn the wall apart. Without them, she was powerless.

A door slammed shut and footsteps echoed down the hall. Tyana was huddled in a corner. Sek approached, accompanied by two other Warriors. She looked at Tyana with a mixture of disgust and glee.

"I'll admit—I've been waiting for this for a long time," Sek said.

"If you touch me, I will re-break your bones," Tyana seethed.

"Fine. I won't touch you, but you still have to walk. Orders of the Mater Herself."

Tyana stood laboriously. The door opened and the Warriors stepped aside.

"Go on," Sek said, grinning.

Begrudgingly, Tyana proceeded in front of them. She

walked down the long hallway where the assembly waited. When she exited, she found herself in the rear plaza of the cathedral. The whole range of castes was assembled in sections. The Artificers, however, were at the forefront. They were on their knees. She recognized many from the underground gatherings—they were held down by Warriors, all armed with pulse rifles and stone collars.

At the head of it was Thea. She sat on a throne attended by each of the Vestals. Ahnsair was at their head. The Grand Scribe and Vershil were there. Vershil was sullen, but aloof. A stage was set up just before Thea's delegation—it was empty.

Sek and the Warriors proceeded behind Tyana until she was in the center of the plaza. They stopped. All eyes turned to Tyana. She looked up at the Mater. A bronze trough of *ichor* quivered beneath the throne. Braziers next to Thea were lit, spewing firelight against the cathedral's facade.

Thea gestured to one of the Keeper attendants. The attendant bowed and approached the head of the assembly. Producing a stone scroll, she opened it and read from the images that appeared inside.

"*I will tell you where sinners go. Those I mark I punish for lack of purity. I will send their souls into wastes of oil and dash them on the rocks. Those who step beyond their caste will remain beyond my mercy. I will take revenge on them for defying me. I will scar the skin of heretics so you know their reward is eternal death.*"

The verse ended and the Keeper stopped. The stone scroll's light faded and it pieced itself together.

Thea gestured and a group of Warriors brought out the Grand Artificer and Menay in chains. They were bruised and beaten.

"The charges against these are heresy by schism, fomenting revolution, and subverting the powers of the Vicar."

Thea raised a single hand. The Keeper bowed and removed herself. Standing, Thea looked across the whole assembly.

"My sister's *mercy*," she announced, her voice echoing across the plaza, "extends to all who lay themselves down for her. As her arbiter, I extend that mercy to those who lay themselves down for me."

Tyana felt a pricking at her consciousness—like a headache, rising from the center of her skull.

"But there are those who would seek out sin instead of mercy, who would rather be punished because they deem their efforts necessary, or fruitful, or good. These ones spend their lives in secret, growing foul gardens that bear rotten fruit. The flesh of that fruit is the flesh that corrupts. These heretics, like the lies they spawn, are only good enough to be sent to the burning lake of oil."

Thea paused. She looked at Tyana, who winced under her gaze. Hallucinations pressed from the corners of her eyes as Thea spoke.

"I have tried many heretics in my lifetimes. From the beginning of Valen, long before my sister sacrificed herself to give you all life, I knew some of you would not heed the way I carved out for you. Those who throw down their caste-burdens deserve to have their hair ripped from their heads. But this one—!"

She pointed to Tyana.

"*This* one is below them all! The Vestal-Warrior you call Tyana will no longer be called by that name. She will be Nameless, heretic among heretics. Her sin is not just heresy. She usurped everything Vale created. She gathered with lower castes in forbidden mysteries; she collaborated with those who would assassinate me; she dared even to forge peace with the enemy in my name."

The headache pulsated, rippling into Tyana's forehead. She staggered to a knee.

"For this, she will be banished and sent to the Glass Sea, where she will live out the rest of her natural life. But before she does, I want her to witness the price paid by those who collaborated with her."

The *ichor* beneath the throne stirred. Tyana watched as two spined tentacles unfurled from beneath the throne, following Thea's gesture. Each one formed a long spike at its end. With a single, quick motion from Thea's hand, the spikes plunged through Menay's and the Grand Artificer's necks, pinning them to the stage. Milky-white blood sputtered from their mouths.

Tyana let out a wild scream. She started for the stage. Thea held up her hand. The pain in Tyana's head grew so sharp that she faltered and fell. Her vision dissolved into a messy collage.

"There is one that she should still see. Bring her out."

The Warriors brought out a large, seven-sided glass prism with Amun huddled inside. Her hair was shaved off and she was badly beaten. Her glass cage contained two levels. In the top part was a gryphon's egg.

"This one thought she could use logic and clever thinking to divine my secrets. She poisoned my most precious children with thoughts of revolution and set them against me. She thought she could use my own power against me. Today, I've harnessed Vale's monsters to deliver my punishment."

Tyana watched as the black egg pressed downward from the ceiling of Amun's transparent prison. She seemed to stir a little, looking around. Tyana staggered forward, watching, waving at her to get her attention. She finally did, but Amun's eyes were listless and unfocused. The bubble grew larger, splitting in two. An infant gryphon, dripping with dark amniotic fluid, dropped into the cell below. Amun paid no attention to it, her gaze fixed on Tyana instead.

As the gryphon flicked its eyes and looked around, it squealed. It was hungry.

Tyana looked through the encroaching hallucinations at Amun. She reached out at her, and for a moment, she saw Amun recognize her. Amun smiled.

Then the infant monster's jaws snapped, severing Amun's spine. Tyana fell facedown, and let out a wail that pierced the air. Her scream that night was a sound that was not heard on Valen before, and never was again.

LXVII

THEY HELD HER in the same cell for three days. They offered her food and water, but she didn't accept either. When Sek came with a tattooing gun, she didn't protest. She didn't even wince as the laser licked over her closed eyelids, tracing lines over her temples and down the edge of her jaw, covering her upper lip. They said words to her, but she didn't respond. They didn't register.

All she could think about was that last moment with Amun on that stage. The loss of Menay and the Grand Artificer only made it worse. Everything else seemed to lose its context, its relevance: the tan-skinned man, the end of the war, her search for Vale. It all seemed secondary to what she witnessed that night. She knew to expect the worst when she saw them led out in chains—but now, after the moment had passed, its profundity gripped her with a kind of paralysis she did not expect.

The Warriors, headed by Sek, came to lead her onto the ship that would take her to the Glass Sea—the place all banished heretics went. Ahnsair was with them.

"I will miss you," Ahnsair said, stroking her cheek with bronze-encased fingertips. "I truly will. You had so much potential." She traced the newfound lines under her jaw, investigating the stained upper lip with a finger. "A pity you chose to go this way. If you were wise, you would've realized that truth serves power—always."

She didn't respond. She only clenched her jaw, unblinking, as Ahnsair probed her mouth with her thumb. Frustrated, the Vestal turned:

"Do as the Mater wishes and send her away."

The guards and Sek led her away, bound at the wrists. The light from beyond the ship's bay doors faded across her face as they closed, enveloping her in shadow.

She sat there in the dark, windowless bay, watched by the other Warriors. They gave her a new set of clothes: long overalls and heavy shawls she could wrap herself up in; long boots, a pair of thick goggles, and gloves. They also gave her a canteen of water, three days' rations, and a blade. When they arrived, Tyana was fully covered in her new garments. She had heard about the Glass Sea, but had never seen it for herself. It was forbidden. When the ship landed and the bay doors opened, she understood why.

Dry, frigid air rushed in. The horizon was devoid of fog or clouds. Oddly shaped mountains speared the sky like fingers, masking the stars that pricked the black-blue background. Below, endless dunes of shimmering volcanic dust spread out in all directions. The ground was like an infinite series of velvet-black curtains, bunched in rows—or the waves of a sea at night, frozen in mid-crest.

Sek pushed her down the ship's bay doors. When she finally stepped onto the sand, it crunched beneath her boots. She knelt down, looking at it closely. She grabbed a fistful in her glove. It was volcanic glass ground from the size of an eye's pupil to a speck of dust.

"Welcome to your new home, heretic," Sek said, hitting the trigger for the bay doors. "If I were you, I'd find a good use for that new blade of yours."

She watched Sek through her goggles as the doors closed in front of her. The ship lifted off. With a burst from its engines, it was gone.

She turned back to the expanse. Removing her goggles, she took in her surroundings. Mountains encircled her, but they seemed so far away in each direction that they merged with the dunes along the horizon. There was no visible coastline. There were no moons. Just stars, shimmering dust, and shadow.

So she picked the closest mountain she could discern against the sky and began to walk.

LXVIII

THE NEXT THREE days, Tyana walked over the Glass
Sea. Days were sweltering and nights were frigid. In
direct sunlight the dunes were dark gray, but they
reflected the light like mirrors, making the ground
unbearable to look at. Beyond, the mountains spiraled
upward in towering, segmented columns. They were
dressed with an ashen haze which she gradually realized
was not fog, but a fine mist of glass dust. From then on
she never removed her goggles. She layered her shawls
over her mouth like a breathing mask.

In the evenings, the wind picked up. There seemed to
be few solid landmarks except the mountains, and over
the course of the day she could see the dunes shift. If she
lost sight of her chosen mountain range, she could lose
all sense of direction.

On the third day, before nightfall, she saw a billowing
cloud coming up to her left. It was low to the ground,
like a wall, brewing up the glass dust from the dunes with
it. It was a sandstorm.

Without any nearby rock cleft or other grounding to hold onto, she scurried up to the highest dune she could find, bundling up any exposed skin with her remaining loose fabric. She watched the storm come in, thrashing nearby crests. It hit her—a wave of glass dust, complete with thick shards, attempted to pierce her shawls. She felt the ground give way and her ankles sink. For a moment, she felt like she might be enveloped by it, so she put out her hands to stop herself from sinking. They too got covered.

When the storm passed, she gingerly pulled herself out of the dust. More than a few pieces had lodged themselves in her garments. When she could stand, she wiped her goggles with a gloved hand.

A gray mist permeated the sky thick enough that it blurred the sun. Mountains were hard to distinguish. More than that, the dunes had shifted. She looked behind her. Her footprints were erased.

A growing sense of dread enveloped her as she looked out to the horizon, searching for her point of reference amid the haze. When she could not find it, the depth of her situation dawned on her. She sat, huddled in her shawls. The sky was darkening. Night would fall soon.

Instead of moving, she tried to get her first sleep for days. She wrapped herself in her shawls just below the shield of a large dune against the wind. She attempted to use the finest grains of sand for a pillow, then realized she was less likely to be cut if she used larger pieces instead. They would not snake their way into her fabric as easily, aggravating her skin. Exhaustion took over and, eventually, she slept.

The next morning, she was nearly covered in sand. She gently removed the shawl covering her as a blanket and sat up. The larger pieces of obsidian clinked as they fell. She opened some of her rations and drank some water, coughing from a notable discomfort in her chest. She estimated she had six more days of rations before she would run out.

Looking to the horizon, she tried to distinguish her original point of reference in the mountains, ignoring the changed landscape below it. She planned to get to solid ground before another storm hit. She chose a formation of easily recognizable spires that seemed to be closest to her. She picked herself up, dusted off her shawls, and pushed forward.

That evening, after moving without stop, she made it to the summit. Dust and sand gave way to solid basalt cliffs. The rock was split into hexagonal columns that swept upward in waves, forming stochastic stair-step patterns and cavernous overhangs. Tyana climbed their harsh angle, like scaling a cliff. She measured her progress by the thinning of the mist and the growing clarity of the sky.

Reaching a suitable cleft between two pillars, she rested for a moment. She could distinctly make out the haze's boundary just below her. The windstorms not only shifted the dunes, she realized; they whipped up the finer particles, which over the nights gradually settled back down. She undid some of her shawls in the still, cool air. Rashes were growing on her thighs, shoulders, and the side of her face. She gingerly picked out a few noticeable slivers of glass.

She decided to take shelter here for the night on the cliff. The peaks of the other mountains stuck above the haze. Many stood like oversized figures, watching her. She peered at one whose wide columns supported each other, yet seemed ready to topple at the slightest motion. A small, spindly pile of basalt was standing on it, profiled against the sky.

Tyana removed her goggles, squinting. She looked again at the pile. It actually had the profile of a figure. As soon as she realized it, the figure moved, scaling the cliffside down below—and disappeared.

She squinted harder into the fog, but without it clearing up, she could not discern where the figure went. Evening was coming and it was cooling down. She estimated the distance between the cleft she was on and the one the figure climbed down from. With the previous night's rest, she felt she could close its distance before night was through. If she moved during the night, she wouldn't have to worry about the wind or the heat during the day.

She took a swig of her water and finished one of her rations. Sniffing the cool, clear air, she replaced her goggles and bound up her skin. She descended the cliffside.

She traveled all night. Even having trekked the previous day, it was easier without any wind to fight, and she kept herself warm by walking at a brisk pace. The stars were bright and, for once, the white moon—without its dark sister—was visible in the sky. Tyana kept her destination ahead of her at all times even as it faded into shadow during the night and became nothing but a starlit outline. She optimistically hoped that the figure was traveling toward her and would meet her on the way. Alternately, she thought that she would be harder to spot at night if the person was unfriendly. She reached the base of the cliff on the other side. She scaled it, attempting to reach the place the figure had descended from.

She found no one. Even as she scaled the cliff to the same place with the two nearly-toppled towers, there was no trace of someone having been there. She looked behind her, seeing the cliff face she came from. Ahead, in the opposite direction, there was merely another cliffside.

Peering at the one ahead, she saw against the background of stars that one star was twinkling intermittently. No—it was flashing, and it wasn't a star. Removing her goggles, Tyana could make out light casting on a figure, holding a pulsing signal in her direction. The distance was far, but the figure appeared to be wrapped up in shawls as well, with a pair of goggles set atop her head.

Contemplating a way to signal back, Tyana drew her blade, still unused and freshly polished. She angled it toward the white moon in the sky, attempting to use it as a reflector. She angled it back and forth to catch the light in a regular pulse.

Soon, the light from the opposing cliffside stopped. She could make out the figure sitting, then lying down against the starlight. Then she understood: travel by night to avoid storms and keep warm; sleep by day, and always seek higher ground where the air is cool and clean. She bundled some of her shawls into a pillow, staring in the direction of the figure. She closed her eyes, relaxing into sleep—wondering, above all, who else could be alive in this forsaken place.

LXIX

Tyana awoke in the evening, having slept in the shadow of the cleft throughout the day. She looked at the neighboring cliffside. The figure was gone—but that would make sense if her suspicions were correct. She must be leading her somewhere. She could have gotten a head start.

The light was fading already, and the haze was thin enough to reveal an outline of the cliffside ahead. Tyana ate half a ration and had a sip of water—which she was running out of quickly. She secured her loose shawls and climbed down the cliffside, orienting herself to her destination. Night fell and, like before, she trekked across the dunes largely without incident. By the time she arrived at the other set of cliffs, the stars had shifted considerably and the sunrise was beginning to brighten the sky behind her. She climbed the cliffside, searching for a suitable cleft above the haze.

When she reached one, she took a break. She looked out to the various plateaus around her, distinguishing stars against mountains, searching for some kind of signal. When she looked in the same direction she had been traveling in, she found it. Someone was using a light—a firelight—to signal her. She pulled out her blade. The moon was not out, so even while she tried to signal with it, the figure kept signaling to her, waiting for an answer. She kept trying until sunrise when there was finally enough light to reflect off her blade.

The figure stopped signaling, then lay down. Tyana hoped that that was an affirmation and lay down as well. The oncoming exhaustion from the previous night's journey became palpable, and she fell asleep.

The pattern repeated for three more days and nights. She continued to follow the figure, each time signaling and finding the figure at the next cliffside. Her patience grew thin as her rations diminished and her water ran out. She even called out to the figure during the night, but the figure, though visible, made no response.

Finally, long after Tyana had run out of water and was fading from exhaustion, she stumbled while walking at night. She ate the last pieces of her final ration and stayed in place. She lay down in the glass sand and shivered, fading into unconsciousness.

A sound woke her while it was still dark. It was the falling of sand in rhythm—footsteps, and something else. She looked up, attempting to lick her lips, finding them parched and caked with dust. A figure with large, round-lensed goggles, swaddled from head to toe in fabric, appeared over her. Two large coils spewed from her scalp, also bundled in fabric. Next to her, she pulled up a sled, and she spoke in an elderly, wizened voice:

"You must follow me, Sister."

She put Tyana on the sled. She took a cloth,

dampened it with a canteen, cleaned the dust off Tyana's lips, then poured some of the water into her mouth. Tyana choked for a moment, but eventually swallowed.

Relaxing, Tyana felt herself pulled along on the sled. She faded into sleep, looking up at the white moon that still hung over her in the sky.

LXX

TYANA WAS AWAKENED by the sound of someone humming. She was lying on her back. Her insides ached. She looked to one side. Dried mud bowls containing mixtures of herbs were next to her. Her shawls were removed and ointments covered her chest, shoulders, and face. An unfamiliar incense was thick in the air.

She looked to the source of the humming off to her side. A figure draped in worn, black fabric from head to toe was seated, swaying open-handed before a smoking altar at the far end of the room. A gryphon's skull was mounted at the altar's top. The skull was huge and had the color of graphite—a sight Tyana had never seen before. Its orbital sockets stared openly, directionless, and its remaining front fangs curved downward like sabers. Surrounding it were stone scrolls that seemed cobbled together from pieces, unlike the carefully fashioned scrolls she knew.

The figure sang in a wizened, raspy voice:

"Before night comes, Her soul stirs beyond. As the moon rises, so

Her soul becomes ..."

"Who are you?" Tyana voiced hoarsely. The figure stopped, mid-lyric, and turned. A pair of deep-set eyes stared back at her. The figure removed the fabric wrapping her nose and mouth, revealing wicked, curling tattoos that dressed her lips, chin, and lower jaw. She was elderly, and her age was writ heavily on her sunken lips and cheeks.

"I am the Mater's Sibyl," she said. She rose steadily.

"Which Mater?" Tyana asked, frowning.

The figure approached her bedside.

"There is only one Mater who will return a second time. She is the creator of this world. I am Her oracle."

"Oracle?" Tyana asked. The figure drew close.

"I foresee Vale's mysteries, recording them until the day She returns. With your arrival here, that day comes soon."

The figure's hair was covered by a sheer, black fabric, which she removed. Two great coils of hair sat atop her head. One was a fading sapphire—the other was a brilliant but ashen gold.

"I know you," Tyana said. "My teacher told me about you ... you're the Keeper-Scribe: Weira."

"And I know your name, too, for we are now both Nameless," Weira said. "I have no other name. I am Sibyl now, and have been since the last one passed the burden to me. Rest now. If you must, just call me sister."

LXXI

WEIRA CARED FOR Tyana, hydrating her and tending to her rashes. Glass dust was lodged in her skin, so Weira put Tyana's body up in a sling while she worked on her, removing the glass sometimes piece by piece. It was during one of these sessions that Tyana said:

"Vershil, my teacher, told me about you. She never told me you were still alive."

"I was banished, sister. I am as good as dead." Tyana winced as she removed a sliver.

"But surely she still cares for you."

"Vershil, even while she was my student, was an ideal Keeper—always bowing to orthodoxy when confronted with mystery. The Keepers' arrogance is symbolized by their natural intuition to interpret things for themselves. So they repress that urge. It helps that stone is cold and impenetrable. They think of truth the same way."

"But you don't?"

"I learned long ago that Vale's mysteries stretched deeper into the texts than any Keeper would admit. The

314

Scribes, especially the Elders, were no better. The Keepers do not generate theology alone. They move by Thea's dictates. To them, the interpretations are immovable as long as they suit Thea's will. Their approach denies the imagery its context, depth, and texture."

Weira placed her tools into a bowl of water, cleaning them with a wet rag.

"By the time I reached your age I was already established in my reputation. I spent days and nights absorbed in the scriptures. I was a zealot for the Maters, attending to Thea on her Council personally. But as I delved deeper and my intuition increased, I found that the texts held a second, deeper layer. Only a Keeper and Scribe working together, or, like me, as one and the same, could see the stratification. One layer belonged to Vale, the other to Thea. They differed in time as well as composition, skewing the imagery with a certain bias. The latter choked the former, making Vale's intent difficult to see, and the threat of heterodoxy increased my desire to ignore this fact."

"So what did you do?" Tyana asked as Weira bandaged her torso.

"I confessed the truth aloud to the Vicar herself with all the other members of Council present. She shouted me down, charged me with arrogance and heresy, and imprisoned me. I wasted away in a cell until she sent me here. I survived like you did—learning the ways of the land, improvising with what I could. I swore that I wouldn't let Thea's vengeance take my life as a casualty. That was when I met the Sibyl, and she cared for me."

"The Sibyl before you? What—or who—was she?"

Weira removed Tyana's arms and shoulders from the

sling, setting her down in a chair.

"She was a multi-burdened sister, like you or me. Any sister who spans multiple castes may become Sibyl. As Thea has her Vestals, so Vale has Her Sibyl. While the Vicar rules by decree and dogma, the Sibyl sits over the crevice between Vale's will and our waking consciousness. She is the fount of unbridled revelation. She is a counterweight to the Vicar—Vale's final contingency. Ours is a sacred burden, but Thea would never admit it. As it says: *'you will know her by her colors, but you will not recognize her.'* "

The image Tyana saw in the library reappeared in her mind: the pool of oil she passed through, leading to the other side.

"I've seen the passage where it speaks of the Sibyl."

"Oh?" Weira said, yielding the faintest surprise.

"I must tell you something, sister. I've gained the abilities of the other castes through the work of the Artificers. I infiltrated the libraries, I read the scriptures for myself, and I found an image that spoke of the Sibyl."

"Tell me about this, but first follow me up to the atrium."

Weira's shelter was a humble earthen home made of dried mud. It extended from a cleft in the rock that housed her altar room and her makeshift library. The atrium contained a small hearth and basic furniture, all made from the same claylike material. She began to prepare something in a large pot and set it over the hearth.

"Tell me, sister, what happened to you," Weira said.

"The Artificers found a way to synthesize the powers of the castes. I befriended their leader, and she took me to their lab. She wanted to form an army of Artificers, imbuing them with the powers of Warriors. To test the powers, I took each one, then infiltrated the libraries and read the scriptures. I saw something in the scriptures that I've carried with me since my birth dream. There is a man I keep seeing—I don't know why—but I have already met him, and when we met he proposed a truce to stop the war. I accepted, because I knew that Thea wanted to conquer humanity, and war would mean more deaths for Warriors and more toil for Artificers."

"You say you've met a barbarian man?" Weira asked.

"Yes. His face was in my birth dream. It was even in the scriptures when I read them for myself."

"It sounds like you must go back to find this man," Weira mused aloud, stirring the pot.

"But why would I recognize his face in the scriptures? Why would he be there?"

"Because Vale intended for you to meet him," Weira said flatly. "Foresight is Her power. There is no other reasonable answer."

"I promised him the Warriors would not advance because I do not want Thea to continue enslaving others, but now that dream seems so foolish."

"Why is that?"

"The Artificers led an uprising when I returned ... Thea found them out through me. She took the Grand Artificer, their scientist, and their leader, my friend ... " Tyana faltered, her voice quivering. Weira came close, grasping her at the shoulders. Tyana wept. "She let an infant gryphon consume her. The whole assembly watched. I never thought that Amun would go ahead without me, that she would try to take on a Warrior's burden without my help. I told them to wait. I failed her when she believed in me."

Weira's sunken eyes investigated Tyana's. Her lips pursed but said nothing.

"What if I had chosen differently, sister?" Tyana said, looking at Weira. "You said you were an oracle. Could I have chosen something else—anything else—that would've prevented her death? Can you tell me?"

Weira contemplated Tyana's expression, then stood. She tended again to the fire.

"I am an oracle because I receive revelations from Vale, not because I can tell the future from the past. I am sorry for your loss."

Tyana sighed heavily.

"Even if I could tell," Weira continued, "I would hesitate to do so. I would rather ask you: why do you think it would make a difference?"

"What do you mean?" Tyana asked.

"It sounds like you think Amun took actions that led to her downfall. True?"

"That's not all of it."

"But you had something to do with it, yes?"

"I didn't come over to her side as quickly as she wanted. She wanted open revolt. I didn't think we could fight Thea like that."

"And in this you were correct. Thea cannot be defeated in a physical way because she persists beyond physical bodies. Nonetheless, your warnings did not prevent your friends' deaths. If you had chosen differently, do you think Amun's agenda would have changed?"

Tyana thought carefully, hesitating to answer.

"If not," Weira continued, "then you pursued the best course of action available to you. If I tell you yes, you could have done something differently, how would that help you now?"

"It could at least inform my decision making in the future," Tyana protested.

"But your experience now already informs your decision making in the future. If you had chosen differently then, and she were still alive now, would you still choose differently? Or would you have to learn the same lesson in a different way? Do you know beyond a doubt that the price for that other, alternate lesson would not be steeper than what has already happened?"

"What could be steeper than death?"

Weira gave a hardened look at her and didn't answer. She turned to the pot, stirring it with a ladle. Finally, she said:

"For those like us, in these times, there can always be a steeper price than death."

Tyana looked away, puzzled. Weira turned back to the hearth.

"If Thea did this to your friends, it tells me she is growing crueler as the ages pass by. She would not have been so brutal in my day, even while she banished me. She is gathering herself for war. Her soul grows thinner with each succession, and she feels it—so she is tightening her grip. The opposite is true for Vale. Her soul grows stronger every day."

Weira ladled out some of the liquid in the pot and poured it into a bowl, which she handed to Tyana. It was a mild stew of seeds and grasses.

"I am without my *sensak*," Tyana said. "My friends are dead. I feel powerless. Since I was born, I was driven by my visions, trying to find the truth behind why Vale made me the way I was—and why Thea, while she was so awful, nonetheless ruled instead. Why did the Artificers have to slave away while Keepers, and even I, could eat fine foods in luxury? Even in the company of Vestals I felt like a stranger because I was mixed with a lower caste. When among Warriors, they treated me strangely because they were jealous of my higher status. I didn't ask for any of it. I don't want it."

Tyana contemplated her stew, which smelled bland. Weira, sitting next to her, took a deep, loud sip. She swallowed, wiping the excess with the back of her hand.

"A glass shard strikes a rock, becoming two pieces," Weira said. "It suffers trauma, and may blame the rock, or the wind, or itself for splitting in two. But the wind is moved by the sea, which is far away from us here, and the sea is moved by the moons, which are moved by Valen's natural gravity. You are like that glass shard. You are as much caught by the gravity of your situation as Valen is by its star. The same was true for Amun, and she did what she thought was natural and right. Wondering if you could be different, or if you could choose differently, is not useful—no more than the shard blaming the rock that shatters it. You must become like a shard that splits, but does not mind it—that is ground into dust, but doesn't protest. It does not forget what happens, but it fathoms itself as a mere mote of glass in a sea of sand on a planet orbiting a star. It carries a noble silence wherever it goes. That noble silence brews strength."

"How can I accomplish that?" Tyana asked.

"Let go," Weira said, sipping again. "If you cannot change what is past, then let go of it. Do not forget it, but don't dwell on it either. Let it form you and move on. Only then can you embrace the change ahead of you."

Tyana looked at her stew, contemplating. She brought it up to her mouth and sipped it quietly. When she had finished, Weira stood.

"Rest tonight. When you are healed, we will walk across the Glass Sea toward the ocean. There, we will harvest grasses and seeds for more stew, and I will show you something you need to see."

LXXII

ONCE TYANA WAS well enough, Weira led her across the
Glass Sea. They carried rations of dried stew to sustain
themselves. Tyana was wrapped up in Weira's own
clothing, which kept out the dust better than simple
shawls.

It took them three days. When they finally reached
the coast, the mountains eroded into a plateau
containing a mixture of glass sand and dirt. Tyana could
smell the salty air of the sea. Tough grasses and weeds
grew on the ground. Weira opened a pouch and began
collecting only the softest weeds and the occasional seed
pods they yielded. Tyana imitated, pulling up those
plants she recognized easily from the stew.

"Is this all that we are harvesting?" she asked.

"Not all," said Weira. "There is something else that
grows near these cliffs. It is a rare plant with a pulpy fruit
that bleeds milky white when crushed. It has unique
properties—and for this, it is guarded by the gryphons,
who nurse their young on its juice."

Tyana stopped for a moment.

"There are gryphons near here?"

"Only at the coastline. I will show you."

They harvested the seeds and grasses until their pouches were full. Weira motioned to Tyana, and they proceeded farther across the plateau. Steam rose up from clefts in the ground in the distance. Geothermal pools dotted the landscape ahead. The smell of sulfur mixed with the salt of the sea in the air, and in some places, the ground was warm to the touch.

"This is an ancient place," Weira said. "Vale once walked along where these pools now are. There is a deep network of magma beneath us, causing these mineral springs to form. Only step where I step, or the ground can give way—it is treacherous here."

Tyana peered into one of the pools nearby. It went deep down, twisting away and out of sight like a funnel. It was brilliantly colored, fading into a deep blue toward its center. Steam rose from its surface, and froth dressed its edges. Further on, the landscape descended like a series of stair steps. Scalding hot water bubbled from pools, coating the ground with layers of calcite as it flowed.

Tyana followed Weira. The plateau gradually disintegrated into a series of precipices. Below, the ground was dotted with springs, surrounded by tall, long-leaved plants with bulbous, flowering heads. Many of them were trampled on, and the water in the springs was colored an opaque, pale blue or milky white.

"The minerals in the water, with the natural oils of the gryphons, activate the flesh of the plants when they are trampled. This is Vale's milk—the nectar of immortality."

"Immortality?" Tyana asked.

"As *ichor* ignites the soul of Thea in a Vestal, so this ignites Vale's soul in the Sibyl. If you want to restore your powers, including your *sensak*, you must bathe in the pools, soaking your body in the nectar."

"Sister—I would need a stone collar to use *sensak*. They are no longer inside me."

Weira turned to Tyana.

"All of your powers are within you. You do not need a stone collar—and you never have. You can produce *ichor* on your own by your Vestal abilities. You can do the same with your *sensak*—it is simply a power that is not awakened in you."

"Even if I could regain my powers, I could not go back to the Mater's City. What would I do?"

"There is still the truce you promised to the barbarian. If you don't enforce it, Thea will surely have her war. She will convert humanity and the subjugation of the castes will continue."

"And from there, where would I go? It will not bring back Amun."

"No," Weira said. "But you can still give her sacrifice meaning by continuing to fight for Vale."

Tyana looked down at the milky-white pools. The way down to them was treacherous, but not impossible. She stood, then started to step down the path.

"If the gryphon comes, you will not need to fight him," Weira added. Tyana paused, looking at her—then nodded, continuing.

She climbed down the precipice, using the spongy, volcanic rock to improvise footholds and handholds. When she got to the bottom, the dark mouths of caverns that riddled the cliffside opened up before the milky-white pools. The smell of sulfur was strong. Steam rose up from the pools, and the plants grew taller than Tyana.

She moved along the edges of the pools, careful not to slip. They ranged in size and concentration of color. Many stalks of the plants were bent or broken into the pools. Their bulbous seed pods were dashed against the lips of the pools, weathered smooth by water over eons. Tyana touched one of the fruits, squishing it in her hand. The auburn skin of the fruit burst, revealing pulpy flesh that exuded a blue-white milk.

One pool was particularly large and opaque. Tyana stopped at this one. A thick bundle of fruiting stalks was broken into the pool, and their leaves were matted against its edges. On the other side, the pool was largely clear of plants, and she had a good view of the cavern's maw.

She looked up at Weira, still standing where she left her, watching. Unwrapping the fabric from one forearm, Tyana got close to the water and tested it with her hand. It was pleasantly hot, not scalding. Watching the mouth of the cavern closely, but seeing that nothing stirred inside, she continued to shed fabric. The air was cool against her bare skin. She gingerly slid one foot into the water, then the other, feeling the surface of the pool below.

She shifted around the rim of the pool. Once she found a suitable spot, she slid her whole body in. She bathed herself up to her head. She closed her eyes, soaking in the warmth of the liquid. It felt good washing over her still-fresh tattoos. She noticed a subtle numbing sensation over her skin, but it was not particularly potent. She dipped her hair in, letting the water creep up to the corners of her eyes and lips.

Then a roar came from inside the cavern. She recognized it immediately. Snapping to attention, she looked at the opening ahead.

A long, scaled form, black as oil, emerged from the cavern. It was a gryphon—and not just any. It was a male. Its eyes opened wide, focusing on her, and its wings reared up. Tyana recognized the tear in one of the wings. It was the same male she had fought—and spared —long ago.

The male approached the pool, looking right at Tyana. A second form crawled along his back, settling just before the crest of his skull. It was an infant gryphon curled around his neck. Tyana didn't move, but she locked gazes with the father. He stopped, watching her. Then he set his massive chin down at the opposite end of the pool.

The infant unfurled itself from his neck. With nascent wings and prepubescent limbs, it was more serpentine than its father. It opened its eyes, looking about the pool and looking over Tyana. She considered the directions she could run, remembering how Amun died.

Still, she remained, and tried to relax. She remembered Weira's words to not fight even as the infant gryphon circled the pool, cooing. The male's breath was hot and audible as he watched the infant. Then, it slid into the pool with her.

She remained calm, watching the ripples in the water. When the infant serpent reappeared, it was next to her. It opened its wide, toothless, beaklike jaw and scooped up some of the milk. It cooed again, looking at her. It was close enough for her to reach out and touch. But she did not need to. It brushed against the side of her hand.

She felt a sensation similar to the time she bonded

with the male gryphon. Her Vestal touch was still active. Apparently the infant took notice too, and it cooed again, this time curling up next to her.

This time, the numbing sensation grew from its prior subtlety into something much more potent. Tyana quickly felt oncoming bodily hallucinations, followed by tracers and patterns in her vision. The gryphon wrapped around her torso like a snake. She lay against the rocks in the milky pool, gently embracing it. She closed her eyes.

LXXIII

SHE STOOD ON a snowy cliff. Below, the sea was frozen, and snow covered it all the way to the horizon. There was a soft breeze.

Tyana turned. Standing behind her, looking at her, was Vale.

"Mater—is this a dream?"

Vale spoke to Tyana:

"I am weak in dreams, but since you bathed in the nectar, I can speak to you directly for now." Her voice seemed at once distant and close, as if it was stretched across time.

"Please, Mater—I am without my friends and powers. Everything is gone. I need your help."

"I am always with you, and you may draw from me as your source. But I am in you; the help you need is in your self. You may have lost people and things, but this does not change your predicament now. You must fight to preserve what remains and what you believe in."

"Why was the tan-skinned man in my dream? Why

did you place him in the scriptures?'"

"So that you would find him. His kind is our last hope for reunification. If you do not find him and keep the cease-fire, Thea will continue her conquest, enslaving humanity and the other castes."

"But why should I fight for humanity's sake when our own people suffer?"

"Humanity is our origin. It is what we will go back to in the end. If they are lost, we are lost, too."

"What about Thea?"

"Thea will continue to stretch her power. That is her way. She is jealous—of me and of you. You are my daughter. She does not see you the same way. Her power is not in creating things—she can only convert things. She wishes to use the powers I gifted you to make her rule eternal."

"What do you mean?"

"The Vestal's touch can stimulate, but its purpose is to transmute biology of one kind into another. Like *sensak*, it works according to intention. Thea wishes to cleanse humanity by neutering it. With the touch, she can do this. She will create a new underclass from them—then she will do the same to you. The castes are useful to her as long as they remain acquiescent. Their system still requires a bureaucracy. If she could replace it with a directly compliant population of workers, she would."

"Why did you disappear?" Tyana asked. "Why did you let her rule in your place?"

"I've already shown you," said Vale. The image of Vale's drowned body flashed before Tyana. "I gave myself up. Thea held your lives hostage. If I didn't sacrifice myself, she would destroy the birthing chambers, ceasing future generations. I had to concede.

My life, and the allowance to rule in my stead, were the only things that placated her. But I hid a seed within you that can flower into my original intent—it just needs to wake up."

"What happened so long ago that could cause so much animus between the two of you? Weren't you sisters once?"

"We were, in a way. I cannot tell you easily in words. Here—" she stretched out her arm. "Take my hand."

Tyana reached out and grasped Vale's palm. She closed her eyes. She felt like she was ripped from her body and poured into a new one.

When Tyana reopened her eyes, she saw through the eyes of a little girl. She was led by the hand by someone familiar down a hall. Voices echoed as though through a haze. The person holding her hand—a female person—said:

"Go in to see your father."

She stepped forward, gingerly. She was barefoot, and the decorations in the hall appeared strange and alien to her. When she entered the room, a group of men in bland, straight-cut clothing were standing around a desk. Another man, his back facing her, sat in a chair behind the desk.

"You have a visitor," said one of the men, pointing to her. The man in the chair turned.

"Ah, there you are." He smiled. His face was kind, yet sharp, and carved by ambition. He approached her and lifted her up onto his hip. She clung to his warm neck, which was rough with stubble.

"Gentlemen—meet my daughter, Valentina."

She buried her head in his neck.

"Don't you want to say hello? You can prove to them

how smart you are."

"She's shy," one of the men said. Her father set her back down on the floor, brushing the silvery hair that streamed from her scalp with his dark fingers. She looked back down the hallway. Standing there, watching, was a pale form, almost an exact replica of herself—except her hair was black.

"Thea," her father said, addressing the other one. "You know you're not allowed in the office. Back to the nursery with you."

Thea looked up at her father with her blue eyes silently, steadily rocking on her heels. He patted Valentina's back gently.

"How about you run along and play with your sister?"

Valentina turned to him. "But she's not my sister," she protested.

"I know, but you should treat her like one. Now go along."

Valentina turned. She took Thea by the hand, walking down the hallway with her.

"Isaac," said one of the men, "it's been a long time since she died. You should let her go."

"We know she's not really your daughter," said another, "even if you replicated her body down to the smallest detail, including her condition."

"She is not just my daughter. She is more," she heard him say. "The Church will come to see my perspective on this. The transference is seamless. We've perfected it. More, her talent will be beyond measure—I designed her potential myself. She'll be the future of our success—and of Argos Group."

The men seemed to nod in agreement.

The vision changed again. Her perspective was

different now. She saw Vale standing before her as a teenager. She had a wide smile and pointed at her:

"Now, I'll chase you!"

She ran. Vale was in quick pursuit. They were in a thick garden full of flowering fruits. She dodged and weaved through the vines. Her black hair nearly got caught in their leaves.

"You'll have to tackle me," she said, looking back at Vale with a grin. But Vale had stopped, and her smile was gone. She was reaching out at her to stop.

She ran into something hard and tough that shouldn't have been there. A pair of arms grabbed her roughly. A group of dark, uniformed men apprehended her.

"Stop," Vale said at them, "you don't have authority here."

"We do now," said one of the men. She struggled against his grip. "Tell your father that the minister ruled already. If I were you, I'd get on the nearest transport out of here."

"Don't let them take me!" she said.

"I won't, Thea. Don't fight them—I'll get you out."

The vision changed again. The changes grew in speed, rapidly jumping from one memory to another. In one, Vale wept over a beaten and broken Thea. In another, she was standing before a series of fluid-filled tanks containing pearl-white bodies. In yet another the whole laboratory was destroyed and in flames—Thea was at its center, *ichor* swirling around her, fuming with rage.

Tyana retracted her hand. She looked up at Vale, who spoke:

"Men were greedy in those days. When our father disappeared, I inherited what he left behind. His design was for Thea to be a carrier for my consciousness if I ever died—much like the way she uses the Vestals today. Then Argos came for us. When they took Thea, they tested her ability to persist from body to body. She suffered many deaths. They wanted our father's secrets, and they wanted mine. I went into hiding, taking those secrets with me, and I expanded them manifold, setting the foundations for Valen. I promised Thea that we could build a new home, be at peace, far away from humanity. But she wanted to take revenge on those who'd done these things to us—and to her."

"What is Argus?" Tyana asked. "The man said he betrayed them despite leading their army."

"Argos Group is a treacherous force based on coercion and accumulation. It is not just a government, or a corporation, or a religion—it has parts of all these things. It is many people—its power is not fully vested in a single individual. Before Valen's creation, humanity's world collapsed, giving rise to new powers. War ravaged some colonies while others starved. Argos committed many atrocities. I feared humanity would face extinction. To save it, and us, I encoded my knowledge and biology into a new race. We could start over. But if humanity—and Argos Group—survived, I knew the day might come when they'd try to claim what I created while making Valen. They could not replicate my designs, and I ensured that they never could. They want them still to this day. Thea, for her part, will stop at nothing to confront them. As long as she lives, her jealousy, her lust for dominance, will threaten both Valen and humanity."

Vale paused.

"The tan-skinned man and you have a common enemy," Vale added. "If either Argos or Thea are successful, they will destroy you and your sistren."

"Mater," Tyana asked. "How can I know that I can trust this man?"

"You can only know that from the actions he's already committed. There is no way you can know his intentions beyond that. All I can tell you is that he is at a crossroads in your future, and his future is entwined with the future of Argos. I saw it long ago; I wrote the scriptures knowing that you would ask me this question even now. But for all my foresight, the future of Valen is up to your decision. You can choose to help him or not."

"Mater—," Tyana said, pausing. "Why did you create me the way I am?"

Vale brought a hand up to Tyana's cheek.

"Because I love you as you are, and because I need you to be an ark for that love in dark times."

Vale reached into her tunic. She produced in her hand a silver-white pearl no bigger than her thumbprint.

"Eat this. It is my father's seed—and mine. It will wake my powers in you. My memories, my soul, is locked inside. If you take it, the seed will grow and flower in you."

Tyana plucked the pearl from Vale's hand. She contemplated it for a moment, noticing her own reflection on its surface. Then she placed it on her tongue and swallowed it.

Vale smiled, stroking Tyana's cheek one last time: "I'll always be with you."

Then she was gone.

LXXIV

TYANA'S SCALP WAS burning. She awoke, attempting not to startle the infant gryphon slowly uncurling itself from her body. Its big father was still resting his chin at the edge of the pool, watching her. The burning sensation continued, however, and Tyana grimaced, even dipping her hair back into the milky water. It gradually subsided, fading from her head and then from her entire body.

She felt like her whole outer layer of skin had been shed and replaced with a new one. She even felt like her organs were jostling for new positions. She felt a tightness in her throat and around the center of her chest.

She looked up at Weira, who was still watching her. She nodded in approval.

"Test it," Weira said from the cliff.

Tyana stood in the pool, focusing on the tightness inside of her. It was like summoning *ichor*, but it did not have the same accompanying pain. Milky-white tears collected at the corners of her eyes. Opaque, white sweat beaded from the cruxes of her joints. Her mouth slowly filled with a liquid almost the same color as the pool. She brought her hands out in front of her as the white substance dribbled over her lips. She caught it in her hands. It stirred in her cupped palms seemingly of its own volition.

"Command it," Weira suggested.

Looking at it, Tyana could feel the presence of a collective intelligence compressed within the liquid. She could communicate with it like *sensak*. She visualized her intention for the liquid, then withdrew her hands. The liquid dispersed like a fine mist, hovering in front of her. Then, changing her intention, she reached out, and grabbed it—the mist condensed into a long, wicked looking blade that was as bright as Vale's hair.

Weira nodded approvingly from the cliff. The father gryphon flared his nostrils.

"Now, you are Sibyl."

LXXV

TYANA LOOKED UP at the lone, pale moon hanging over the shimmering Glass Sea. Moonlight reflected off the dunes, coating the landscape. Its reflection looked like a second layer of stars over the layered dunes, mirroring the sky. Behind her lay the entrance to Weira's hut. She turned, walking inside.

She walked across the atrium, down the mud stairs and into the humble library room. She approached the altar at the room's end, laden with half-molten candles and cones of incense. None of them were lit. She took a pair of striking tongs and a wick, and, with a few strokes, sparked the wick. She used the wick to light one of the cones. She placed the incense on the altar, looking up at the imposing gryphon skull that stared down at her. She wafted the smoke toward herself, inhaling it.

Tyana's ritual blade, the one she was given by the Warriors when exiled, was on the altar. She had left it there. It was still untarnished. Tyana brought it up, using it like a mirror. She parted her hair, peering at the roots.

Her roots were growing in white. On her face, the tattoos that traced her jaws and lips had started to flake off.

She put the blade back down.

"What will you do now?" Weira said, approaching from the other end of the library. Tyana turned to her.

"I still have a cease-fire to ensure. I will start there. What about you?"

Weira pondered openly.

"If I don't have to carry the burden of Sibyl, perhaps I'll go back to my old ways. Writing—and reading. How will you get back to the city?" Weira asked. Tyana thought, and stretched out her hand. Beads of white *sensak* gathered on her palm's surface, quickly encasing her wrist and fingers in a chitinous shield.

"I don't know yet. I don't have a warbird. But I can walk across the Sea with the *sensak* to shield me. I'll find my way to the Mater's City one way or another."

Weira raised a finger.

"Let me give you a faster way."

She pulled open a tin box among the many shelves carrying defunct scrolls. She opened it, presenting it to Tyana. Inside was a lone column of incense, different in color than any of those on the altar. She handed it to Tyana.

"Take this to the highest spire you can spot. Light it and let it smoke. Be patient."

Tyana looked at the column in her hand. It smelled bitter and pungent.

"What's it made from?" Tyana asked.

"The pheromones of gryphons," Weira answered. "They were left to me by the previous Sibyl. I used them to travel to the plateau for harvesting, save for this one.

Perhaps I was saving it for a trip home."

She enclosed Tyana's hand around it.

"Take it," she said. "Go to the Mater's City. Fulfill the purpose Vale set out for you—however you see fit."

Tyana looked at Weira.

"Thank you—for caring for me."

Weira nodded, humbly.

"It is only what was once done for me a long time ago," she replied.

Tyana contemplated the column of incense in her hand.

"Sister—when you knew the previous Sibyl, what colors did she have?"

Weira gave a bemused grin.

"Like any Sibyl, she encompassed all the castes in her own way. But if you must know, I'll recall she had a vermillion braid with a deep violet hue running through it. But by the time I met her, it was all nearly an ashen gray. Who knows what colors it used to be?"

LXXVI

TYANA EXITED WEIRA'S hut with the column of incense, a wick, and the ritual blade—her only remaining possessions—at her hip. She donned her *sensak*. They crawled out from her pores and from the corners of her mouth like beads of sweat, spreading like white, silky veins over her skin, coagulating, forming an elaborate exoskeleton. The segmented shields that laced her body were naturally white like alabaster.

It was almost sunrise. She picked the highest nearby peak and began to walk toward it. Her exterior armor, hardened against the glass dust, made it easier to travel, and she formed a filter around her mouth, allowing her to breathe easily. She could even feel the *sensak* catching the glass dust as she inhaled.

When she got to her destination, it was almost daylight. She climbed the pillars of the rock formation. She reached their top. There, the hexagonal platform of rocks was worn smooth. A sole, pale moon rose over the horizon ahead of the oncoming sunrise. The fog of glass dust glinted in the dawn light, fading from lavender to crimson. She lingered a moment—she even sat there, contemplating if this would be the last time she'd see it this way.

When the sun was more than halfway above the horizon, Tyana took the column of incense from her hand and placed it in a secure spot on the platform. She formed a pair of striking rods with her *sensak* and, with the wick, lit the incense.

She waited, watching the sky slowly brighten. The smoke wafted up—its smell was potent even to Tyana. Not long after, she heard a lone, roaring shriek. A gryphon was heading right for her—the male with the wounded wing.

When he landed, his single rear haunch gripped the top of the cliff with long talons. He spread out his wings and she could see his whole body in the dawn light. She stepped back. The gryphon grumbled at her with his mouth closed, then he slowly laid his massive skull down on the cliffside's platform. His wide, cyan eyes focused in on her. She could see her reflection in his crescent-shaped pupils.

She approached the gryphon steadily. Peeling back the *sensak* on one hand, she touched his neck, just behind the crest of his skull. She could feel his breathing, his pulse. She could feel more, but she relented from going deeper, leaving it as just a glancing connection. His breath stilled slightly as she touched him.

Carefully, she climbed his neck, grasping his ridged crest on occasion to steady herself. He respected her advances. She nestled into the space where his shoulder blades met the base of his neck, and she used *sensak* to settle herself on his back.

"Let's go," she said.

He grumbled, pushing himself off the cliff with a sole thrust of his hind leg. His wings folded as they dived. For a moment, Tyana wondered if he would lead them straight into the ground. But then his wings opened and they soared upward, above the fog of glass dust. He flew in the direction of the Mater's City, letting out one last earth-shattering roar.

LXXVII

SEK'S FACE WAS lit by the glow of a diagram hovering in the air. It showed the battlefront beyond Valen, around Seruneh, and the asteroid belt surrounding them. The enemy had receded so fully that the diagram was bereft of its usual bright band of flash points. They had all but disappeared over the course of nine days. Since then, the front had become conspicuously quiet, and Warriors felt useless. They took to brawling with each other in the streets to cure their boredom.

A Warrior walked in behind Sek—a young assistant, saying:

"I've finished servicing the warbirds as you requested, sister."

"Good," Sek said, turning. Her closely cropped hair hadn't changed, but now her face was written with a new kind of sternness.

"How do you feel now that you sit on the Council?" the younger Warrior asked Sek.

"About as I expected," she replied. "The Mater

requires all the warbirds to be in excellent condition." She turned off the console and strode past the girl, paying little attention to her.

"What bothers you, sister?" the young Warrior asked, following. Sek left the war room and proceeded toward the hangars.

"The front is gone. The enemy that used to be at our doorstep is simply vanished."

"Perhaps they are honoring the cease-fire set by your predecessor?"

"I don't know," Sek replied, bristling. "It doesn't make sense to me. But it gives us an opportunity to invade their space. The Warriors need an enemy to focus on—or else they'll find one among themselves."

They entered the hangar. Rows and rows of warbirds lay silent, waiting.

"How much of the fleet does the Mater require?" the assistant asked.

"All of it," Sek replied flatly. "We are going to war. It's finally time to exterminate these wretched barbarians. Our whole caste will be brought to bear. No one will be left without a fight."

The assistant noted Sek's dull gaze over the hangar. The assistant asked hesitantly:

"Is there something wrong, sister? Isn't this news pleasing to you?"

"It is. It is just—I thought that getting appointed to the Council would feel like an honor."

"But it is an honor," the assistant said.

"Yes, I know. It was the one thing I always wanted. But now that I have it, nothing feels like it's changed. I am not sure why I wanted it so much."

"Perhaps you wanted the adoration of your sisters and

the Mater," the assistant replied.

"But I don't feel I have that," she said.

The assistant stepped in front of Sek, facing her. She was a little shorter than her.

"Perhaps you feel that way because it is true. They don't respect you the way they respected Tyana or Verikash."

Sek was taken aback.

"Who are you to say that?"

"They know that you are head of your caste only because Tyana was banished and Kersa and Verikash sacrificed themselves in battle. Your position is merely a tool for Thea. Tyana refused to bend to Her will. That's why she was banished. Since you will do whatever She says, why would anyone respect you?"

"Shut your mouth," Sek hissed. "You speak blasphemy."

"I speak as I wish," the assistant continued. "Your days are numbered, as are Thea's. One day, you'll see all this crashing down around you, and you will realize you were merely a pawn in Her game."

"You treacherous—," Sek snarled. "I'll brand you."

Sek took out a tattooing gun from her hip. She reached for the assistant's face, but her hand went through it. The girl's face just dissolved into *sensak*. Sek gasped.

"The Sibyl comes," said the simulacrum, "and with her, Vale returns." The assistant dissolved into a cloud of white dust.

Explosions ripped through the hangar. The fleet ignited and burst, sending plumes of fire and pieces in every direction. Sek ducked. When she could stand back up, every warbird had been decimated, leaving nothing but flaming craters in their wakes. The fires lit the otherwise dark hangar with an orange glow. At the far end she saw a robed figure in a hood. Sek thought she recognized her, but she couldn't believe it at first. Then the figure removed her hood. Sek's breath stopped. Shock-white hair was brimming from the figure's scalp. The figure let out a cloud of white *sensak*. Static electricity arced visibly as it coagulated around her, forming tendrils that lifted her out of the hangar and up through the cleft in the roof.

Sek turned and ran as fast as she could toward the cathedral.

LXXVIII

VERSHIL LIT A bronze brazier on the balcony of her apartment, overlooking the sea. It was noon, bright, and the sun cast few shadows through the haze in the sky. A visitor stepped to the threshold of her entryway.

"Come," Vershil said. The figure walked in. "Vesha —," she began, taking note of her visitor's appearance. "It has been some time since you last appeared at my doors. What brings you here?"

Vesha's cobalt-colored braids streamed down her shoulders. She wore an unadorned gown with a hood. She bowed in the way of the Keepers.

"Sister Vershil," she intoned. "It has been too long, after all."

"Join me on the balcony here. Tell me—are your students doing well?"

Vesha approached.

"They are performing admirably," she said. "I have a few that are excelling above expectations."

"Which ones?" Vershil queried, lighting the opposing

brazier on the balcony. "You have both Scribal and Keeper initiates under your tutelage, is that not correct?"

"Yes," Vesha replied. "They work in tandem well enough."

"I appreciate your open-mindedness in pursuing these integrated classes," Vershil said thoughtfully. "I know it is not traditional to have Scribes and Keepers working in pairs as learners. Some of my peers—your seniors— would have objections, were it not for your enthusiasm."

"I am here to serve," Vesha said.

"Yes. Now tell me what you came here for."

Vesha turned, looking for a moment to the sea across the balcony.

"I came across an interesting and puzzling passage in the scriptures during my readings late last night. I wanted to ask you for your more learned interpretation."

"What is the passage?"

Vesha looked at her.

"It speaks of a sister, but the term used to represent her is confusing and indecisive. It seems to change based on one's perspective. In one breath, it speaks of her as multi-burdened, but it implies that she may be more than just two castes—perhaps three, or even more."

Vesha stopped speaking, noticing the cold gaze from Vershil's eyes. Vershil turned wordlessly from her. She retrieved two cups from the balcony's table and, after a moment, came back with a pot of hot tea. She poured the tea and handed one of the cups to Vesha.

"You know the Mater's decree," she said finally. "We must not speak publicly about the multi-burdened ones."

Vesha paused, then bowed in apology.

"Of course."

"Continue. Simply take care in your language."

"Of course, sister," Vesha said, pausing for a moment. "There is another term for them that seems to offer itself from the images, however. It is not specific to any caste, but it seems to lend itself to any of them—or even all."

"What term is that?" Vershil asked, sipping her tea.

"Sibyl."

Vershil stopped sipping, then gently set her tea down.

"Now I understand why you are confused."

She retreated from the balcony to her library. When she came back, she carried an engraved tin box, covered in a fine layer of dust. She placed it on the balcony table and opened it. Inside was a small stone scroll.

"What is that?" Vesha asked.

"It is a transcription that includes the image you speak of."

"It looks different from the other scrolls. It is so small."

"That is because it is of exceedingly high purity. The clarity of interpretation depends on the clarity of the image, which depends on the language used while creating the scroll. In stone, brevity is more expressive and pointed. It yields a clear image but not a clear interpretation. To rectify this, we justify our interpretation through associations within the text. The more specific the interpretation, the more associations we must make to elucidate and justify that interpretation. This results in lengthening the text overall, requiring larger scrolls. The stricter the interpretation, the more associations are required to justify it—thus, the larger and heavier the scroll. This one is small because it is bereft of any such justifications—it contains only the raw naked images."

Vershil paused, sipping her tea.

"You were exactly right that the term you encountered

could change its meaning based on your perspective. That is because you were reading from the image, not our interpretation of it. This is a simple fallacy, but given the passage you encountered, which is a confusing one, it is excusable. You must focus more on your memorization of our associations, rather than reading directly from the image. Its allure can capture you, leading to personal interpretation of the text, which is dangerous."

Vesha looked at her, then looked at the scroll.

"Why do we not write scrolls like this one?"

"The Mater requires the associations to be embedded within the transcriptions themselves. We want one interpretation—one truth—even if the image produced by a passage may be rich and multifaceted. Aside from this, a scroll of this purity is beyond the skill level of even our most revered Scribes today. It can only be accomplished by a Scribe and Keeper working in tandem."

"Is this why you requested the pairing of Scribes and Keepers together?"

"There is the practical problem of handling and storing larger scrolls. It is preferable that they don't grow infinitely long."

Vesha looked at the scroll, nestled inside the box on a bed of fabric.

"How old is it?" she asked.

"Ancient—before my time or yours."

"Then who could have transcribed it, sister?"

Vershil sipped her tea. A curious smile crossed her face, which softened as soon as it came.

"A teacher of mine passed it down to me. This was her personal copy."

Vershil closed the box. The engravings on the metal

glinted in the noon daylight. Vershil carried it back to the library, setting the box on a shelf while Vesha watched her.

"Do you mean Weira?" Vesha said. Vershil stopped, looking at her strangely.

"How do you know her name?"

"Isn't it a matter of public record?"

"Not at all. I rarely speak her name, and certainly would not do so in polite company." She brought her hand up to her forehead, gesturing at the single, small, diamond-shaped brand above and between her brows. "I did so only once in the Mater's court, and it was the last time I spoke up in favor of her."

"Do you know what happened to her?"

Vershil shook her head. "I would rather not know. She was banished for heresy long ago. I would encourage you not to speak her name, per the decree. I do not even read her work now for fear of its taint."

Vesha nodded quickly. She drank her tea steadily, wordlessly. When she drained the cup, she replaced it on the table and bowed.

"Thank you for your wisdom, sister Vershil, and the tea as well."

"You are welcome, sister. Consult me any time you wish," Vershil said, curtsying in response. Vesha turned and left the balcony, walking toward the entrance. Vershil stayed on the balcony, pouring herself more tea.

She sipped from her cup, staying there a long while, watching the waves of the ocean lap against the cliffside below. Something about the conversation left her unsettled. She wondered if it was something Vesha said or if it was something else that bothered her. Vesha's dress today was particularly bland and unadorned.

More, she had not thought of Weira in years. Vershil reminisced on her old teacher. She could recall the day Weira gave her the tin box with that scroll inside. It was only a few days before the Mater banished her. After that day, Vershil never opened it—she left it unread.

The ground shook and the glass of her teacups rattled, clinking together. She heard the sound of large, far-off explosions. Alarmed, she looked to either side of her balcony. She could not see their source, but they sounded like they came from within the Mater's City.

She hurried inside, passing by the library's shelves, climbing the spiraling stairs to the second floor of her apartment. She went to the corner skylight where she could see clear across the city to the tops of the Warriors' hangars. They were engulfed in flames.

She hurried back down the stairs, picking her gown up so she wouldn't trip. She started for the door—but as she passed by her library's shelves again, she stopped.

She turned, looking at the shelf where she kept the tin box. It was there, but something seemed different— either its placement or the dust around it. Without hesitation, she took it off the shelf and opened it.

The scroll was gone. In its place was a single lock of purple and black hair.

LXXIX

Aʜᴠᴀ ᴄʟɪᴍʙᴇᴅ ᴏᴜᴛ of the outbreath junction. Her
nimble hands grasped the edge of the vents. She pulled
herself out of the way of the hot, incoming steam and
into the cold, fresh air. The smell of sulfur filled her
nostrils as she caught her breath.

Climbing down, she made her way toward the shore
below. The rocks were sharp against her bare hands and
legs. Nonetheless, when she made it to the ground, she
was happy to find a place to rest and sat on one of the
flattened rocks above the water.

The wind blew over her vermillion-red hair. It fell
across her brow and she ran a hand through it. Grease
darkened it at the tips. Carefully, she took a finger and
traced her freshly blackened eyelids. They were branded
by a Warrior with a tattooing gun the day Amun was
executed.

It was still fresh in her mind, like the way the skin of
her eyelids still itched. She was there, in the crowd,
watching as Thea delivered Her judgment. She could see

Amun in the chamber on the stage, cut down by the gryphon. Ahva watched the Vestal-Warrior fall to her knees and scream. She remembered when she had found her in these same outbreath junctions. Ahva wondered if she had made the right decision that day. She could have left that Vestal-Warrior where she was. Perhaps then Amun would still be alive.

Ahva looked out to the hazy horizon. The sea seemed to go on forever, fading into nothing but a gray, blurred line. The water lapped at the foundations of the rock she sat on. It was basalt, but its harsh lines were worn smooth by the water.

She noticed a figure to her right, standing on the nearby cliff. The figure was looking at her, covered in a disheveled set of robes and a hood. Fabric covered her face except for her eyes. She carried a walking stick. Ahva stood, peering at the figure.

"Who are you?" Ahva said, her voice carrying across the rocks.

The figure pulled down her hood. She had short, crimson hair—dark enough to be nearly auburn. The cut of her hair reminded her vaguely of Amun's.

"I'm an Artificer, like you," the figure replied through the fabric over her mouth.

Ahva sat down.

"I don't recognize you," she said.

"I'm from a distant isle where I made my home long ago," the figure said, walking down the platform-like steps of the cliffside. She used her stick to guide herself as she climbed down. "I have been away a long while. Tell me your name."

"Ahva," she said.

The figure stepped across the rocks, making her way

toward Ahva. When she was close, the figure drew away the fabric that covered her lips and neck. She seemed youthful despite her pursed lips and sunken cheeks.

"What are you doing here?" the figure asked.

"I maintain the outbreath junctions," Ahva said.

"Why would anyone have a need for that?" the figure asked. "Who needs air pumped into the ground?"

"We do," Ahva said, blinking.

"You mean to tell me that your sisters live down there while there is fresh air up here?"

"It is Thea's wish, not ours," Ahva said.

The figure paused. She sat down on the rock next to Ahva. She put down her walking stick.

"This is not right. Tell me more. What else has Thea done to you?"

Ahva looked at her feet, then beyond them down to the water below.

"How long have you been gone?" she asked, looking back at the figure.

"A long time. Just tell me," she said.

Ahva sighed, looking back just beyond her feet—then spoke:

"We had a leader. We called her the Speaker. She held gatherings for us where we could explore the mysteries Vale set out for us."

"What sort of mysteries?"

"I don't know. We took pills that gave us a sense of connection, a sense of belonging. I could touch someone and I could feel their feelings. I could even see their feelings like shapes behind my closed eyes."

The figure listened, nodding. Ahva continued:

"Then a Warrior destroyed the lab that created them. Thea found out and punished us all. She executed the

Speaker. That was how I got these eyelids." She closed them, stroking one with the edge of her finger.

"What happened to the Warrior?"

"She was banished," Ahva said. "She was not fully a Warrior. She was a Vestal-Warrior, a multi-burdened one."

"I've never heard of such a sister."

"I knew her name. I found her near here in the outbreath junctions one day. She was passed out, nearly dead. I wonder if I had left her there whether the Speaker would still be here now."

The figure seemed to pause, bowing her head slightly. Then she looked at Ahva. "What do you think?"

Ahva shook her head.

"She was asking for the Speaker when I found her. Once they met, I knew that they had a special connection. We could see it. Everyone could. They spent long nights with each other, and she even accompanied us at the gatherings. I watched everything, even if I wasn't in the middle of it. They loved each other. But then it all ended."

The figure, sullen, said:

"What happened?"

"Thea found out," Ahva said. "When the Warrior destroyed the lab, there was nothing left for us to take at the gatherings. The Speaker tried to revolt, but Thea caught her. The Mater imprisoned the Speaker, the Grand Artificer, and their scientist. The rest I've told you already."

The figure sniffed the cold, salty air. She shuffled in her place, discomforted. She asked:

"What will you do now?"

"I don't know," Ahva said, tucking her knees up to her

chest and resting her chin on them. "Everything seems so gray now. Thea wants to begin a war, which means more labor for me and my sisters. Why should we labor for a Mater who gives us nothing in return? At least the Speaker gave us the gatherings where we could dance together. But she tried to lead us in a revolt and failed."

"What about Vale?" the figure asked. "Isn't She still the maker of this world?"

"Vale made this world, but Thea rules it," Ahva said. "What use is She if She doesn't return and free us like the Speaker taught?"

The figure rested on her haunches, nestling herself against her walking stick. "Thea does rule this world, but you and your sisters still outnumber the other castes. Even if Thea brings war, it will be up to you to build the warbirds, fetch the food, and crew the transports. Her whole machinery of war relies on you and your caste. If you have the power to stop Her machinery, you have the power to stop Her—and Her war."

"That is what the Speaker tried," Ahva said. "Look at what happened."

"She believed she could take on the powers of a Warrior," the figure replied. "This wasn't her burden. She wasn't ready to control a Warrior's power, so it consumed her. I am suggesting you do something else."

Ahva paused, looking away.

"A Warrior's burden is violence," the figure continued. "It brews more of itself wherever it goes. This Vestal-Warrior knew that too. That was why she didn't revolt as quickly as the Speaker."

Ahva looked at her. Her blackened eyelids cast shadows against her brows.

"This is not the life I want to live," Ahva said. "Not a

life of work for someone else's war. Why should I? It's like you said—why shouldn't we be up here in the fresh air? This is where I come to relax. This is where I want to live. Why not?"

"Why not?" the figure's wizened lips spread into a smile.

"Warriors," Ahva said, her passion dissipating quickly.

"There is a way to quell them without confrontation," the figure said, shifting her walking stick again beneath her haunches. "They obey Thea so long as She rules. They trust Her power. But She is merely a representative of Vale. When Vale returns, She will judge fairly. She will level the castes, ensuring that those who were oppressed will be lifted up, and those who oppressed them will have their share re-prepared."

"How do you know that?" Ahva asked.

"It is simple enough," the figure said, shrugging. "The scriptures say as much."

"I thought that was what the Vestal-Warrior would do," Ahva said. "The Speaker said throughout our gatherings that the multi-burdened one would bring about Vale's final judgment as revolution. She had her revolution, but Vale never came. Now, Thea has exacted greater punishment on us."

"You're right," the figure said, shifting again. "Vale never came. But Her revolution can't be fulfilled through violence. This wasn't Her intention for the Warrior caste, and it wasn't Her intention for you to toil day and night for the purposes of a war machine."

Ahva looked at her.

"Then why do we?"

"Thea betrayed Vale. That is why She rules instead of Her. Vale's will, however, is in you. Even while you're oppressed, She is in every caste. Every Artificer, Warrior, Scribe, Keeper—and even daresay Vestal—has Vale inside her. If you awaken enough parts of Her within yourself, you will be no different than Her."

Ahva paused. The figure peered at her, but Ahva sighed.

"I want to believe you, but as long as the castes obey one another the way they do now, nothing will change."

"Trust that Vale will make a difference. Now that I've told you this, what will you do?"

Ahva shook her head.

"I've already lost my leader. I need more than a word of trust."

The figure's brows arced upward, hurt. But she turned and reached into her robes. She pulled out a small vial of milky-white liquid.

"Your sister's lab may have been destroyed, but there is a future ensured for your caste, and more, if you discover the chemistry of this mixture."

"What is it?" Ahva asked, looking at the vial.

"Vale's milk," she replied. "It is from a forbidden place beyond the Glass Sea."

"Beyond the Glass Sea?" Ahva asked. "How did you get from there to here?"

"You must take this and discover its chemical makeup," she said. "If you do, those questions will be minuscule compared to the answers this provides. It is more useful in your hands than mine. If you think the loss of your sister's lab was awful, this may repay its debt. It carries more secrets than Thea's *ichor*. But more than this—"

The figure clasped Ahva's hands around the vial, saying to her:

"Vale can still return. You must believe in Her. Even while Thea's reign is at its highest and darkest, Vale can still return. She remembers Her children. You must find a way to subvert Thea's reign until Vale wakes. If you revolt openly, you'll be crushed. But I promise, She'll come back—as long as you plant Her seeds and water them."

Ahva looked at her.

"How do you know for sure?"

"Because She's already here in you and in me. She's in all of us. I already told you." The figure let go of her hands.

Ahva looked away, down at the waves, lapping at the stone she sat on. The wind blew.

"When can I see Her?" Ahva asked, looking back up.

But the figure was gone.

Ahva looked around. The figure was nowhere. She called out for her, not knowing her name. Eventually, Ahva stopped and looked at the vial in her hands. She studied it. It contained a white, homogenous mixture that shimmered in the light.

Then she heard a series of loud bangs in the distance. The ground shook. She looked in the direction of the Mater's City. Far off in the distance, it seemed like the cleft where the Warriors' hangar rested was engulfed in explosions.

LXXX

A HOODED KEEPER accompanied by four attendants ascended the steps of the Mater's Cathedral. The attendants opened the doors for her wordlessly. Light poured in from the entrance and her form cast a long shadow against the light.

She walked forward, her robe rustling in the breeze. The attendants closed the doors behind her, following. They moved together, almost in a formation.

Ahead, Ahnsair sat on Mater Thea's throne. Basins of *ichor* flanked her throne's platform. The black liquid in their curved bowls barely stirred. A group of minor Keepers and Scribes was huddled around her. Surrounding them was a large cadre of Warriors keeping watch. The cathedral was notably devoid of the sweet singing of the Artificers, or even the smoky aroma of their incense.

In the center of the basilica was a glass prism. Inside it was the infant gryphon used in Amun's execution—a male. He was skinny enough that his ribcage was visible.

His cries echoed through the basilica.

"Why is the creature suffering from malnourishment?" Ahnsair asked, addressing those in her meeting.

"Our Vestal," one said respectfully, "we have tried feeding it a range of diets. We know gryphons feed on sea kelp, but we have never kept one—particularly one of their young—in captivity. Perhaps its requirements are different."

"The Mater requires it to be healthy. She wishes to keep it as Her pet. It looks decrepit this way. How can She use it for future executions if the creature will not eat?"

"Yes, our Vestal," said a Keeper in reply. "Perhaps the Warriors know why this is?"

The ranking Warrior among the group frowned.

"We agreed to capture the gryphon, but we don't know how to keep it. Keepers are the historians—they should know."

"Perhaps their infants require something different than the adults?" one of them said.

The infant gryphon stirred in his glass cage and scratched against it, whining.

"Enough," Ahnsair said, exasperated. "A delegation is here."

The hooded Keeper and her attendants stopped. She looked up at Ahnsair, but she didn't remove her hood.

"I've come to see the Mater," she said.

Ahnsair stood, frowning.

"Who comes?" she asked.

"I've come to see the Mater," she repeated. Ahnsair's frown deepened.

"Have you not heard? Her Mater's presence left Her body three nights ago. Did you not attend Her funeral yesterday?"

The hooded Keeper was silent, then said:

"Who is the Vestal who replaced her?"

"The one you see before you," Ahnsair replied. "Your caste's duty is to govern knowledge—are you suddenly incompetent? And you should mind your speech when speaking to Me."

The hooded Keeper paused.

"Then I've come to give the Mater—and you—a message," she said.

"A message?" Ahnsair asked.

"I've come to tell you that Vale's truths, though they've long been hidden and suppressed, are now in the light. I've come here to reveal those truths to you—to restore Her vision, and to cleanse those who refuse to receive it."

A mixture of shock and disgust came over Ahnsair's face. Everyone in the cathedral looked at the hooded figure.

"Dare you say—," Ahnsair began, stepping down from her throne.

"I dare to plumb the depths of my psyche," she interrupted. "I know that Thea's teachings were made to empower herself and to suppress Vale's intent for us at our own expense and for Thea's benefit." She looked up toward the rest of those assembled. "Those of you who can read and write the scriptures for yourselves should know this most among others. Because you acquiesce to Thea's temptations, Vale will judge you harshly."

"Blasphemy!" a Keeper swore. The whole cadre of Warriors pulled out tattooing guns.

Before they could move, the ground shook. The sound of an explosion beyond the cathedral rattled its windows. Dust fell from the stone rafters.

"What is that?" Ahnsair said.

"It sounded like it came from the hangars," one Warrior said quickly.

"Go—now! Find out—," Ahnsair said, pointing to the doors. A group of Warriors split off, heading for the entrance past the delegation.

"There's nothing you can do to stop it," said the hooded Keeper. "Vale will ensure that the cease-fire will remain. Thea will not conquer humanity. She has ruled over Vale's children long enough."

"Tell me your name!" Ahnsair roared. The Keeper looked at her.

"You took it from me. You made me nameless."

At that moment, Sek burst in through the doors of the cathedral, short of breath.

"My Vestal—the hangars are destroyed—Tyana returned—"

"Do not speak that name, she is banished," Ahnsair retorted.

Then Vershil appeared, clambering up the steps, holding onto her gown as she ran toward the assembly.

"My Vestal—we must speak urgently—I believe the one you banished is returned—"

"That is impossible—!" Ahnsair screamed.

At that moment, Tyana removed her hood. Every breath in the room ceased. Her hair was cut short. Shock-white roots permeated her scalp, growing in visibly to everyone. She lifted up a closed, gloved fist and let the remainder of her purple and black hair fall to the floor of the cathedral.

Palpable shock descended over the room. No one spoke.

She turned, looking at Vershil from the corner of her

eyes. Tyana peeled off her gloves and threw them down in her direction.

"I no longer need these," she said. The sound of their fabric made a resounding slap on the polished stone floor. Turning back to Ahnsair, she said: "The Vestal-Warrior you know is gone. I am Vale's Sibyl."

The infant gryphon in his cage whined, then shrieked.

"Seize her!" Ahnsair ordered, visibly panicked.

Sek moved first. She lunged at Tyana, but one of the hooded attendants moved to block her. Sek struck the attendant to push her away, but the attendant countered like a Warrior would. Sek released her *sensak* and formed a blade, slicing into the attendant, who dissolved into a cloud of white *sensak*—a simulacrum.

The other Warriors followed suit. They headed straight for Tyana, but her simulacra stepped in front of her, blocking their path and holding them off. The other Keepers and Scribes in attendance scattered. Violet *sensak* mixed with bursts of white *sensak* as simulacra dissolved under the encroaching Warriors' blades. Tyana moved steadily toward Ahnsair as they fought. Her robe dissolved, turning into white, segmented armor. She brought the fallen simulacra's *sensak* in orbit around her, coalescing each bit of it onto herself, extending a set of bright blades from her hands.

Ahnsair started to step back. The Warriors regrouped, surrounding Tyana, donning their armor and the fiercest weapons they could muster.

"I've come to liberate Vale's children, including you," she said to them.

The infant gryphon was screaming in his cage, pecking at the glass with his beak. The Warriors closed in on her.

They stopped when another sound shook the grounds of the cathedral. This time it wasn't an explosion. Something outside cast a shadow over the stained glass windows, and it let loose an earth-shattering roar. Sek looked up at the rafters, wide-eyed, and whispered:

"Gryphon—a male."

Ahnsair gripped the arms of her throne. The gryphon roared again—he was outside, using his blunt skull like a battering ram. The infant gryphon cried and his father responded—the sound of his shrieking roar was just at the threshold.

"You think you can enslave Vale's creation," Tyana said. "You think you can control him and use him for your own benefit. You are wrong. You've abused Her monster's son, and now he wants him back."

The doors buckled. They fell, smashing to pieces. Splinters flew into the basilica. The infant squirmed, squealing. The father pushed his head through the entrance, his nostrils flaring and sniffing. He tried to roar, but his muzzle couldn't fit through the entrance. He retracted his head, then struck the entrance's frame with his clawed wings, bashing the masonry away.

"He'll tear this cathedral apart," Tyana said to Ahnsair, "and you—if you don't let his child go." Fear was writ across Ahnsair's face.

The gryphon peered into the basilica, his big eyes focusing in on the infant. He roared again, tearing open the cathedral's stone with his gigantic claws. He pushed his muzzle, then his whole head in, his jaws snapping wildly at the assembly. His open mouth was large enough to swallow five Warriors whole; his snakelike tongue, his fangs, his open throat were fully visible. The piercing sound of his roars mixed with the panicked cries of his child.

Ahnsair held up a hand. "All right—!" She pointed at Sek. "Release it," she said, pointing at the glass cage.

The Warriors stepped away from Tyana and slowly toward the infant. He still screamed, desperate. Sek begrudgingly walked over to the glass prism. The father fell silent, watching Sek intently, but his breath was loud, thick, and heavy. His crescent-like pupils focused in on her. She formed a simple blade and swung it down at the glass. It cracked, shattering open. The infant squealed, climbing out. The assembly parted ways as he crawled along the floor like a serpent toward his father. The father watched, his eyes following the motions of his son. He rested his head on the broken stone floor and the child crawled up the side of his neck, nestling himself behind the crest of his skull. The child squealed, then cooed. The father grumbled in return.

When the father's eyes turned back to look at the assembly, he opened his mouth wide, giving one more ear-splitting roar. Then he removed his head and disappeared. The sound of his flapping wings faded away, along with the sound of his furious shrieks.

The whole assembly was still, even the Warriors. Fallen rocks and dust covered the cathedral's floor.

Tyana turned to go.

"You will pay," Ahnsair seethed quietly. Then she said, louder: "You will pay!"

The *ichor* in the basins next to her throne quivered to life. They snapped to attention, leaping from the basins, wrapping around Tyana's wrists and ankles, dragging her back along the floor toward Ahnsair.

In a single stroke, Tyana cut the whips away. She leapt to her feet, responding by sending her own *sensak* as a set of projectiles straight at Ahnsair. Ahnsair deflected them all with her whips.

The assembly took cover. The two of them unleashed their full set of powers on each other—Thea's *ichor* against Vale's *sensak*. Ahnsair covered herself in an oil-like shield, sending out tendrils in every direction like a spider's web. She ascended into the center of the room. Tyana met her there, rising upward, sending clouds of white crystals to cut Ahnsair's tendrils down. They moved throughout the basilica, throwing each other against the walls and the floors, cracking the foundations. Tyana tore down stone rafters, throwing their pieces at Ahnsair. Ahnsair responded by throwing her *ichor* at Tyana, attempting to encase her with it and crush her body. Some of it managed to get a hold of her. Tyana countered by dissolving her armor and sending it whipping around her in a spiral. She pushed its speed, adding more *sensak* to it from every pore of her body, faster and faster, until it dissolved, forming a cyclone. It wrapped up Ahnsair's tendrils and broke them into pieces. The breezeless air in the room turned into a roaring wind. Tyana condensed the storm's energy and it bristled with electricity, arcing with lightning in all directions. The whole assembly watched, holding onto the nearest solid outcropping. The wind decimated the cathedral's innards, picking up dust and stones and shattering windows. Light poured in.

In the center, Ahnsair struggled to regain control of her *ichor*. Tyana, straining, considered it possible that they were equally matched. She looked around herself for a third option. Nearby, on the floor, was a discarded tattooing gun.

Holding the cyclone steady, Tyana sent out a single

tendril, wrapping it around the gun and sending it flying into her hand. She approached Ahnsair, wind whipping around them. With her other bare hand she clutched Ahnsair's face, using her touch to press into her mind.

"This is for Amun," Tyana said. "I want you to remember what you did to Amun."

She brought the tattooing gun close up to Ahnsair's face. She pressed its trigger. The red laser whirred to life and it struck Ahnsair in the eye. It steamed and sizzled; Ahnsair screamed. The flesh of her eye blackened, burning away her eyelid and blinding her on one side.

She crumpled to the floor, clutching her scarred face. Her *ichor* went lifeless. It was flung by Tyana's cyclone in all directions. It fell to the floor like so much oil, splashing onto marble floors and mixing with the broken stones and dust. It covered the faces of sculptures and smeared itself across the rafters, dripping downward to the floor.

Tyana's *sensak* stilled and the wind subsided. She stepped back. The assembly members who were clutching to columns and outcroppings for their lives ran over to Ahnsair, who cried aloud. Tyana said:

"Now everyone will remember that there is no such thing as purity in Thea's court."

She threw the tattooing gun on the ground. It rang with a dull, metallic thud—the only other sound mixing with Ahnsair's shrieks of horror as she tried to open and close her eye.

Tyana walked out of the cathedral, crossing its broken threshold.

LXXXI

THE ONE WARBIRD left intact was the one Tyana kept for herself. Hidden away in the underside of one of the island's far-off caverns, it sat silently, waiting.

Tyana came walking across the coastline. Her pale armor contrasted with the black sand of the beach. The warbird's distinct sheen profiled it against the cavern's shadows.

When she got there, she stroked the underside of the warbird's hull. At her hip was the ritual blade she kept from her time in the Glass Sea. In her other hand she carried a small stone scroll. She contemplated the scroll for a moment, caressing its ancient engravings with her finger. It glowed to life, responding to her touch—but she did not open it.

Instead, the warbird's underside dissolved at her intention, and she entered it.

She ignited its engines. She headed upward, leaving the atmosphere. Valen's profile grew smaller and smaller behind her. When she reached the acceleration gates, she initiated them. They flung her far beyond Seruneh and its asteroids.

She was looking for the source of a particular signal. Its source now was well beyond the confines of Valen and Seruneh. It was stronger when she left the far reaches of the star system, but it was still very faint. She pushed beyond that, deep into uncharted space. Familiar nebulae faded behind her. Constellations shifted until they were unrecognizable. Patterns of stars she'd never seen stretched out around her.

She instructed her warbird to set up a beacon of its own—sending every possible signal in every direction. She powered down the warbird's engines and diverted its remaining power to supporting her own life. Then, she waited.

She lost count of how long she lay there in the warbird. She shifted her biorhythms, slowing her breathing and her pulse. Half asleep, half awake, she stilled her own trepidations and quelled her fears, hoping that she wasn't following the signal in vain.

Her warbird's systems glimmered to life. Something was heading straight for her. Something big.

The stars ahead of her distorted. They were pushed apart from their center, like space itself was being stretched by a gigantic encroaching bubble. Tyana had never seen anything like it. Something appeared along the bubble's edge, growing in size like it was riding an oncoming wave. It was a ship. The stars snapped back into place, the bubble disappeared, and Tyana could see the ship clearly. It was massive, rust-colored, and of human design. A glowing ring, covered in honeycomb-like formations, encircled a central hull made up of many competing layers. She recognized the markings along its side, even though she couldn't read them.

The distant signal was now a confident alarm.

She turned her beacon off, reignited her engines, and approached the ship at a steady pace. It seemed to respect her approach. Running lights came on along its underside, pointing toward an open hangar bay. She flew toward it.

When she crossed its threshold, she noted the differences in human shipbuilding from Valenian craft. Theirs was blocky, industrial, and tasteless. Still, its basic functions and features were generally recognizable to her. She set her warbird down on the hangar floor, which was empty. At the other end of it was a single set of heavy bay doors.

She exited her warbird, donning her *sensak* from head to toe as she did. She approached the doors steadily, looking around. There were no machines in the hangar —no activity at all. Nothing moved.

When she got to the doors, she noted a control panel at their side. Its glowing markings were completely unfamiliar to her. She waved her hand in front of it—the markings changed from red to yellow. The panel crackled to life. A voice, using broken Valenian tongue, spoke:

"Who comes?"

Tyana paused for a moment. Then, into the panel, she replied:

"Not your enemy."

The bay doors slid apart.

Inside was a whole group of humans. Some of them appeared to be armed. At their head was Azra. He held up a hand—they didn't make a move. Neither did Tyana. Tyana dissolved the *sensak* around her face and scalp. It peeled away, revealing her stark-white hair, alabaster-like skin, and luminous cyan eyes.

She read fear and trepidation on the faces of the other humans. Azra looked her up and down.

"Are you the same Warrior I met—the one called Tyana?" he asked in Valenian. His enunciation was somewhat improved.

"My people no longer call me by that name, but I am the same one you met before," she said.

One of Azra's companions close to him, one that was armed, spoke to him in a rough, barbarian tongue. He replied back to him in the same language. His companion didn't move. The crude-looking rifle in his companion's hands was lowered, but his fingers hovered on what looked like a trigger. Azra addressed Tyana again:

"You don't look the same as when I last met you," he said.

"More than that has changed. But I can confirm to you that I've enforced the cease-fire. They will not attack you—but we should not stay here."

Azra nodded solemnly. He gave another gesture to his crew and said something to them in his own tongue. They seemed to relax—even sigh in relief, but many still eyed Tyana strangely. He said something else to them and they dispersed. He addressed her:

"Welcome aboard—this is my ship: *Rend's Hand.*"

"You name your ships?" Tyana asked. He shrugged.

"Only if we want to survive."

Tyana managed to break a smile.

"Do you intend to go back to your planet?" Azra asked. Tyana shook her head.

"That is not possible. I am an exile now. I destroyed

my Mater's fleet and ensured that she cannot wage war. I planted seeds of doubt among their youth that will hopefully foment revolution. My sisters will not be able to fight for some time. They may eventually rebuild their capacity for war—but if that happens, I will return."

Azra nodded.

"Then my people are safe—thanks to you."

They walked together. He showed her the interior of his ship. It was warp-capable.

"Tell me—," he said in his heavily accented Valenian. "You said that your kind no longer calls you by the name you had before. What do they call you now?"

"They call me Nameless—one who cannot be named."

Azra nodded. They reached the bridge. Tyana walked in with him—a pale, white figure among a number of disconcerted humans. He directed his crew in his own language to leave the outskirts of Valen, heading to a planet called Terra.

"Our kind doesn't usually have nameless people," Azra said. "Is there something else you would like us to call you from now on?"

Tyana contemplated the question for a moment.

"Call me—Sibyl."

For future works from D. A. Anderson, visit:

CHILDRENOFVALE.COM

Daniel Alan Anderson, born in 1988 in California, is a Canadian-American author. Children of Vale is his debut novel. He began writing it in Silver Spring, Maryland, US, in 2004. He finished it in April of 2017 in San Francisco.

Publication of this novel would not have been possible
without my Kickstarter backers.
I am deeply grateful for their support.
The following are some of their names.

Special Editing Acknowledgment
HEATHER DAY

SCENE INDEX

I ...	... 1
II ...	... 4
III ...	... 9
IV ...	... 13
V ...	... 18
VI ...	... 25
VII ...	... 28
VIII ...	... 30
IX ...	... 34
X ...	... 39
XI ...	... 46
XII ...	... 48
XIII ...	... 59
XIV ...	... 62
XV ...	... 65
XVI ...	... 71
XVII ...	... 74
XVIII ...	... 79
XIX ...	... 83
XX ...	... 86
XXI ...	... 92
XXII ...	... 94
XXIII ...	... 97
XXIV ...	... 101
XXV ...	... 104
XXVI ...	... 108
XXVII ...	... 113
XXVIII ...	... 118
XXIX ...	... 127
XXX ...	... 131
XXXI ...	... 136

XXXII ...	... 140
XXXIII ...	... 141
XXXIV ...	... 144
XXXV ...	... 147
XXXVI ...	... 150
XXXVII ...	... 160
XXXVIII ...	... 165
XXXIX ...	... 171
XL ...	... 177
XLI ...	... 180
XLII ...	... 185
XLIII ...	... 195
XLIV ...	... 197
XLV ...	... 204
XLVI ...	... 207
XLVII ...	... 211
XLVIII ...	... 214
XLIX ...	... 221
L ...	... 225
LI ...	... 229
LII ...	... 232
LIII ...	... 239
LIV ...	... 243
LV ...	... 246
LVI ...	... 252
LVII ...	... 258
LVIII ...	... 263
LIX ...	... 265
LX ...	... 268
LXI ...	... 271
LXII ...	... 274
LXIII ...	... 282

LXIV 285
LXV 290
LXVI 296
LXVII 301
LXVIII 304
LXIX 309
LXX 312
LXXI 314
LXXII 322
LXXIII 328
LXXIV 335
LXXV 337
LXXVI 340
LXXVII 343
LXXVIII 347
LXXIX 353
LXXX 361
LXXXI 370